The Art of Wag

Susan C. Daffron

An Alpine Grove Romantic Comedy

Book 3

 Published by Magic Fur Press
An imprint of Logical Expressions, Inc.
P.O. Box 383
Ponderay, ID 83852

The Art of Wag

Copyright © 2014 by Susan C. Daffron
All rights reserved.

ISBN: 978-1-61038-025-6 (paperback)
        978-1-61038-026-3 (EPUB)

Like all of my books, *The Art of Wag* is dedicated to
my husband James Byrd,
my best friend and biggest supporter.
Thanks for everything!

Chapter 1

Sweet Nothings

Even though she was wearing heavy leather welding gloves, Tracy Sullivan could feel the 17-pound gray tabby's muscles twitch under her grasp. She was holding the cat by the scruff of the neck while her other hand rested on his back. Although she was cooing sweet nothings to the feline, he didn't seem to appreciate the sentiments. A low growl from deep within the chest cavity of the cat rose to a high-pitched squall as he tensed all of his muscles at once and launched straight up off the examination table.

"Get back! Don't let him bite you!" the veterinarian, Dr. Karen Cassidy, shouted as the two women jumped back from the shiny stainless steel table.

The cat landed with a thud back on the table, made a horrific screeching noise, and jumped down to the floor, scurrying around the room looking for an exit.

Fortunately, Tracy had closed the doors before the exam, so the cat had nowhere to go after his bout of kitty performance art. The large feline continued to circle the room and then settled in a corner, growling menacingly. Squiggy was a beautiful cat with the type of swirled, contoured tabby markings that reminded Tracy of van Gogh's famous "Starry Night" painting. At the moment though, the cat seemed to have discarded the peace and tranquility of the impressionists in favor of a more expressionist work like Edvard Munch's "The Scream."

Tracy looked over at the tall, slim veterinarian in the room with her. "Should we bag him?"

Karen Cassidy ran her fingers through her curly brown hair, pushing it back off her forehead. "Yes. I guess we'll have to. Could you grab the net, too?"

Tracy reached for the fishing net hanging on the wall and then grabbed a bright blue zippered nylon bag off a hook. "Were you able to figure out what's wrong with him? This smell is really starting to get to me."

"He just seems to have a case of, ah, extreme flatulence."

Tracy's straight blonde hair brushed her chin as she shook her head. "I hate Mondays. Why is it that we always get patients like Squiggy, the gigantic farting cat, on Mondays? What do people do to their animals when the clinic is closed on Sunday? It's like there's a full moon every weekend and people sprinkle their critters with wacko dust so they can drop them off here bright and early."

Dr. Cassidy smiled. "I don't know, but it does seem to be a trend, doesn't it? We need to catch this guy, so I can get to surgery. I have all those strays to neuter today."

"We're going to give those ferals some happy, sleepy drugs, right? Because after Squiggy's meltdown, my hands are shaking." Tracy held up a quavering hand horizontally in front of her face to demonstrate. "At this point, I'm not up for dealing with semi-nuclear wild kitties."

The vet crouched down in front of the cat. "I was hoping we wouldn't have to sedate Squiggy, since his owner said he's a big 'love bug,' but it looks like we'll have to, after all."

Squiggy growled more loudly from his corner to emphasize his displeasure and readiness to leave the room.

Tracy looked down at the cat's scowling face. "Yeah, sure. You're a real love bug."

The two woman worked together to catch Squiggy and put him into the "cat bag," a zippered bag uniquely designed to confine a feline, so the animal isn't able to easily scratch large swaths of skin off a veterinary professional.

Tracy held onto the cat again while Dr. Cassidy gave Squiggy a shot "to take the edge off," as she liked to say. After the injection, Squiggy was significantly less cranky. Tracy looked up at the vet."This smell is starting to make me feel a little ill. Are you almost done?"

The veterinarian looked up from her ministrations. "Yes. In addition to his flatulence, he does seem a little dehydrated. I'd like to give him some fluids and see if the owners would be willing to let us keep him for a few hours so we can keep an eye on him."

Tracy nodded. For suffering through eau d'Squiggy, she was being paid six whole dollars an hour, the going rate for veterinary assistants in Alpine Grove. Given that she was the only assistant at the only vet clinic in town, it must be the going rate. Becoming a certified vet tech would pay more, but taking all the required courses was far beyond her means. On the Chinese Zodiac, 1995 was the year of the pig, but that clearly had nothing to do with bringing home lots of bacon for her extremely lean piggy bank.

Although Tracy loved animals, working two jobs was starting to get to her. She worked as a veterinary assistant from seven thirty in the morning until three in the afternoon, ran home, took her dachshund Roxy for a walk, grabbed a shower, changed into the required idiotic outfit, and worked from four to ten in the evening as a hostess at the local Italian restaurant.

Being clawed and shed upon during the day by dogs and cats and then groped in the evenings by drunken male tourists meant she could afford her rent. And food. Most of the time. But job opportunities in Alpine Grove were scarce. On her best days, Tracy was grateful to have any job. But this wasn't one of her best days. Today, all she felt was exhausted and annoyed.

Cradling the large stinky and now sleepy cat in her arms, Tracy carried him back to the row of stainless steel cages. She closed the cage door firmly and mentally acknowledged the metal clang, indicating the lock was in place and the cat was securely confined. With any luck, Squiggy would still be feeling a little sleepy when his owner arrived later that afternoon.

Dr. Cassidy had wasted no time and already had a small feral cat anesthetized and on the surgery table for his neutering. It was amazing how quickly the veterinarian worked. None of her movements were wasted and she could neuter a cat in minutes.

Tracy stood next to the table and monitored the anesthesia machine while the vet worked. "I'd like to take a couple of days off. Is that okay? I got a free pass to an art class. It's a weekend class about a computer program called Photoshop. My friend Shelby got some special deal and gave it to me. The price is right. Free works for me."

Dr. Cassidy looked up from the cat. "Sure. No problem. Gail can cover your shifts. She's always wanting more hours, anyway."

"Don't we all? I agonized about going, but it's been a long time since I've done anything like this. Plus Shelby is going to let me stay with her at her place in the city. It could be fun. I could use a weekend away from here." Noting the movement of the anesthesia machine's reservoir bag, which inflated and deflated like a balloon, she gave it a squeeze. What would it feel like to go up in a brightly colored hot-air balloon and soar through the sky like Dorothy in *The Wizard of Oz*? She'd never been on a plane, much less a balloon.

Dr. Cassidy finished up and passed the little orange tabby to Tracy. "This one is done. Could you put him in a cage and grab the next one?"

Tracy snuggled the sleeping cat to her chest and looked down at his striped face. "Okay, little fella, let's go. Your opportunity to be a daddy is over now."

The sound of furious barking came from within the tiny studio apartment as Tracy walked up the stairs and opened the door. The scuffed hardwood floor was littered with clothes and art supplies. Tracy's long-haired dachshund Roxy ran up to her, deftly dodging an empty laundry basket, a half-painted canvas, and a box filled with crumpled tubes of acrylic paint.

"I guess it's laundry day, huh? Even I am starting to think it's a little messy in here."

Seeming to agree with the assessment and delighted to see Tracy, Roxy continued yipping happily. Tracy picked up the dog, sat on the couch, and placed Roxy next to her. "How was your day, little dog? Mine has been a pain so far. Are you ready for your walk?" She stroked the dog's silky fur as Roxy danced around her on the sofa pillow. "Okay, okay. I just need to change my shoes." She reached for her sneakers and bent down to tie the laces.

Tracy grabbed the leash, clipped it onto the dog's collar, and picked her up. "I think I want to make it a short one today Rox, so I can fit in a tiny nap before work. Squiggy really wore me out."

They went down the stairs to the street and Tracy placed the dog on the ground. Roxy wagged her feathered tail like a flag behind her as she checked out her favorite sniff spots. Even though the dog had only three legs, she motored along quickly down the sidewalk.

When Tracy had started work at the vet clinic, Dr. Cassidy had cautioned her that sometimes animals would come in that were injured and their owners wouldn't want the vet to treat the animal. Tracy didn't realize what that warning meant until the day a woman dropped off a young dachshund with a terribly mangled back leg. The story of how the dog's leg was hurt wasn't clear, and the owner didn't stick around for the exam to provide details. In the end, the damage to the leg was too extensive to repair. When Dr. Cassidy called the owner and suggested amputation to save the dog's life, the owner wanted nothing to do with that idea. She had proclaimed that she didn't want a "defective dog," and said they could put Roxy to sleep or find her another home.

Tracy normally tried to think the best of people; in fact, her mother called her a "total softie." But when Elise Palmer walked out on her injured dog, a little part of Tracy's heart hardened. She hoped there was a special fiery place in the afterlife for people who didn't care for their animals. Maybe karma would take care of Elise. In her next life, the woman might come back as something small and disgusting. Like a fat slug creeping around a garden, eating defenseless seedlings, until it was consumed by a hungry robin for breakfast. Whenever Tracy saw Elise in the grocery store, she imagined a little slime trail following the woman through the aisles indicating where she'd been.

After caring for Roxy at the clinic during her convalescence, Tracy fell in love with the little dog's independent personality, so she adopted her. Once Roxy was restored to health, the dachshund was definitely a force to be reckoned with, but Tracy never regretted her decision.

As she followed Roxy to a small grassy spot, Tracy marveled at how well Roxy had healed. The dog didn't know or care that she had only three legs. Tracy glanced through the storefront window and waved at her mother, who was standing behind the counter helping a customer. Tracy's apartment was located above her mother's gift store. Bea Haven Gifts had been a prime stop for Alpine Grove tourists for years. Tracy's mom Bea loved everything about running a store—meeting the people who were traveling through town, ordering touristy tchotchkes, talking to sales people, and setting up all her pretty seasonal displays. Her enthusiasm was infectious and past customers always made a point of stopping by whenever they were in town.

Roxy led the way as they wandered down the main street of town, passing a number of real estate offices with enticing photos scattered across the windows. Tracy sighed. The odds of her ever owning a house or even a falling-down shack out in the sticks were slim to none, unless she figured out another way to earn a living that paid a lot better.

After spending so much time in her mother's shop while she was growing up, Tracy discovered that she had no passion for retail. Playing with the merchandise in Mom's store had been fun when she was a kid, but actually working at the store was a different story. Mom found the tourists interesting and funny. Tracy found them tiresome and exhausting. She had spent a lot of time in the back room hiding out, pretending to price merchandise.

Although she clearly had no future in retail, Tracy's short-lived attempt at insurance had been even worse. Her father owned an insurance agency in town, and after Tracy dropped out of college the second time, she had tried working there. During her stint at the office, she discovered a deep loathing for the insurance industry, forms, filing, and the depressing gray cubicles in the dreary old brick office building on the outskirts of town.

Tracy's mother waved off Tracy's failed experiments into gainful employment, saying that Tracy just hadn't "found her bliss" yet and that it would come in time. Her father was markedly less sympathetic, particularly after her failed forays into higher education. Tracy had tried college more than once. Her dream since she was a little girl had always been to become a veterinarian. She loved animals and it seemed like a natural fit. And she tried really hard to like biology, chemistry, and math. She really did. But her brain just couldn't do numbers. It didn't work that way and it never had. Who was she kidding? All that math was just too much. She tried different classes and switching majors, but nothing really panned out. Discouraged and depressed, she returned to Alpine Grove. Tracy's former college roommate Shelby had a theory that Alpine Grove had some bizarre elastic pull.

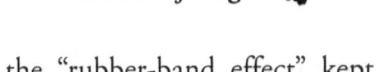

Once you had lived there, the "rubber-band effect" kept bringing you back.

After dropping out yet again and then a demoralizing few months of unemployment living at home with Mom and Dad, Tracy finally got the job at the vet clinic. Dr. Cassidy was a fantastic vet. The only bad thing was that working up-close-and-personal with a veterinarian was a real dream killer. If Tracy had actually possessed the math skills to get into vet school and make it through the program, she knew she would have relegated herself to a lifetime of stress.

As the only veterinarian in town, Dr. Karen Cassidy was on call all the time. Tracy felt bad for the woman sometimes, because she seemed perpetually exhausted. Although the vet evidently didn't mind all the charged, high-stress moments, Tracy knew that personally, she was too soft-hearted and emotionally wimpy to handle the day-to-day life of a veterinarian. Going out in the middle of the night and having to make life-and-death decisions related to someone's cherished pet would have made her miserable. Sometimes those little-girl dreams weren't quite what they were cracked up to be.

Even though she lived an economical and somewhat Spartan existence, Tracy liked her tiny apartment above the store. Mom had used it as a storage area for years and stuffed it full of extra merchandise and supplies, but after a particularly unpleasant argument with her father, everyone in the family agreed that Tracy needed to move out of the house.

Yes, Tracy was a slob. No one disputed that. But when Dad put the contents of her bedroom on the front lawn next to a "free" sign, he really crossed a line. He was a pretty mellow person when it came to most things. Sure he had a habit of getting angry once in a while about things Tracy had done, but that incident hit a new level of parental reprimand.

If she hadn't had the store, Bea would have made a fantastic mediator. She always said that Tracy and her father were just too much alike. Tracy didn't buy that explanation, but obviously it had been time for her to move out. Plus, after you reached a certain age, continuing to live with your parents was just pathetic, anyway. When her mom had suggested Tracy could live in the apartment, she jumped at the idea.

After Tracy cleaned out the space above her Mom's store, she discovered that the tiny bathroom and kitchen were workable and even sort of cute in a vintage, shabby-chic kind of way. She had painted the apartment with cheap, brightly colored paint from the "oops" bin at the hardware store. Most of the walls were done, except for the one near the kitchen. She'd get to that eventually. Although it was basically just a single room with the kitchen and the bathroom on the far end, the space worked, and now it was her home. And Roxy's home too. In an effort to meet his criteria for being a responsible adult, Tracy dutifully paid her father the small rent he requested every month. Well, most months, anyway.

Tracy stood and waited for Roxy to finish her activities and waved feebly at Larry Lowell, who was standing outside his law office on the other side of the street, grinning at her. She would undoubtedly see Larry later tonight when he came in for dinner at the restaurant. Although he was a nice-enough guy, she wished he'd get over his little-boy crush on her. After all this time, most of the residents of Alpine Grove were aware that Larry had the hots for her. It was getting embarrassing. A few months ago, she was thrilled to see him eating with some other women at the restaurant from time to time. He'd had more than one actual date. It was a miracle. But then all those romantic aspirations appeared to fail, and now he was alone again, spending way too much time loitering around her hostess stand. Larry had to be the most regular of the restaurant's regular customers. Apparently, the man never, ever, ate at home.

Sometimes living in a small town felt like being an animal in a zoo. Everyone could see when you did everything. The fact that Tracy was practically the only person her age living here was also a little disconcerting. All her friends from high school were gone, so most people she knew were either significantly older or younger than she was. The local chamber of commerce held seminars about how the town might attract younger people, so it wouldn't end up turning into a retirement community. There was a lot of hand-wringing about "brain drain" as high school students graduated and moved away to find jobs elsewhere. Tracy knew why. By now, the rest of her classmates with real jobs probably weren't eating ramen noodles or living in a 300-square-foot studio above a gift store.

Tracy turned around and looked down at the little dog at her feet. "Okay Roxy. I hope you're done, because I really don't want Larry to run across the street for a little afternoon rendezvous. We're picking up the pace and getting outta here. I need my nap."

~

After a short but restorative nap, Tracy put on her much-loathed hostess uniform and went to work at job number two. At most restaurants, employees were asked to wear something simple like black pants and a white shirt. But no, at this place, the owner had other ideas. Tracy detested the short skirt that was held up by green-and-red suspenders, but the ruffle-laden blouse was even worse. She looked like a deranged Italian oompa-loompa.

She opened the back door to the kitchen of the Italian restaurant and found Lou, the cook, stirring a marinara sauce that was simmering in a stainless-steel vat on the huge commercial stove. The rich, savory aroma of basil and oregano permeated the room. The large balding man waved his spoon at her. "You aren't gonna like it."

Tracy turned to face Lou. "Like what?"

"Jerry's on a rampage." Lou's face was red and it probably wasn't just from the heat of the stove.

"Don't you mean Giovanni?" Tracy said with a smirk. The owner of the restaurant had no Italian heritage whatsoever, but that didn't stop him from pretending he did.

"I have a lotta things I could call him, but you're too young to hear that type of language. I'm just letting you know he's cranky and sharing the *amore* with everyone nearby."

Tracy nodded. "Thanks for the warning and for protecting my tender sensibilities. I'll try and stay out of his way."

"Oh, and Jenny is pissed at you because she thinks you gave Anna more tables last night. She whined to Jerry when she got here to do prep, which probably didn't improve his mood. Then she marked up the seating chart with a red pen."

Tracy looked over at the chart on the wall and took note of the many angry-looking scribbles on the table layout. Sometimes she added colorful happy doodles to the wall chart, but the skull and crossbones was definitely not Tracy's work. Great. "I don't know what Jenny's problem is. It's not like I get creative with the table rotation. You get the two-top when it's open. You get the four-top when the slowpoke campers finally turn over and get out of here. And it wasn't my fault that the huge guy from Topeka couldn't fit in that booth." That had certainly been a difficult conversation.

Lou wagged his spoon at her again. "She thinks you skipped her on purpose."

"I can see it's going to be a very long evening. Maybe I'll double-up Jenny's tables and see how she does."

"Now you're just being mean. You know she'll yell at you."

"She's going to scream at me anyway, but at least she'll be more tired and have more tips in her pocket, right?"

Lou waved his spoon in a shooing motion. "Go on. Get outta here. You got stuff to do."

Tracy grabbed a cloth so she could wipe down tables, and then she reached out and gave the gruff older man a hug. "You know you love me. Thanks for giving me the heads-up."

Later, Tracy was standing at the hostess stand rolling silverware into napkins when Larry Lowell walked in. Was he stalking her? He hung around her hostess stand all the time when the restaurant was open, but this was new. Bordering on creepy. She looked down at the reservation book. "Hi Larry. I have your reservation for your usual table at 6:30, but you're a little early. We're not open yet." She tried to look extra busy by laying some silverware rolls into a star design on the end table next to her. Maybe he'd go away.

Larry clasped his hands together in front of him. "I wanted to talk to you before anyone else is here." He looked like he was praying to the gods of Italian food.

Tracy plastered on her best customer-service smile. "Do you want to change your reservation? Or are you bringing someone with you tonight? I'd be happy to help you if there's a surprise for someone special."

Larry's hands tightened, causing his knuckles to turn white. "Well. Yes. Actually, it's something I've wanted to ask you for a very long time, but I think you may consider it somewhat forward."

"Forward?" Who used the word forward? Was Larry trapped in the 1800s or something?

"My law school reunion is coming up. It's a rather important occasion and I was hoping you would be able to attend with me."

Tracy put down the roll of silverware she was holding and took a step back from the hostess stand. "I don't think that would be a good idea." Not on a bet.

"It's in Los Angeles; I'd pay for everything. You'd have your own spacious room at the event hotel. And free meals. It could be an enjoyable vacation. You work very hard and I'm sure you could use a bit of a holiday."

Larry wasn't wrong that she needed a vacation, but there was no way she was going to La-La Land with him. "You're right, I could use a break, but I am already going to be taking a class, so I really can't take any more time off right now."

Larry dropped his hands and gazed down at his loafers. "Are you sure?"

"Yes. I'm sorry. I thought you had a girlfriend, anyway. The woman with the big curly hair?"

Larry looked back up at her. "That didn't work out. She said I was too much of a lawyer."

"But you *are* a lawyer."

"I know." He shook his head. "It was a confusing conversation. But in the end, we agreed to terminate our relationship."

Tracy picked up another roll of silverware and added it to her star design. "I'm very sorry to hear that. But right now, I really need to get back to work. I have a lot of tables to set up before we open."

"I think I'll just cancel my reservation for tonight." Larry stepped back, away from her. "I have something I need to do."

Tracy looked down at the appointment book. "That's fine. No problem." At least she would be faced with one less uncomfortable conversation later tonight.

Larry nodded. "Have a good evening." He turned and quickly moved out the door, capering out to the street like an antelope fleeing from a starving tiger.

Tracy started moving the silverware rolls into a big basket so she could start setting up tables. Larry had made it pretty obvious he'd had a crush on her for ages, but the idea of actually going on date—much less a trip—with the guy was alarming. She'd witnessed enough of his dates here at the restaurant to know exactly what it would be like. No way.

∼

Tracy looked at her watch. A half hour until they opened. She grabbed the silverware basket and went out into the dining area, setting up tables as quickly as she could. The door to the kitchen swung open and slammed against the wall. Jerry stomped through the doors, making at beeline for the table Tracy was setting up. He didn't look happy. Uh-oh.

The thin, small-boned man stopped in front of her and threw a pile of menus down on the table. He ran his hand over his slicked-back hair, making sure every ebony strand was in place. With his beady eyes and long nose, it was easy to see why Lou often referred to Jerry as "The Weasel."

Tracy straightened. "Hi Jerry. Is there a problem with the menus?"

"It's Giovanni! My name is Giovanni. You need to call me that."

"Okay Jerry. I'll keep that in mind." His voice was like fingernails on a chalkboard. The guy brought out the absolute worst in her.

A flush rose on Jerry's sallow face. It looked like he might explode. "Are you being smart with me? Where did the lawyer go? He's one of our best customers. And why aren't you at the stand? I see you out here at the tables too much. You need to be at the hostess stand at all times!"

Tracy gripped the silverware roll she was holding more tightly. "It's physically impossible for me to simultaneously stand at the podium and set up tables. Or walk customers to their tables. Or get booster seats or high chairs for the kids. Unless I were cloned. If you need someone to stand at the podium at all times, you need to have two hostesses." Sure. Like that was ever going to happen. As her salary and the level of employee turnover amply indicated, Jerry was the biggest cheapskate in Alpine Grove.

He pointed his long index finger toward the kitchen. "Get Jenny to do that! She's the waitress."

"Jenny and Anna are busy serving food. That's what they do." When they weren't whining about tips or snacking on bread sticks.

"Are you being a smart-ass?" Jerry waved his arms toward the seating area. "You'd better not be talking to customers like that. And I saw on your receipts that you're spelling your name wrong again. How many times do I have to tell you? You need to end your name with an "i" and put a little heart above it. Customers like it and it's good for business."

"That's not how I spell my name. It's T-r-a-c-y. There is no 'i.' Sorry." And the hearts were stupid. What was this, sixth grade?

"I don't care. It helps business. And you get more tips."

"Perhaps you've forgotten, Jerry, but as the hostess I don't get tips. If you'd like to start splitting some of the tip revenue with me, I'd be happy to accept it." What she was being paid barely covered the cost of Roxy's dog food.

"Stop calling me Jerry. And you didn't answer me. Where's the lawyer? Did you drive him away?"

"I'm not rude to customers. Ever. Take last night, for example. Even when that kid threw 7,000 Cheerios on the floor, I just picked them up and smiled after Jenny told me to 'get my ass' over to table four. And then Anna took one of Jenny's tables."

"See! You are supposed to be up here all the time!" Jerry was practically jumping up and down now.

"Then who was supposed to clean up the Cheerio disaster?"

"We don't serve cereal. Why are you letting customers bring their own food? What is wrong with you?"

Tracy dropped her silverware roll in the basket and leaned forward, putting both hands on the table. "I don't frisk the customers before seating them. Do you know what kids can do to Cheerios? It's totally disgusting. I don't want them bringing cereal in here any more than you do. But if Mom has stashed a box in her purse and smuggled it in, there's nothing I can do about it."

"You keep changing the subject. What did you do to the lawyer? I looked through the kitchen door and saw him leave. He looked unhappy. You'd better make it right when he comes back tonight for dinner."

Tracy looked down at the silverware basket. Jerry wasn't going to like this. "Larry canceled his reservation. He said he had something to do."

The color in Jerry's cheeks intensified and it looked like he might explode into little quivering weasel pieces. "*What? The lawyer eats here almost every night!*"

"If you must know, he asked me to go to a reunion with him. I have another trip planned, so I told him no."

Jerry raised his arms and gazed at the ceiling as if imploring a higher power to give him strength. "What have you done? Do you know how much money that man spends here?"

"He'll be back. It's just one night. Like I said, Larry said he had something to do this evening." Obviously the guy couldn't or wouldn't cook and there were only so many places to eat in Alpine Grove. He didn't have a lot of options.

Jerry lowered his arms and glared at her. "That man has nothing to do and you know it! You've driven him away forever. You're fired."

Tracy grabbed the handle of the basket. "You're firing me because I won't go on a date with a customer? You're not my pimp."

Jerry pointed at the door. "Get out!"

"Fine!" She let go of the basket and put out her hands in front of her. "*Ciao*, and have a lovely evening." She wasn't going to miss saying that 25 times every night. Or much of anything about this place. But paying her bills this month was going to be tricky.

Chapter 2

Exit Stage Right

Tracy walked slowly down the street back to her apartment. On the one hand, she would never have to go back to a job she hated. The endless conflict and stress of working at the restaurant had been exhausting. On the other hand, now she had exited yet another job. This was not going to look good on her already miserable excuse for a résumé. She could just imagine what her father would have to say about her latest employment implosion. He already thought she was an underachiever. Now that she'd been fired from the lowest-wage entry-level job at a restaurant, she'd hit a new all-time career low.

Tracy opened the door to her apartment. Nothing had changed in the two hours she'd been gone. It was still a mess, but now she'd have more time to clean up. Maybe tomorrow. But where was Roxy? She wasn't doing the hiding thing again, was she?

"Roxy? Come on out. I'm really not in the mood for this tonight."

A small scrabbling noise came from behind the sofa. Tracy turned and said, "Okay, Roxy. Did you get stuck again? This isn't cute. Or funny. It's really not."

Tracy bent down to haul the ugly plaid sofa away from the wall. An old beat-up bedspread that normally covered the hideous 70s-era pattern dragged behind the sofa as she yanked it across the wood floor. Tracy shoved some books aside with her foot to clear a space, and Roxy shot out from underneath the sofa toward the kitchen. One of the cabinet doors slammed and some metal pots crashed together. Sometimes having a burrowing dog was a challenge. Tracy kept thinking she should get something to hold the cabinet doors closed, but cabinet locks were absurdly expensive. And she'd just bought some new acrylic paints, which blew all her extra cash.

Tracy stood up. "Roxy! Come on now. Don't do this. You know you don't like it when I pull you out of there." Her shoulders slumped and she put her arms against her sides. "I changed my mind. I'm not extracting you. Not this time. You can just sit in there and pretend to be a stock pot, for all I care. I'm tired and I'm going to watch TV. On the sofa. By myself."

She turned around, shoved the sofa back against the wall, and replaced the bedspread. Grabbing the remote from the pile of clutter on the coffee table, Tracy sat down, put her feet up on the table, and turned on the tiny black-and-white TV. Settling in, she sighed and called out toward the kitchen. "You can stay in there forever, for all I care. I'm here on the nice, warm sofa if you need me." The only response was a metallic clank as the dachshund readjusted herself among the pots and pans.

Tracy flipped through the channels and found a whole lot of nothing on TV. Even relaxation was frustrating. She leaned back and stared at the ceiling. The cracks in the paint looked like lightning bolts shooting across a dingy sky. Did astronauts see lightning from the other side when they shot off into space? The patterns and textures of multiple bolts would have to be remarkable.

As the familiar sounds of a particularly stupid commercial jingle came on, she clicked off the TV and picked up the phone. Since life here in Alpine Grove was depressing, it was time to focus on her trip. She dialed her friend Shelby's number and smiled when she heard the woman's sugary southern drawl on the other end of the line.

"Hey honey, what's up?"

Tracy slumped down into the sofa. "I got fired."

"From which job? I hope it was the restaurant one. Because that was not a good fit for you, and you know it."

"Yeah. Jerry canned me."

"You mean Giovanni?"

Tracy grinned. "Yeah. During our little chat, I kept calling him Jerry. I thought he was going to blow a gasket."

"You shouldn't mess with people like that. It never ends well." Shelby sighed. "You know I love you, but the cute, perky blonde thing you have going only gets you so far. You just can't be blurting out the first thing that comes into your head all the time."

"I know. But I couldn't help myself." Tracy twirled the phone cord around her finger. "I got fired because I wouldn't go out on a date with Larry. I mean, that's probably grounds for a lawsuit isn't it? That's gotta be some type of harassment if my boss is trying to pimp me out to customers. Yuck!"

"I'm not sure you have a case, darlin'. You just turned down the only lawyer in Alpine Grove."

Tracy grimaced. "Good point. I don't want to talk about that anymore. Let's talk about my trip. It's still okay if I stay with you, right? I really gotta get out of this town."

"What are you going to do about Roxy? You know she can't stay with me. Billy Bob is just too much cat for her to handle." Shelby's cat Billy Bob outweighed Roxy by probably twelve pounds. The giant feline spent a lot of time sitting on the sofa cleaning his ample gut and he didn't like a nosy dachshund interrupting his personal time.

"I know. I talked to Dr. Cassidy about the days off, but I forgot to ask about Roxy. Maybe she'll have some ideas."

"On the bright side, at least you don't have to worry about Jerry now."

"Yeah, although I don't want to talk to my parents about my rent again. I'm really not up for another lecture from my dad about how I'm not responsible. I told you about the whole incident that happened with Roxy the last time she stayed at my parents place, so we all know she can't stay at there again. That was a mistake. Dr. Cassidy banished Roxy from the vet clinic too. After being there as a patient, Roxy took issue with staying there. It was bad. But maybe Dr. C knows someone." Roxy's reputation as a troublemaker was spreading. It was getting seriously depressing.

Shelby said cheerfully, "You'll get it figured out. You always do. I'm looking forward to seeing you. It's been too long! Maybe we can study together after your class."

"Oh boy, that just sounds like a whirlwind of fun. But I don't think it would work. The class I'm taking is about art software and I doubt you'd have it on your computer, unless you suddenly decided to chuck that whole idea of getting your PhD in Comparative Literature. Do you have any coloring books? I could play with Crayolas while you work on your dissertation."

"I suppose I could take a night off from it." Shelby sighed. "Just one night wouldn't hurt."

Tracy methodically chipped at a piece of desiccated cereal on the bedspread, placing the crumbly pieces in a pile on the coffee table. "I'd love to go out someplace where I don't recognize every single person I meet. Being anonymous in a large city is underrated. You can miss one night of study. I promise I won't corrupt you with my idle ways."

Shelby laughed. "If you couldn't corrupt me in college, it's way too late now."

~

The next morning, the alarm went off promptly at six o'clock. With a groan, Tracy rolled over in bed and whapped the snooze button. It had been a long night after Roxy decided to emerge from her hiding place at two in the morning. The dog had crashed out of the kitchen cabinet with a yelp, clanking the pots and pans all over the kitchen. Worried that the dog might have hurt herself, Tracy hauled herself up to investigate. Roxy was fine, but then Tracy couldn't get back to sleep. The financial implications of losing the restaurant job swirled around in her sleep-deprived brain. What was she going to do? Leaving town for this class was stupid, since gas cost money. She should start asking around town for employment possibilities. But she really wanted this weekend away.

After several more arguments with the snooze alarm, Tracy finally dragged herself out of bed, fed and walked Roxy, and actually made it into the vet clinic on time.

Dr. Cassidy looked up from the chart she was holding and appraised Tracy's unkempt appearance. "What happened to you?"

"My dog has a really irritating sense of humor. I thought she killed herself getting out of her latest hidey-hole. Then I couldn't sleep and I didn't have time for a shower. I figure the dogs will just find me more interesting this way."

The veterinarian pulled a file from the cabinet. "That's probably true. Maybe you could comb your hair before the clients come in, though."

Tracy reached up and tried to run her fingers through her hair. Yikes. "Sorry about that. I ran out of the apartment before I looked in the mirror." She walked into to the bathroom to try to do something about her appearance. She looked at herself in the tiny mirror. It was like Buffy the Vampire Slayer had gotten herself chomped. The undead look was decidedly unattractive.

After the morning rush of clients had dropped off their animals for surgery, Tracy stood next to the vet as she worked to drain a large abscess on a cat's neck. Tracy stuck out her tongue and made a face. "That's nasty."

"I know. Sorry. It's not like this is Tigger's first abscess either."

Tracy averted her eyes, opting to study the gauges on the anesthesia machine instead. "I know I asked you about getting the weekend off, but I was wondering if there's any way Roxy could stay here."

"No. You know that didn't work out well. We talked about that."

"I know." Tracy sighed. "It's just that I really want to get out of town. Do you know anyone who might be able to take her? It's only for two days. She can't come with me. My friend Shelby's cat and Roxy have issues."

"Roxy has a lot of issues. Could you grab a needle?"

"I know. But I love her." Tracy peeled open a sterile needle package so the vet could grab the needle with her gloved hand. "I can't just leave Roxy in my apartment."

The vet shook her head. "Well, maybe the boarding place could take her. Remember Kat Stevens?"

"Oh yeah. She has the huge dog that barfed all over you." That had been quite a memorable performance.

"Yes. That's her. I heard she's opening a boarding kennel."

"That's great! I'll get her name from the file and give her a call."

Kat sounded nice on the phone and was remarkably amenable to taking Roxy on such short notice, as long as it was okay that the dog stayed in the house. Tracy agreed to drop off Roxy in the afternoon, so she could still make it to Shelby's place that night.

After work, Tracy loaded Roxy and her crate into the car, which was an ancient brown Subaru station wagon that her father referred to as "The Turd." The story was that it had been used by commune members in the mid-seventies until the car died an ignoble death in a pasture and was left to rot.

Tracy's parents almost never talked about their years living in the Alpine Grove commune, but Tracy remembered the hippie life fondly. When she was a little kid, she had spent a lot of time outside and there had always been someone to play with. It had been fun, but she never told anyone now that her hippie name was Rainbow. And yet, every once in a while, she met someone who remembered. In a small town, there were no secrets. People knew *everything*.

When she was in high school, she had convinced her father to let her boyfriend Neil drag The Turd out of the pasture, and give him a shot at getting the car to run again. Although Neil wasn't the greatest boyfriend for a number of reasons, he was a fairly decent mechanic. Through a complicated negotiation with the DMV, she was able to get a title on the formerly junked vehicle, and she'd been driving it ever since. The Turd made a lot of noise and sometimes opted not to run at all, but she never had to worry about anyone stealing it.

Tracy nosed the ancient car down the winding gravel driveway toward Kat's house, cautiously picking her way around the deepest holes, since the car still had a long journey ahead of it tonight. Roxy was looking annoyed at all the bumps and barked a few times to express her displeasure.

"Sorry Roxy. We're almost there. You have to be good while I'm gone. Kat is being really nice about taking you today. I hope this works out. Please, please be good."

Roxy just looked out the window at the passing pine trees, ostensibly immune to the pleas for good behavior.

Tracy pulled the car under a tree and cut the engine. The car coughed out a final burst of exhaust before quivering into silence. A huge hairy brown dog ran from behind the house, skidded to stop by the old car, and began sniffing the tires as Tracy got out. "Hi Linus. Do you remember me?"

The big dog wagged his tail at the friendly visitor and was soon joined by a small black-and-white border collie. Tracy bent to pet the dogs and noticed the sound of a chain saw whining somewhere in the distance. Fall had definitely arrived, so it must be time to get the wood in. Out here in the middle of the forest finding firewood certainly wouldn't be an issue. The front door of the house opened and a petite woman with long, wavy brown hair started down the front steps.

Tracy waved. "Hi, Kat. It's good to see Linus looking so healthy. Who is the border collie?"

"That's Lori. Two other dogs, Tessa and Chelsey, are in the house and Lady is out in the woods with Joel somewhere."

"Is he the one making all the noise?"

"Yes. He finished fixing the roof of the house. Now he's working on the firewood program, so we don't freeze this winter."

Tracy smiled. "Yes, him and everyone else. It's like they say—there are two seasons: winter and getting ready for winter."

"I haven't experienced winter yet. I'm not sure I'm up for chopping firewood. But Joel doesn't seem to mind, so I'm going with it. Where's Roxy?"

Tracy turned toward the car. "She's in there. Let me get her out. She's only got three legs, so it's better if I don't let her try and get out herself."

Kat nodded and stroked Linus's head slowly as Tracy extracted Roxy from the car. Linus leaned on Kat in an effort to soak up as much affection as possible. She looked down at the dog. "Listen, Big Guy, you're going to knock me over. Cut that out."

Tracy put Roxy on the ground and the little dog started barking furiously at Linus, who looked distressed at the outburst. "Roxy, no! Quiet!"

Roxy started marching off toward the forest until she reached the end of her leash, and turned to glare at Tracy. Kat said, "Maybe we should take her for a little walk to help her get acclimated?"

"Yes. Roxy tends to be a bit opinionated. Also, I know I told you about this on the phone, but don't forget about her hiding thing. I'm not sure if she'll do it here at your place, but she thinks she's really funny. Hiding in my pots and pans cabinet is getting old.

Kat nodded. "I'll keep that in mind."

Roxy started barking again and was practically levitating in her state of hysteria, yanking at the leash. A tall man wearing bright orange chaps and a hard hat emerged from a break in the forest. He was carrying a large orange chain saw. A brown-and-black collie mix walked by his side. Seeing the dachshund, the dog ran ahead to say 'hi.'

All of the dogs circled and sniffed each other in an elaborate, complicated greeting ritual. Roxy allowed herself to be sniffed, yipping occasionally at any impolite transgressions. The man removed his hard hat and waved. "Hi Tracy. I guess that's Roxy?"

Tracy waved back. "Hi Joel. Nice chaps."

"Kevlar. It's not just for bulletproof vests anymore. I'm fond of my legs."

Kat grinned. "So am I. And I've watched way too many chain-saw-massacre movies. So I'm all for Kevlar everything."

Joel waved toward the house "I'm covered with sawdust and wood chips, so I'm going to go take a shower. It was nice seeing you again, Tracy."

As he walked away, Tracy turned to Kat. "Wow, he sure looks different."

Kat turned to look back at Joel's retreating form. "What do you mean? He looks the same to me."

"He's going native, isn't he?" Tracy nodded. "Yeah, this happens when men stay in Alpine Grove too long. They get hairier. Then they start losing teeth."

"Eww. His teeth are fine. But I suppose he does need a haircut. I kinda like the longer hair, though."

"Is he growing a beard? When was the last time he shaved?"

"I'm not sure. Maybe a couple weeks ago. At least it's past the scuzzy stage. I'm trying to remain open-minded, but I told him if he starts looking like any one of the members of ZZ Top, we have a problem."

Tracy shook her head. "It's a slippery slope. The last time I saw him, he was gorgeous. Like every other woman in this town, I had a huge crush on him. But then he had the super-model girlfriend." Seeing the look on Kat's face, Tracy cringed inwardly. Shelby was right. She needed to learn to shut up once in a while.

Kat looked down at Roxy. "Um, well, that's been over for some time."

"Roxy, stop that." Tracy pulled back on the leash. "I'm sorry. I didn't mean to bring that up. But everyone *was* hoping that girlfriend would get lost. It's a big event when a good-looking guy arrives in town. There was a long line of women wanting to date him."

Kat looked up and smiled slightly. "I think I cut in line."

"Yeah, well, I'm sure they'll back off. He's going native now."

"I guess that's good news for me, since I'd prefer that he stay right here."

~

After Tracy left, Kat carried Roxy up the steps into the house. She put the dog down on the floor and Roxy ran around her legs, effectively hog-tying her. Kat bent to disentangle herself from the leash. "Okay Roxy. This is the house. I've heard about your wily ways and I'm going to stay leashed to you for a while, so you can learn where everything is."

Roxy glared at Kat and then charged toward the living room. "Okay. So you want to see what the sofa is like? I wouldn't mind going back to my novel. It was just getting good."

Kat sat down on the sofa and lifted Roxy up to join her. Like most small dogs, Roxy was used to being picked up and carried around. She seemed to view humans as large servants, ready to do her bidding. Clearly worn out from the excitement of the drive, she turned around a few times and curled up next to Kat to settle in for her afternoon nap.

Joel emerged from the bathroom wearing a towel around his waist, and Kat looked up to admire the view as he walked to the bedroom. Spending time out in the forest chopping wood certainly was doing marvelous things to his shoulder muscles, which already were mighty fine. She picked up Roxy and placed her back on the floor.

The dog started motoring back toward the kitchen. Kat tugged on the leash. "Nope. We're going to go see what the half-naked man is up to."

She leaned in the doorway of the bedroom and watched as Joel yanked a t-shirt over his head. He tugged the shirt down over his stomach and looked over at her. "Something wrong?"

"Did you brush your teeth?"

Joel grinned, emphatically flashing his pearly whites at her. "Yes. What has prompted your concern for my dental hygiene all of a sudden?"

"Tracy says you're going native."

"What?"

"She says that men who live in Alpine Grove too long get hairier and lose their teeth. It's no big deal if you don't want to get a haircut, but the toothless thing is definitely *not* sexy." Kat had seen enough Alpine Grove men to know that some of them weren't making dental care a priority. Tracy was definitely not wrong about that.

Joel laughed. "I'll keep that in mind. Tracy has lived here her whole life, so she should know."

Kat walked over to him, pulling Roxy behind her. She looped the leash over her arm and ran her hand under his shirt and up his chest, spreading her fingers across his muscles and enjoying the feel of his skin. "Would you be willing to bring in Roxy's crate? It's at the bottom of the front steps."

"You seem to be attached to that dog. Literally."

Kat wrapped her arms around Joel's waist, leaned her head against his chest, and looked down at Roxy. "I'm trying to keep her close, so she doesn't disappear. Tracy says Roxy thinks hiding is funny. I'm not amused by that sort of thing, particularly after the last dog we had here kept escaping. And Roxy is so tiny that I might never find her again. What if she got hurt? She's already only got three legs."

"Okay. But you'll have to let go of me first."

Kat looked up into his face. "You feel good. Maybe I could put the dog in her crate for her nap. Then I would be free to do other things."

He bent to kiss her. "Will I like these things?"

"I'm pretty sure you will."

Later, Kat was lying snuggled next to Joel with her head resting below his collarbone. She stroked his forearm absently. Now that he was in a good mood, she should get this conversation over with. "So um, my mother called today."

Joel opened his eyes and stared at the ceiling. "Uh-oh."

"She was nicer than usual; it was sort of strange. Maybe something is going on…I think she wants to visit. But I haven't, um, exactly mentioned that you're living here. I didn't suggest that she come up here, but it seemed like she was angling for an invitation."

Joel rolled over to look at Kat. "I thought she hated the fact that you live in Alpine Grove. She wants you to move back to the city and get a real job, right?"

"That was when she was trying to keep my family ancestry a secret. Now that everyone knows the whole complicated story about how I was adopted, I think she doesn't care that I live here anymore. Maybe she's curious to see the house again…I have no idea." The workings of her mother's mind were a mystery to just about everyone, particularly Kat.

He tilted his head. "Do you want to see her?"

"I'm not sure. She's my mother. But as you know, we don't exactly get along. And I think that the level of dirt and dog hair here might send her into some sort of neat-freak apoplectic seizure. She's really not good with dust. Or my boyfriends. At least the past ones, anyway." That was an understatement.

Joel sat up and rearranged the pillows. He gripped the back of his neck with his hand and leaned back. "Your family has a long history of secrecy. Am I now one of those secrets?"

"No. Well, not really, anyway. I just try to avoid discussing my personal life with my mother, since it usually doesn't end well. But it's going to be pretty obvious I'm not alone here if she shows up."

"I'm not sure what you're saying here. Do you want me to move out?"

Kat's heart skipped in her chest. "What? No. Definitely not." Could she possibly screw up this conversation any more than she already had?

"My place is just sitting there empty. It's not like I don't have somewhere I can go."

"That's not what I meant." She gripped his hand. "I just wanted you to know, that's all. There's a chance my mother could show up. I mean, I hope not, but you never know with her. She could just decide to drive up here and there she'd be, just standing there on my doorstep. I mean *our* doorstep." Kat groaned. "And that would be awful on so many levels."

Joel reached over and caressed her cheek with his fingertips. "Sometimes you confuse me."

"I know. Sometimes I confuse myself."

Chapter 3

Black Berets

The Turd made it to the city without any automotive incidents, which was nothing short of a miracle. Tracy knew it was a risk taking the ancient car on a road trip, because there was always the possibility that it would have some type of anxiety attack under the hood and decide that remaining in motion was just too much for its tender sensibilities. With a great sense of relief, Tracy collapsed that night at Shelby's apartment. The next morning, they took the bus to campus and Shelby pointed Tracy in the right direction to make it to her class.

Tracy walked into the room and zeroed in on a place to sit. Tables were set up with two computers sitting on each one. She took a seat at one of the empty tables and examined the machine in front of her. When was the last time she'd even used a computer? It would be totally humiliating if she killed it. The professor didn't appear to have arrived yet. Tracy put her hands in her lap and looked around the room at her fellow classmates. She couldn't hurt the computer while it was off, anyway.

All the other students in the room seemed to know what they were doing. Every one of them was dressed in black. Who wore a black turtleneck in sunny Southern California, anyway? Probably they were all art majors. Maybe all the art snobs had gone digital by now.

In her college art classes, Tracy had discovered that many art majors spent far more time ruminating on the aesthetic and social value of art, rather than actually producing art. Because they tended to wear all black all the time, she referred to them as the "black-beret crowd." The most pretentious black berets focused on brush strokes and the importance of the medium in "the work." But did brush strokes even exist in digital artwork? What would they talk about now?

Tracy sighed. This class was likely to be strange and awkward. She shouldn't have come. Who was she kidding? One weekend class wasn't going to give her enough information to get a job doing this stuff. And what she really needed was a job, not flashbacks to the days of blundering aimlessly through college art classes.

Tracy turned in her chair and looked at the door. Shelby would be so disappointed if she just bailed out on this class. A tall, lanky man wearing baggy pants and a light-blue shirt that didn't fit quite right scuttled through the doorway and upon spotting the empty seat next to Tracy, strode across the room and put his backpack down on the table with a *thunk*. He smiled at Tracy and pushed his glasses farther up on his nose. "Hi. This is the Photoshop class, right?"

Tracy nodded. "Yes. But I don't think the instructor is here yet. Maybe she is running late."

"That's a relief." He sat down in the chair next to her. "I couldn't find a parking place anywhere. I felt like I was walking for miles, and then I ended up at the wrong building. It's been a long morning."

"A friend showed me which building to go to, so that helped a lot. I'm sure I would have gotten lost." Tracy tried to smile sympathetically. "But you made it." And sat next to her. Perfect. So much for all that extra table space.

The man took off his glasses and rubbed the bridge of his nose. He pulled a notepad and pencils out of his backpack and paused to turn and put out his hand. "I'm Rob."

Tracy shook his hand. "I'm Tracy. Do you know much about this software?"

Rob shook his head. "Not really. At my job, I set up computer networks and satellite services. My boss wanted a web site, so I created one for the company. But he thought it was ugly, so they're sending me to this class so I can fix it."

"How bad could it be?" She wouldn't know a good web site from a bad one.

"I guess it needs more graphics. And my boss called the colors I selected *horrifying*, which I thought was a little harsh." He looked down at his row of pencils and picked one up to study it. "I warned them before I started that everything I've ever tried to draw ends up looking like a three-year-old's rendition of a pig. I'm not really artistic at all, so I'm not sure how much this class is going to help."

Tracy leaned forward and put her elbows on the table. "I took some art classes in college, but I don't have a computer, so I'm not sure about this either. My friend gave me a free coupon so I could take the class, which was really nice of her, since normally it's pretty expensive. But without a computer of my own, I'm not going to be able to try out anything we learn here. So it's probably all kind of pointless." Why was she telling this guy all this? It was time to shut up now.

Rob put on his glasses again and looked around the room. "I think we may be the only ones here who are old enough to drink."

"Thanks for bringing that up." Tracy noted the row of pencils and notepad neatly arranged on Rob's side of the table. She probably should have brought something to write on. Maybe they'd have handouts. She rummaged in her bag and pulled out a tiny notepad that she used for grocery lists.

Rob handed her the perfectly sharpened pencil he was holding. "Do you need something to write with? I brought a bunch."

"Thanks." She looked around the room again. "Where do you suppose the instructor is?"

"I don't know. I hope she shows up. A lot of people ask me about web sites. It would be great if I can learn enough here that I can create web sites that aren't hideous. Then I could get out of the networking business. At least creating web sites would be inside work. Crawling around on ladders to attach satellite dishes on buildings is starting to get to me."

"Yeah, I guess that would be harsh. At least, it's warm here. It could be worse. You could live in Alaska or something." Tracy wanted to laugh at his earnest expression. She could certainly relate to the desire for a career change. He was kind of goofy–looking, with unruly brows and a long face. The overall disheveled look kind of reminded her of Shaggy in *Scooby-Doo*. Behind the wire-rimmed glasses, he had tawny hazel eyes, which were surprisingly expressive. Right now, he was so intent on what he was saying, it softened the overall Shaggy impression. But if he said "Zoinks," she really would burst out laughing.

A large woman charged into the room and the door slammed behind her. She had a black beret jauntily placed on her wild curly black hair and wore thick glasses with severe black frames. Setting her books on the desk at the front of the room, she exclaimed, "Ladies and gentlemen, turn on your computers. It's time to make art!"

Along with everyone else in the room, Tracy and Rob straightened in their chairs and rummaged around to find the power switch on the computer. Class had begun.

~

After class, Tracy took the bus back to Shelby's apartment. Her brain felt like mush after a whole day of learning about paths, masks, filters, and layers. Who knew messing around with a bunch of pixels could be so complicated?

On the other hand, she had learned enough to create a pretty cool drawing of Roxy. She had also discovered why Rob's boss might have considered his color choices "horrifying." Maybe Rob wasn't just nearsighted. He might actually be color-blind. It seemed to be the only possible explanation for the grotesque creations she saw on his monitor.

Maybe she'd sit next to someone else tomorrow. Perhaps she'd just taken a lot of art classes, but Rob seemed to have the aesthetic sensibilities of a goat. He also didn't seem to realize that what he was creating was repellent. To her credit, the instructor, Ms. Melina, had tried to remain encouraging, but the expression on her face was telling. As she squinted through the heavy lenses of her glasses at his creations on the screen, she looked like she'd eaten a rotten lemon.

Shelby had given Tracy the key to her place, so she let herself in and was greeted by Billy Bob, the jumbo cat. Even Squiggy, the stinky gray tabby at the vet clinic the other day, was small by comparison. Billy Bob was a proud orange member of the 20-pounder club. It wasn't just that he was fat, which he was, but he was also tall, burly, and extremely furry, which added to his imposing feline presence. The cat lumbered toward Tracy, his prodigious gut swinging back and forth as he approached.

Tracy crouched down to say hello. "Hey, Billy Bob. How's the mega-cat?"

Billy Bob flopped over on his back and exposed his pale orange-and-white underbelly for Tracy to rub. He curled his paws up to his chest and closed his eyes, obviously expecting Tracy to comply with his demand for affection.

At the sound of the door unlocking, Tracy stood and turned. Shelby walked into the room and threw her book bag on the entry table. She looked down at the expanse of orange cat. "So are you falling for the charms of that big ole lug? That fine figure of a feline, Billy Bob, obviously has you trained."

"Yes. He's a sweetheart, although I didn't appreciate finding him on my head this morning when I woke up. Breakfast is clearly an important part of his day."

At the comment, Billy Bob stood up to his full height, stretched, and bellowed a throaty meow.

Shelby chuckled. "Yes my liege, I'll get right on that cat-food program."

"So what's in the bag?"

Shelby looked down at the grocery sack she was holding. "I stopped by the store. I know you wanted to go out somewhere, but let's face it—you know neither of us can afford that. I took that cash you lent me for lunch and bought dinner. We're eating in."

"Yeah, I suppose you're right. It's my last chance to see the big city and I'm broke. I hate this."

"Oh, it won't be so bad darlin'." Shelby put down the bag on the kitchen counter. "I edited a paper for another grad student and she was so happy that she gave me a bottle of wine." She pulled a bottle out of the bag and presented it to Tracy with a flourish.

Tracy examined the label. "Hmm. Do you suppose *last* year was a *good* year?"

"Don't look gift hooch in the mouth. It's better than no year, which is what we had before."

Tracy put the bottle down. "That's true. So what's for dinner?"

"I know you've been eating that nasty packaged pasta stuff, so I'm gonna get some good Southern food into you. It will help your brain power. You just watch."

"At my place, we refer to that packaged pasta stuff as dinner."

Shelby paused in her kitchen organizing. "I know. And that's just sad. So tonight we're having black-eyed peas, greens, and my famous homemade corn bread. It's good for you, and the total cost for both of us is less than five dollars."

"Greens? You know how I feel about vegetables." Tracy picked up the evil bundle of leaves. "At least it's not grits."

"This food is part of my heritage. And you know you love my corn bread."

"That's true. It is amazing. You have won over countless men with that recipe. They date you just to get more of the stuff." That and the fact that Shelby was beautiful in an elfin way. She had a round face and a sweet smile that seemed to turn men into a puddle of quivering gelatinous goo.

"My grandma's corn bread recipe is my secret weapon." The corner of Shelby's mouth turned up in a small, knowing smile. "You could learn a thing or two from watching me cook, you know."

"I suppose. I hope you're right about my brain power too. Today I thought my brain would explode. Why do they make software so complicated? It's like it's out to get me."

Shelby poured some of the wine into two glasses and handed one to Tracy. "Cheers! Don't think of the software as complicated. Think of it as empowering. Remember how you struggled with paints? You can't erase paint with just a click."

"My apartment is ample proof of that. I'm hoping my mother doesn't stop by. There was a cerulean blue incident that it's probably better she not know about."

"So other than the software being complicated, did you enjoy the class?"

"Sort of. At first, the guy I was sitting next to was afraid the instructor wouldn't show."

Shelby tilted her glass toward Tracy. "Guy? Is there something you aren't telling me?"

"No. I tried to make myself look large like I needed the whole table to myself, but it didn't work. He spotted the empty seat. I guess he was harmless enough. At least he wasn't some art snob. I created a picture of Roxy that I thought was okay. The layering effects you can create are cool. Once I figured out how to do some stuff, the time flew by."

Shelby sipped her wine. "See! That's great. You're so talented. I wish you'd stayed around here and gotten an art degree."

"It wasn't meant to be." Tracy twirled the wine in her glass. It was a deep, rich burgundy color that almost looked velvety as it swirled around. "After I dropped out twice and pretty much flunked the biology program, effectively killing the idea of vet school, my father said there was no way he'd pay for any more college. And he told me an art degree would be useless as far as getting a job. You know I've never had enough money to try and go back myself. I can barely pay my tiny rent. Now, it all just seems pointless. I can paint by myself whenever I want, after all. So what do I need a degree for, anyway? Plus, I don't miss the black-beret crowd."

Shelby shook her head. "It just bothers me that you didn't pursue something you enjoy. That's what school is for."

"Not according to my father." Tracy put down her glass and leaned on the counter toward Shelby. "Oh, you'll be amused to note, my instructor actually was wearing a black beret when she walked in. I almost laughed out loud!"

"Maybe it's a uniform. So you can pick artists out of a crowd. It's like at home in Alabama where you can spot the biggest loser rednecks because they wear their baseball hats turned backwards. And then they're shading their eyes with their hand. There's some comedian who calls the backwards hat the "stupid sign." All I know is that it's helpful when you're driving. You see a guy with a stupid sign and you know you gotta give him a wide berth. Because you never know what dumbass maneuver he's gonna pull in that rusty ole Ford pickup of his."

Tracy laughed. "Remind me not to visit your home town. Alpine Grove is bad enough. The hunters are all out in their rusty pickups. But they're wearing camo gear, so they think you can't see them."

~

Joel stood in front of the open pantry in the kitchen. "Kat, could you come here for a minute?"

Kat put down her novel, got up from the sofa, and was followed by three dogs. She stood next to Joel. "What's wrong?" The canines—Lori, Lady, and Linus—stared into the pantry lovingly. The huge wooden box full of human food was always a source of great interest.

Joel pointed at a huge plastic jug in the cabinet. "What is that?"

"Mustard."

"I know that. It's a lot of mustard. No one needs this much mustard, except maybe a baseball concession stand."

Kat shook her head. "The grocery store has a new restaurant-supply aisle. Maria thought it was incredible. I didn't notice that she'd grabbed this until we were checking out."

"How can you not notice when your friend puts a six-pound jar of mustard into your cart?"

"I was trying to keep her from buying any more Twinkies. We have more than enough."

"That's for sure." Joel sighed. "Could you return the mustard? It's not opened. Just because something is a good deal doesn't mean it's a good idea."

"All right. I discovered it when she was here and I didn't want to hurt her feelings. She did buy a lot of food for us."

"Mustard is a fine condiment, but it's not something we can live on. What do you want for dinner?"

Kat gazed at the pantry and then grinned at him. "Well you've ruled out mustard and Twinkies. That really limits our options, you know."

Joel grabbed some cans and walked to the kitchen. "I'll wing it. Would you chop up some carrots for me?"

Kat headed for the refrigerator, followed by the three dogs. "I'm on it."

Joel started opening cans and dumping them into a pot. "You have a parade of large dogs following you. What did you do with the little one? Where's the dachshund?"

Kat looked around her. "She was right next to me." She bent down to look under Linus's hairy body. "Okay guys. Where is Roxy?" All three dogs wagged, but none of them gave any indication that they had any clue where the dachshund had gone.

"You didn't lose the dog, did you?"

Kat stood up and put her hands on her hips. "*Lose* is such a strong word. Roxy is here somewhere. I'll look around." She went back to the living room and looked under the sofa and end tables. Lori licked her ear. "Yuck. Lori, why do you *always* have to do that?"

A small yip noise came from the direction of the kitchen. Kat pushed Lori away and stood up. "Did you hear that?"

Joel stopped chopping carrots. "I heard something. Was it the dog?"

Kat started back toward the kitchen. There was a louder woof and all the dogs ran back to the kitchen and stared at the walls and cabinets.

Joel put down the knife and leaned back against the counter. "Was it from inside or outside? She didn't get out, did she?"

Kat's shoulders slumped. "I hope not. She doesn't really do stairs, but I'll go look, just in case." She waved at the dogs. "Let's go, everyone." It was pouring rain and Kat grabbed an umbrella and a raincoat on her way out. The dogs thundered down the front steps and then turned to glare at Kat. She waved at them. "I know. Yes, it's raining. Get over it. Look for Roxy. You're dogs. Use your noses. Sniff her out."

Linus shook his huge body, spewing water on the other dogs, who leapt away from him. They all sniffed around half-heartedly for a few moments. Lori and Lady were not fans of wet weather, so they went back up the steps and stood on the front landing, looking soggy and annoyed.

Linus followed Kat around the yard as she called for Roxy. His tail drooped and water dripped off his long brown coat. Kat looked down at him. "Sorry, Big Guy. I hope Roxy wasn't stupid enough to go out in this. We'll never find her."

The front door opened and Kat turned at the sound of Lady's and Lori's scrabbling claws as they ran back inside the house. Joel stood on the landing and said, "I think you're right. I don't think she's out there. She barked again and I'm pretty sure it came from inside somewhere. It was too close."

Kat patted Linus's head. "Thank goodness. It's horrible out here."

Back in the house, Kat pulled off her sodden coat and walked into the kitchen. "That is a seriously cold rain. I'm freezing."

Joel smiled and put his arms around her. "Look at the bright side. It's not snow. Now you know why I'm so motivated to get firewood."

Kat shuddered and huddled in closer. "I'm not sure I'm cut out for winter." At the sound of another yipping noise, she pulled her head away from his chest. "Was that Roxy?"

"Presumably. Somewhere."

Kat looked up into his face. "She's in the kitchen. Could she have gotten into the cabinets? Tracy told me she got into her pots and pans. But how could I not hear that? I was *right* here." She walked over to the kitchen and crouched down. "Roxy? Are you in there?"

A little yip noise came from the corner cabinet. Kat opened it and sat cross-legged on the floor, pulling pots and pans off the lazy Susan. "Roxy? It's okay. Where are you?"

Joel crouched down and looked over her shoulder. "There's no dog in there."

"But I heard her. She's in there somewhere. What's behind the cabinet?"

"A wall? Move over and let me look."

Kat picked up the pots and pans and put them on the counter while Joel reached around in the back of the corner cabinet. "There's a loose piece of wood here behind the lazy Susan, but I can't get at it."

Kat said sweetly, "Oh Roxeeey, are you in there?" and received a small *yip* in reply. "Uh-oh."

Joel stood up and turned off the burner for the soup on the stove. "I think dinner may be delayed. I'll go get my tools."

Kat sat in front of the corner cabinet. "Are you okay, Roxy? Don't worry. Joel is good at getting animals out of small spaces. He's had lots of practice. You'll be okay."

Joel returned and sat in front of the cabinet, next to Kat. "I need to take the lazy Susan out first. Then I might need to lift the counter." He positioned himself on his back inside the cabinet so his head and shoulders were inside. "Could you shine the flashlight in here?"

Kat complied. "If you have to kill the kitchen to get this dog, I'm going to be depressed."

Joel mumbled something unintelligible and began removing pieces of the lazy Susan mechanism and handing them to Kat. Finally, he extricated himself from the cabinet and sat on the floor next to her. "I can hear Roxy scrabbling around back there. I think there's a strip of wood that she was able to push in, but then it wouldn't go the other way, so she can't get out."

Kat put the flashlight in her lap. "What is it with the animals here? It's like they become possessed and need to explore the deepest recesses of this house."

Joel shook his head and shoved aside the pieces of the cabinet on the floor, so he could reorient himself in the cabinet again. He grabbed a saw and stretched out on his stomach with his head and shoulders inside the cabinet. "I think I can avoid messing with the counter if I just cut out this piece of wood. Look out, Roxy."

Kat peered over his shoulder. "Be good, Roxy. Watch out for any blades you might see go by."

After slowly and methodically sawing for a few minutes, Joel yanked on the piece of wood, which gave way with a crack. The dog jumped up over his arm and ran down his back into the kitchen. Joel jerked away, whacked his arm on the cabinet, and yelled a long string of descriptive phrases about Roxy's heritage.

Kat grinned. "Wow, you have a bigger vocabulary than I thought."

"Just get the dog, please," he said through clenched teeth.

"Okay, I'm on it."

Chapter 4

Nothing to Hide

Tracy got to the second day of class a little late. By the time she arrived, the typical educational social dynamic had come into play and everyone had already claimed the same seats they had been in the day before. Tracy sat down at the table in the seat next to Rob, who gave her a friendly smile in welcome.

After an evening talking to Shelby about the dangers of feline obesity and her various artistic endeavors, Tracy was feeling better about coming to class this morning. Dr. Cassidy would be proud of her for giving Shelby the fat-cat lecture, because Billy Bob really did need to lose some weight. And unlike Tracy's parents, Shelby was supportive of Tracy's interest in art. Shelby even had one of Tracy's paintings hanging on her wall as a show of solidarity. Since it was her friend who had insisted that she finish the piece, it was fitting that she should have it.

The instructor, Ms. Melina, told everyone to open their files from yesterday. Tracy looked at her drawing of Roxy and missed her little dog. She had captured Roxy's somewhat aloof and demanding personality in the expression on her face and the jaunty tilt of her head. Part of today's class was to print the image. All the printouts would be hung on the wall and then each student would explain how the drawing was created. Other people then could make suggestions about how the artwork could be improved. Fortunately, as an art-class veteran, Tracy wasn't as afraid of critiques as she used to be. And at least her image of Roxy was better than the thing Rob had created.

Tracy jumped in her chair as Ms. Melina bellowed, "It's time to make art! Start a new file!" After hurriedly clicking on some menus, Tracy was greeted by a blank white screen. The instructor rattled off a list of instructions and Tracy clicked furiously, trying to keep up. She turned and peeked at Rob, who looked a little disturbed. He raised his eyebrows at her and Tracy shook her head slightly.

The entire class seemed to vibrate in unison as a loud siren went off. The screeching noise was insufferable, yet Ms. Melina managed to yell over the din, "Save your files now. We have to leave the building."

Tracy clicked and at the very moment she pressed the *OK* button, her stomach clenched. Where had her detailed digital painting of Roxy gone? She had spent all of yesterday slaving over that thing. Did she now have only an almost-blank image with two black lines on it? How could she be so completely stupid? She slumped in her chair and closed her eyes as her classmates all rushed to gather their things.

Rob reached over and tapped her shoulder. "Come on. We've gotta go. I think I actually smell smoke."

Tracy shut off the computer. "Okay, I'm coming." She grabbed her bag and followed Rob toward the door and mumbled, "Stupid computer. I hope you fry."

Everyone filed out of the building and gathered on the lawn. Tracy stood next to Rob and placed her bag on the ground. The students stared at the windows, looking for any sign of smoke or flames. The jangling sound of the siren was starting to get to Tracy and she bent to pick up her bag, and took a few steps back to get farther away. Rob gave her a sidelong glance, then looked away. Was he checking out her butt? Ignoring him, she looked up at the sky, watching the clouds swirl around. One of them looked like an African elephant talking to a refrigerator. How long did they have to stand out here? Couldn't they leave yet?

Ms. Melina waved at the students, who were slowly starting to disperse across the grassy area. "Wait! You can't go. Everyone come over here, next to this tree."

Once all of the students had reassembled in front of her, the instructor said, "I haven't heard what's going on, but I have counted and it seems you're all here and not burning up into little cinders inside. So let's just take our lunch break early. Meet back here at two o'clock. I hope I don't have to tell you that if the building is truly on fire, please do not go inside. We'll reschedule the class. However, since I don't see smoke, I'm betting someone just wanted to get out of a test. I'll see you here in two hours."

Relieved to finally be able to get away from the awful noise, Tracy turned and started walking away from the din. There had to be a convenience store around here somewhere. She had two dollars budgeted for a lunch of pretzels, crackers, and a soda, but now she really wanted to get some aspirin too. That was going to cut into her funds.

Rob ran up alongside her. "Hi. Since we have some time, would you like to go to lunch with me?"

Tracy shook her head. "I was just going to get something at a quick mart somewhere. Have you seen anything like a 7-Eleven nearby?"

"No. There's a great deli, though. And we actually have time to eat lunch, thanks to the alarm, so we don't have to rush."

"Sorry. This might sound like a lame excuse, but I can't afford that." With the exception of the last two dollars, she'd given her cash to Shelby again so her friend could have lunch.

Rob's bushy brows came together momentarily and then his expression lightened. "Don't worry about that! It's my treat. I want to talk to you about your drawing yesterday." He pointed toward a building. "The place is right over there."

Tracy smiled at his enthusiasm. "Well, okay. If you don't mind paying, I don't mind eating. I thought the drawing we did yesterday was fun, didn't you?"

"Not exactly." He readjusted his backpack on his shoulder, hunching over like a turtle retreating into its shell. "I know guys aren't supposed to cry, but that thing I drew was enough to make a grown man weep. Even I could see that."

"What was it? Or was it an abstract?" All artists knew that the term "abstract" could be used to tactfully indicate that a piece of art had no resemblance to anything in the real world. Sometimes abstracts were created on purpose. And sometimes not. Fortunately, Rob probably wasn't aware of that little verbal nuance.

Rob gestured toward the sky. "It was going to be a sunset. Then I changed my mind and it was going to be an ocean scene. Then I deleted something and it just got worse."

"The colors were...interesting."

"I know. Nothing like that exists in nature. Well, maybe after the apocalypse it might, but not now."

Tracy laughed. "Thank goodness for that! At least you don't seem too worried about it."

Rob opened the door at the deli for Tracy. "I was hoping I could talk to you about that. But first, what do you want to eat?"

They perused the menu, ordered, and sat down at a table with their sandwiches. Rob had been right; the place was great and Tracy dug into her huge avocado-filled veggie sandwich with gusto. She paused to pick a wayward clover sprout off her chin. "This is so good. Thank you! So you wanted to talk about your artwork for the class. Is there anything I can do to help?"

Rob put down his sandwich and leaned forward. "Well, last night after I got home, I had a message from someone who wants a huge web site. From a technical standpoint, it's really exciting, with lots of back-end databases."

"Uh, you think databases are exciting?" Was he kidding? And what was a back-end database? Something dirty? The Internet was supposed to be full of porn, after all. Ick.

"When it comes to web sites, including database technology like that means it is going to cost money. Lots of money. They even want to tie in the real-estate multiple-listing databases so people can look at houses online. A real-estate web site for a tourist area could be a big deal. Businesses could advertise. There isn't much like that out there now. It would be leading-edge."

Tracy tried not to roll her eyes at all the techno-zeal. "So it's not porn. That's good. But what does that have to do with your artwork for this class?"

Rob took a sip of water. "You've seen what I can—and mostly can't—do in Photoshop. There's no way I can even talk about design with these guys without sounding like a complete idiot. Maybe you could help me?"

Tracy picked up her last potato chip and waved it at him. "I don't think so. How could I do that? I told you, I don't even have a computer. I can't talk about databases. No way. Plus, you don't even know me." She popped the chip into her mouth and looked up at the clock on the wall. "Hey, we should be getting back."

Rob readjusted his glasses, glanced at the clock, and pushed his chair back to stand up. "I know you have an eye for design. Maybe we can talk about this a little after class?"

Tracy stood up and gathered her tray. "Yeah, maybe. I have to figure out what I'm going to do for the rest of class. I think I killed my drawing from yesterday."

"How could you have killed it? It was great."

"I saved the stupid lines we drew this morning and then my drawing from yesterday was just gone. I'm kind of hoping that the computer died in the fire so I don't flunk the course." She was doing it again. Why did she continually blab to Rob about everything? She needed some type of electronic zapper to get herself to shut up.

He grabbed his backpack and turned to her. "Depending on what happened, I might be able to find the file for you and get it back. If I can do that, will you at least talk to me a little more about this project?"

Tracy inclined her head in a mock bow and twirled her hands in an elaborate supplicant wave. "If you can get my image back, you'll be my geek hero."

"Okay. I'm fine with that."

∼

Although there was a slight smoky smell in the building, whatever fire had set off the alarm must have been small and localized, so class resumed after all. Rob sat in front of Tracy's computer and pecked at the keys. "I got it."

Tracy leaned over his shoulder to look at the monitor. "That's fantastic!" She squeezed his shoulders with both hands. "You *are* my geek hero. I might not flunk!" For a geek, he had surprisingly muscular shoulders.

His lip curved in a half smile and he looked at her out of the corner of his eye. "No, you definitely won't. I might. But you won't."

Ms. Melina walked in and said, "Everyone sit down. It's time to make art!"

Tracy and Rob rearranged themselves so they were in front of their own computers again. Tracy smiled at her image of Roxy. What a relief. She slowly and carefully saved the file and then saved it again with another name that included the word "backup" so she'd have more than one copy, in case the inevitable happened and she screwed something up.

After some final instructions about creating Photoshop brushes, it was time for the critique. Tracy printed her picture of Roxy and carried it over to the wall. She hung it up and smiled again. Something about the dog's expression and the colors she'd used made Tracy unreasonably happy.

All the students pulled up chairs and arranged them in a semicircle in front of the images hanging on the wall. When it was her turn, Tracy explained her process. When she was done, the class fell into silence. No one said anything for what seemed like forever and Tracy's heart sank. Everyone hated it. Just like every other thing she'd tried, she couldn't do this either. She cleared her throat, "Um, well, I know it could be improved. I should have added shading under Roxy's chin. Roxy is my dog, by the way. I just drew it from memory. It's not really that good. Maybe if I'd had a photograph to work from I could have made it better."

Ms. Melina's black curls bobbed back and forth as she shook her head. "No. This is your artistic vision. It's not supposed to look like a photograph. It's your vision of your pet in your heart. It's very honest. I love it. I can't think of any way you could improve it. Frankly, I'm impressed. Given how difficult some of the tools in Photoshop are to use, I think you've done a brilliant job. What does everyone else think?"

At the many mumbles of assent, Tracy sat up straight in her chair. "Really? Thank you. That means a lot."

Ms. Melina pointed at the student next to Tracy. "Okay, next. John, please tell us how you created this image."

For Tracy, the rest of the critique passed in a blur. She made some suggestions to some of the other students on their artwork, but she kept looking back at her own drawing of Roxy. She had created something other people liked. It was looking like she'd pass the course and get her certificate of completion, after all.

After class, she asked Ms. Melina if she could print a couple more copies of her image. Once she had saved multiple copies of her files on a disk and had her printouts, Tracy was ready to head back to Shelby's place. She couldn't wait to show the drawing to her friend. Maybe she could buy a frame and give one of the copies to her as a thank you. As she gathered up her things, Tracy was almost giddy at the idea. Shelby would love it!

Rob stood next to Tracy, slowly collecting his notebook and pencils. As he jammed his printout into his backpack, the expression on his face was decidedly unhappy. The other students had quite a bit to say about his artwork and the discussion took such a negative turn that Tracy started to feel bad for him. He was a nice guy and she'd been in that situation before. It could be upsetting to have your creative work verbally dissected and analyzed.

Rob paused in his packing to push his glasses back up to the bridge of his nose. He gave her a sidelong glance and asked in a somber voice, "Do you still have time to talk? I did find your file for you."

"Yes, you did!" Tracy reached over and squeezed his arm. "I'm forever grateful. Do you want to have a cup of coffee or something at the deli? Since you paid for lunch, I've still got two dollars burning a hole in my pocket."

The expression on his face brightened. "Sure, that sounds great." He threw his backpack over his shoulder and they went outside. As they made their way across the lawn, he seemed to shrug off the events of the last few hours. "I think I told you that I have this big potential web site contract. What I was hoping is that you could go to a meeting with me."

Tracy glanced at him. He was clutching the strap of the backpack with both hands and looking down at the grass as he walked. She said, "I don't live around here. And I have a job." Sadly, it was just one job now. At least she still had one source of income left, so she wasn't completely unemployed and destitute yet.

Rob kicked a rock with his sneaker, causing it to skitter across the sidewalk. "Where do you live?"

"Alpine Grove. It's a little town."

"Oh, I know it. That's perfect. It's not that far away. Couldn't you come back here for the meeting?"

Tracy gripped the handle of her bag more tightly. "I have to work. And at the risk of sounding like I'm financially challenged, I can't skip out on work again, because I need the money. I can't take any more time off. My boss will kill me." *Financially challenged* was a far more pleasant way to say she was totally broke and almost homeless.

"I'd just need you for this meeting. Whether or not I get the contract, you're off the hook. If I get it, I'll have money to hire a freelancer to actually do the work."

Tracy stopped in front of the deli and turned to face him. "Is this something unethical? Or illegal? Because I don't want any part of it, if that's the case."

Rob opened the door for her. "No, not really. Well, maybe it's a little deceitful to imply that you'd be doing the design later, I guess. But that happens all the time with this type of contract. People hire freelancers that come and go. You said you don't do that type of work anyway, right? But I know you can talk about color theory and contrast and all that artsy stuff. All you have to do is pretend to be an artist for one meeting. It will be great!"

Tracy was busy rummaging in her purse for her two dollars, but paused to look at him. "*Great* is definitely not the first word that comes to mind here."

They got their coffee and carried it to a table. Tracy sat down and encircled the mug with her hands. "So why should I do this? I don't even know you."

"I'll pay you. How about $500?"

Tracy gripped the mug more tightly. That would pay her rent and then some. She could buy something other than fire-sale bulk boxes of ramen noodles at the grocery store.

"Um. Well, that makes it more interesting. I'd need to talk to some people first. But I still don't know anything about you."

"What do you want to know?"

Tracy stirred some sugar into her coffee. "I don't know. What is your shoe size?"

He took a sip of coffee. "Really? That's the best you can do? Thirteen."

She peered under the table. "Those are some big feet!" He had large hands too. Was it true what they said about that? Hmm. "Okay. Are you afraid of the dark?"

"No. Are you?"

Tracy shook her finger at him. "Hey, I'm asking the questions here. It depends on where I am. If I were in an old cemetery in a scary neighborhood with alien neon werewolves creeping around, then yes. But if I'm walking around downtown Alpine Grove, no."

"Anything else? How are my shoe size and neon werewolves related to the meeting?"

"Fine. Where did you grow up?"

"A galaxy far, far away."

Tracy scowled. "Oh, come on. That's not helpful. How am I supposed to know you're not some creepy serial killer or something?"

Rob waved his hands in front of himself. "Do I *look* like a serial killer to you?"

"Not really, but serial killers never do, right? And if you were one, would you tell me?"

"I have nothing to hide." Rob rummaged around in his backpack and pulled out his wallet. He held up a stack of cards and began laying them on the table. "Here's my driver's license. And a business card for the networking company I work for with my phone number and e-mail address. This is my library card. And here's my American Express card."

Tracy flashed a grin at him. "Oooh, a gold card. You didn't leave home without it. I don't think a serial killer would show me his gold card." She pointed at his chest. "And the logo on the business card is the same as the one embroidered on your shirt."

He looked down and pulled the shirt away from his body to examine the logo. "I could have stolen the shirt."

"I don't think so. No one steals logo wear." She waved at the cards on the table. "Fine. You have convinced me you're really Robert J. Thompson, a networking guy with big feet who reads books. I suppose I can go to this meeting if you want. But I need to talk to my friend Shelby. I'm staying with her while I'm taking this class, and I'd have to do that again. And I need to talk to my boss at work. When is the meeting?"

"They said they want to talk sometime next week. I can ask them if we can do it Friday afternoon so you can come down for the weekend again. Would that work?"

"I guess so."

"Great! I'll give you a call this week with the details after I get it set up."

After finishing their coffee, they exchanged phone numbers and shook hands. Tracy went to the bus stop and sat down on the bench to wait for her public transportation to arrive. She still didn't have a completely good feeling about this arrangement. Rob seemed nice enough. And five-hundred dollars was five-hundred dollars. But what if she screwed up this meeting? It wouldn't be the first time she'd choked under pressure. But hey, Rob had asked her to do this, even after seeing how pathetic she was at saving and finding computer files. The guy knew what he was getting into.

~

Tracy drove The Turd down the driveway toward Kat's house. After grabbing her stuff from Shelby's place, she had experienced a long, unpleasant drive through horrible city traffic. In a way, bumping slowly through the potholes littered throughout the driveway was a relief. At least she was away from other drivers intent on going eighty miles an hour. The freeway was a scary place for a car that couldn't go faster than sixty. Or okay, maybe fifty-five. Here deep in the forest, it was pitch dark and pouring rain, which made the giant road craters difficult to spot until the front end of the car splashed into one of the swampy lakes. But the old car was a veteran of far worse rural roads, so it didn't really matter. It wasn't like the thing could get any uglier or more beat up.

At last, the lights of the house appeared through the foggy darkness. The muddy smears on the windshield made the view look like a poorly done painting you might find above the bed at a cheap motel. Tracy parked as close to the front of the house as she could. She leaped out of the car, slammed the door, and ran up the steps to the landing. Fortunately, there was a roof over the area, but she still huddled as close as she could to the door and rapped her knuckles on the tongue-and-groove wood.

Kat opened the door, let Tracy in, and said, "You made it! Roxy is going to be so glad to see you."

Tracy rushed through the door and stood dripping in the entryway. "Ugh, it's just pouring out there. The fall rains have arrived. And it's only going to get worse."

"Please come in. Why don't you take off that wet coat and warm up while I go get Roxy? Joel finally fired up the wood stove because he got tired of listening to me whine about being cold."

Tracy took off her coat and walked into the kitchen, where it was significantly warmer. "I'm not a big fan of cold either. I think you and I may be in trouble when winter arrives for real."

Kat walked toward the back of the house and disappeared into the bedroom. The crate door clanged and Roxy came rushing out. Tracy bent down and gathered the little dog in her arms. "Hi there! Were you good?"

The two women loaded Roxy and the crate into the car. They came back inside and stood in the entryway as Tracy rummaged around in her bag for her check. She looked up. "So where is Joel?"

Kat waved in the general direction of the stairs down to the basement. "He's in his office doing nerdy stuff, I think. There was...ah...a little problem and he hurt his arm, which is slowing down his typing, I guess."

"What happened? It wasn't while he was out cutting wood, was it? Is he okay?"

"I wasn't going to bring it up, but he had to get Roxy out of a cabinet. You were right. She has a thing for kitchenware."

"Oh no. I'm sorry." Tracy looked down at the floor. "I guess you're not going to be willing to board her again, are you? That's not unusual, really. No one wants to take care of Roxy after the first time. I can't leave her with my parents and I can't bring her with me to Shelby's place either. Both of them have banished Roxy from their premises. My mom and dad have farm dogs and work all day. The last time I left Roxy at their place, it was bad. They lost her under the woodshed for a while. Roxy thought the whole experience was really fun. Mom was less amused. Dad even less so. In fact, I think he's still mad." He still referred to Roxy as "that long hairy rodent."

Kat leaned against the door. "And your friend won't let her stay either?"

"No. Shelby's cat Billy Bob is bigger than Roxy and they really don't get along. You probably know this, but interspecies disagreements are extremely unpleasant. And a little scary, even. Shelby is my best friend, but she said she'd let me rot out on the street—to use her words—rather than let Roxy in her apartment again."

Kat gestured toward the kitchen. "I guess it's a little comforting to know it's not just me. I suppose it wasn't really that bad. I should have been watching Roxy more closely. She's really good in her crate and she was so sweet sitting next to me on the sofa while I was reading. I guess I got complacent."

Tracy chuckled. "Yeah, that's her M.O. You think, oh what an adorable little dog. She won't do anything. Then half your kitchen is all over the floor."

"Actually, I took the pots and pans out of the cabinet, so I can't blame her for that. Roxy got behind the cabinet and Joel had to take it apart to get her out. That's when he hurt his arm. On a positive note, she can't get back there again. Joel put in a new board and reassembled the lazy Susan one-handed. It was pretty tricky. He was definitely not in a good mood, though. After I put all the pots and pans back in the cabinet, I decided to lay low."

Tracy reached out and touched Kat's forearm. "I'm so sorry. That doesn't sound good. I hate to ask this after what happened, but would you be able to board Roxy again? It would only be one night. This Friday I am supposed to go to a meeting in the city."

The expression on Kat's face was impassive and hard to read, but after an uncomfortably long pause, she finally said, "Okay. It will be fine. I'll talk to Joel."

Tracy let out the breath she'd been holding. "Thank you so much! I'll bring her by here on Friday morning." She'd already mentally spent the $500 Rob was supposed to give her. Rent, food, an oil change for The Turd before winter. Maybe a new coat too.

Tracy left the house before Kat could change her mind. She rushed down the steps through the driving rain and got into the car, where Roxy was contentedly snoozing in the back seat. Tracy turned the heater on full blast, listening to the engine warm up in its sickly, sputtery way. At least the stupid thing started. If it got any colder, the car was going to stage a rebellion.

She turned around in the seat to look at the dog. "Listen here, Roxy, you need to get over this kitchen thing." The dog raised her head. "Yeah, don't look all innocent at me. I found out what you did. And no matter what you think, it was definitely not funny." Roxy wagged the tip of her feathery tail lightly. "No. I don't think they like you. Right now, I'm pretty sure I don't like you. And you had *better* be a good dog on Friday." Roxy put her head down and closed her eyes.

Tracy sighed. The word was getting out about Roxy. Soon no one in Alpine Grove would be willing to take this dog off her hands, even for a weekend. She'd never be able to take a vacation again. Not that she could afford one. She could be trapped here forever.

~

Kat closed the door and leaned back against it. Having Roxy out of the house was a relief. Joel was going to kill her for letting Tracy drop the dog off again on Friday. Linus came over and leaned his large body against her. She stroked the smooth fur on his head. "Yeah, Big Guy. I know. I have to tell him. Let's go downstairs and get it over with."

Linus wagged eagerly and charged down the stairs. Kat followed more slowly and significantly less enthusiastically. She leaned in the doorway of Joel's office. Linus settled into a spot on the floor next to Lady, who was curled up in a tight furry ball. Joel was sitting at his computer, frowning at the monitor. His left hand was grasped around his right forearm, holding it up against his stomach. He looked over his shoulder at her. "Is Roxy gone?"

"Yes. She's Tracy's problem again. Are you feeling any better?"

"I'm okay."

"You don't look okay. You have a death grip on your arm. Shouldn't you go to a doctor?"

"I hate doctors. I'll just take some more aspirin. It's fine."

Kat walked over and stood behind the chair, putting her hands on his broad shoulders. "How do you know your arm isn't broken?"

He looked back up into her face. "You realize you're being a nag about this, right? It's just a bruise. I'm fine."

Kat scowled. The macho thing could be so annoying. "I am not being a nag. I'm just worried. If you broke your arm, you might need a cast or something. It could get worse."

"It's not broken. If it were, when it happened, my arm would have swollen more and been a lot more painful."

Kat ran her fingers through the hair that was curling down past his collar. "How do you know? Have you broken a bone before?"

"Yes."

She trailed her index finger behind his ear. "Would you care to share that story?"

"No."

"Are you sure you're okay? You seem, um, grumpy."

"Pain makes me grumpy."

Kat bent to kiss his cheek. "I'm sorry." She patted his shoulder. "Since you're obviously not in a talkative mood, I'll just share this little tidbit before I go back upstairs. Roxy is returning on Friday."

Joel swiveled the chair around to face her. "You're kidding, right?"

"No. I caved. It's just for one night. I promise I'll keep her attached to me or in her crate. Really."

Kat walked back upstairs followed by Linus, Tessa, and Chelsey. When had Joel broken a bone? She'd make it her mission to find out sooner or later. But right now she had enough other things to worry about. Time for some escapist reading. She settled onto the sofa with her novel. The dogs all flopped on the floor for their evening nap. The phone rang and Kat jumped up. After navigating the canine obstacle course littering the floor, she grabbed the receiver off the ancient harvest-gold wall phone and was greeted by her friend Maria's voice on the other end of the line.

"Hey girlfriend, what's up?"

Kat sat down at the table. "Just another hopping night in Alpine Grove. How's the new place? Better than Melrose?" Maria had just moved to a new apartment. The prior complex where she'd lived had been so filled with neighborhood drama that she'd taken to referring to it as Melrose Place.

"So far, so good. I'm glad to be outta Melrose, that's for sure. I got those weirdo Dungeons and Dragons dudes in the mail room to help me move my stuff. It's amazing what twenty-two-year-old fantasy nerds will do for a slice of pizza. I'm thinking they don't get out much."

"Uh, no. When I worked there, that skinny guy Duncan used to have a creepy way of staring at me."

"I know. When he was lifting boxes, I thought he was gonna kill himself because he wasn't looking where he was going. I had to have some words with him. I told him, 'listen here, they're boobs. Fifty percent of the population has them. I have them. Get over it.' Actually I think I embarrassed him, if you want to know the truth."

"So did he stop the creepy staring?"

"Not really. But these guys probably don't get an up-close look at a fine woman like me very often, so I couldn't blame them too much."

Kat leaned back in her chair and put her feet up on another one. "So now that you're all moved into the new place, have you returned to the job quest?"

"Yes I have. And I need resume help. That's why I'm calling. You're the writer. I am not having much luck getting across my personal abilities in this document. It's too limiting. I need more flexibility, so I can express myself."

"Resumes are about facts, not free expression."

"Whatever. If I send what I have to you, will you look at it?"

"Sure. No problem."

"So how's the sexy engineer?"

Kat dropped her feet off the chair, leaned her elbows on the table and sighed. "I think he might have broken his arm, but he says he didn't."

"What did you two do? Do I even want to know this? Is it something kinky? Or some country-living thing? That rural life you've got going there is dangerous, you know. Farm animals weren't involved, were they?"

"No. You know I only deal with dogs and cats. It's a long story, but basically Joel had to take apart a cabinet and he hit his arm. He got kind of mad about the whole thing." And he was still mad. Silent and surly was not a lot of fun to be around.

"That's probably not doing much for your sex life."

Kat sighed. "No. But thank you for your concern."

"Speaking of your extracurricular activities, how's Aunt Flo? Has she arrived at the station yet?"

Kat leaned her forehead on the table and stared down at her feet on the floor. "No. I don't want to talk about it. And come on, *Aunt Flo*? Who even says that?"

"I was trying to be discreet. You'd prefer Cousin Red? Red tide? Woman trouble? Wait, you're just trying to distract me. It's not me you need to talk to about this, girlfriend. First you need to go to the drugstore and get the little tester thingie. Then, depending on what you find out, you need to bring the engineer in on your little secret. If Kat is having a kitten, he's in a definite need-to-know situation."

Kat sat back up. "I really don't want to talk about... kittens. I mean we're unbelievably careful. When it comes to the perils of unprotected sex, my family tree is filled with a lot of seriously poor role models. I'm completely neurotic about this particular subject. Why me?"

"Don't freak out. You don't know anything yet. Maybe you're just late. Go to the drugstore. Promise me you'll do it."

"Okay. But I'm going to have to drive to some other town somewhere. Because you know someone will see me buying...that. There are no secrets in Alpine Grove. None."

At the sound of footsteps on the stairs, Kat jumped up from her chair. "Oops, I gotta go."

"Engineer alert?"

"Exactly. I'll talk to you later, after I, um, well, you know. But I'll let you know."

"You'd better."

Chapter 5

Plans and Arrivals

Later in the week, after a long day at work at the vet clinic, Tracy was sitting in her apartment watching the tiny TV with Roxy by her side. Even though Tracy had spent her day dealing with an extremely rambunctious Akita, it was still a luxury to not be working at the restaurant anymore. She finally was able to catch up on her sleep and felt better than she had in more than a year.

The phone rang and Tracy stubbed her toe on the box of paints on her way to answer it. Ouch. Now that she had more time, maybe she should clean up this place. Maybe tomorrow.

As promised, Rob was calling with details about the meeting on Friday. Tracy had already asked Shelby if she could freeload again. Her friend had been far more positive about the big meeting than Tracy was herself. Shelby thought it was a great opportunity, but Tracy wasn't so sure. However, given her perpetually precarious financial situation, it was hard to argue with five-hundred bucks, so she wasn't going to dwell on her doubts too much.

Rob sounded different on the phone. His voice was deep and pleasant to listen to, like a mellow radio DJ. He sounded less geeky and more like a grown–up, somehow. As he relayed the details, Tracy fiddled with the coat hanger wire she used to hold together an old lamp. The fix mostly worked, but sometimes it needed a bit of adjustment. Should she suggest To Rob that he leave his backpack at home for the meeting? Of course, that brought up a dreadful question: what was *she* going to wear?

Tracy closed her eyes and tried to focus on what Rob was saying instead of her broken lamp and meager wardrobe. "Okay, so you'll pick me up on Friday at Shelby's place. I'll leave here early, in case traffic is bad again."

Rob said, "That sounds good. I'll pick you up, then we can go to lunch and talk a little more about the project before the meeting."

"Well, maybe you could give me some information now. I have no idea what I'm supposed to be doing. What is this web site even going to be about? You said it is supposed to have real estate listings on it?"

"Yes, that's part of it. The idea is that it will be a tourist destination site with everything that you need to know if you want to visit or move to Alpine Grove."

"What? Alpine Grove? It's about...here?" Tracy glanced at the windows of her apartment, which faced the street.

"Yes. It's so great that you live there! You can bring a local perspective, since you know the area. That will help us sell the deal."

"I'm not sure I'm a great advertisement, but it is my home town, I guess. I'll try to smile and say nice things." Even if there was no way to earn a living, it was a beautiful area.

Rob cleared his throat. "Do you have any pictures you could bring?"

"Maybe. I have snapshots I've taken on camping trips with my family and stuff. A lot of them are kind of old, though." And kind of odd. But it would be hilarious to put a photo of her dad in his hippie garb online. It would serve him right for being such a jerk about the whole moving out thing.

"Please bring whatever photographs you can find. Maybe we can create some history pages. And if you have anything that shows some of the local attractions, that would be perfect. Isn't there a waterfall trail or something?"

"Yes. Everyone knows about that and the lake, of course."

"Not yet. That's why we need the web site!"

Tracy looked at Roxy and rolled her eyes melodramatically at her. Oh brother. "Okay. I'll go through my pictures and see what I can find. My mom owns the gift store in town and my father took some pictures of the area that he got enlarged to hang on the walls for decoration. I'll see if I can grab some of those too. Some of them are pretty good."

"This is so great. I'm going to draw up some rough page layouts to show where menus and stuff might go. I'll bring them to lunch and we can talk about it."

Tracy sat down on the box of paints. "So um, what should I wear?"

Rob paused and she could hear the muffled sound of him coughing in the background. He cleared his throat again. "Well, I'm not an expert at women's clothes."

"Okay, what are you going to wear? A suit? Tie? I'm guessing you're not going to wear what you wore to class, right?"

"I hadn't really thought about it."

Tracy tried not to sigh too loudly into his ear. "Well, think about it now. It's a business meeting. Shouldn't you look business-like?"

"I guess so. I do have a suit. I could wear that."

Tracy bent over to pet Roxy, who was sleeping on the floor next to her. "You might want to leave the backpack at home too." There, she said it.

"But what will I carry my stuff in?"

"A briefcase?"

"I guess I could get one of those."

Tracy pulled a tuft of hair off Roxy's ruff. The fall shedding season had begun. "Hey, I'm just making suggestions here. If you want this contract, you should look like a professional."

"Well, what are you going to wear?"

"I have an interview suit that I bought a while ago." It was sitting in Shelby's closet, since she had let her friend borrow it for her grad-school interviews ages ago. The suit had been much luckier for Shelby than it had been for Tracy. Hopefully it still fit. If not, she was going to have a serious wardrobe crisis. The nursing scrubs she wore as a vet assistant, while good at repelling fur and animal excrement, probably didn't qualify as business casual.

Rob paused to cough again. "That sounds nice. I'm glad I talked to you about this stuff. I didn't really think about it."

"It's a girl thing. Women tend to think about clothes. Our options are more complicated than yours. As a guy, all you have to do is put on a suit and you're good. We have to figure out jewelry, makeup, shoes, accessories. It's all quite complex and interrelated."

Rob half-laughed, half-coughed. "I guess that's true. I appreciate the suggestions, though. If I get this contract, it could change my career. It's all really exciting!"

"Yeah, we'll see how it goes. I'll see you Friday." Although she didn't share Rob's level of enthusiasm, she had to admit that being able to pay her rent this month definitely fell into the category of exciting.

~

Kat sat at her computer staring at the blank screen on the monitor. Her editor had loved the last article she had written for the design magazine so much that she assigned Kat another one. Already. Now Kat was back at square one, facing the evil demon writer's block again. She was not thinking about the software she was supposed to be writing about. No, she was reflecting upon her conversation with Maria about kittens, and not getting anywhere.

The phone rang and she reached to answer it. After months of running up the stairs, Joel had installed phone jacks in each of their downstairs offices. Kat wasn't getting as much exercise, but she missed a lot fewer calls this way.

Kat mentally cringed when she heard her mother's sharp voice at the other end of the line. She made an effort to sound cheerful. "Hi Mom. How are you?"

"I'm fine, dear."

Kat closed her eyes, hoping maybe the awkward pause would end soon. Nope. No dice. It never worked. Her mother could wait out anyone. "Um, so what's new?"

"I'm at that lovely gift shop, Bea Haven."

Kat opened her eyes and sat up straight in her chair. "You mean you're in Alpine Grove?"

"Yes, dear. And I can't quite remember how to get out to the house. It's been many years since I saw it back when Abigail lived there. Could you give me directions?"

As she rattled off the directions, Kat mentally cataloged the things she could do to make the house less of a pig sty before her mother arrived in the next twenty-five to thirty-five minutes. "Okay, that's how you get here. Just make sure to go slowly on the driveway. I guess I'll see you in a little while, then." *Help*!

Kat hung up the phone, leaped out of her chair, and ran across the hall to Joel's office, followed by a parade of canines who had been startled from their afternoon naps. "Emergency alert! DEFCON 1! My mother is in beautiful downtown Alpine Grove at the gift store right now. And she's headed this way. I need your help."

Joel swiveled his chair away from his computer and turned toward her. "This isn't good, is it?"

"No. This place is a mess! There are books all over your office. She's going to freak out!"

He turned his head to survey the office, which did have books lying on most of the available surfaces. "It's not any different than it ever is. Those are just reference books. I need them."

"You don't know my mother. This is a nightmare." Kat ran out of the office and back into hers, frantically grabbing books off her own desk and throwing them into the closet. Joel walked in and stood in the doorway. "You do realize that you don't have enough time to do much of anything, right? This is one of those 'accept the things you cannot change' moments."

Kat heaved one last book onto the shelves in the closet and her shoulders slumped. "I wonder how long she's staying. It's probably rude for that to be the first thing I ask when she arrives, isn't it?"

Joel put an arm around her, pulled her close, and kissed the top of her head. "I'm afraid Emily Post would not approve. Let's go upstairs. Maybe we can dust something before she gets here."

Kat laughed mirthlessly. "Yeah, like that will help."

While Joel was attempting to forage food for dinner, Kat spent some cathartic time putting away a few morsels of clutter upstairs. By the time her mother knocked on the door, Kat had calmed down somewhat. All five dogs started barking hysterically at the interloper and Kat weaved her way through the furry bodies to get to the door. She opened it and found her mother, Mary Stevens, standing on the landing with a pinched expression on her face. The clear plastic rain bonnet that she usually kept carefully folded up in her purse was covering her Miss Clairol light caramel brown curls.

Kat shooed the dogs back out of the entryway. "Hello Mother. Come in."

"This rain is dreadful. Finding this place in the dark was unnerving. Are there wild animals out in the forest?" All five dogs started slowly moving back into the entryway to get a sniff at the new person as Mary fussed at removing her bonnet. She shook it out and looked up. "Oh my heavens. How many dogs do you have here? Goodness, that one is just enormous!"

"There are five." Kat pointed at the dogs, "The big one is Linus, the black-and-white border collie is Lori, and Tessa is the golden retriever. The brown–and-white one that looks like an Australian shepherd is Chelsey and Lady is the black-and-brown collie mix. She is Joel's dog.

Mary stared at Kat. "Joel? Who is Joel?"

Kat turned and stepped out of the entryway into the kitchen, where Joel was leaning on the sink. She gestured toward him. "That's Joel."

Joel waved. "Nice to meet you."

Mary grabbed Kat's arm, yanked her back into the entryway, and whispered at her. "Who is that man? And why is he here?"

"He lives here."

"Since when? And why in heaven's name didn't you tell me this?"

Kat shrugged her arm out of her mother's grasp. "It never really came up in conversation. I think you needed to vacuum or something."

"Humph. Does this mean you are living in sin?"

Kat turned to her. "Oh please. No, we are not married. And before you ask, yes, we sleep in the same room. In the same bed."

"Katherine! I can't believe you didn't tell me. This is terribly awkward."

"Only if you make it that way. Joel is a nice person. He's helped me with more things around here than I can even count. Can we please move into the house now? Why don't you take off your raincoat?"

Mary slowly unbuttoned her London Fog and handed it to Kat, who hung it up in the entryway closet and followed Mary into the kitchen. "Would you like to sit down and have something to drink?"

Mary settled into a chair and looked around the room. The walls were log and the open living and dining area had a high tongue-and-groove cathedral ceiling. Pieces of shiny white new replacement boards stood out among the older weathered wood. "The place looks different."

"It smells better too." Kat leaned on the counter next to Joel and crossed her arms. "How was the drive?"

"It was fine up until I hit the mountain road. I forgot how winding it is. Then it started to rain and the visibility was bad, which was exhausting." Mary jumped as Linus put his large head on her thigh. She waved her hands in front of her. "Oh dear. Please make it go away. It's getting hair on my slacks."

"He's just being friendly. Come over here, Big Guy." Linus obliged, wandering over toward Kat. He leaned on her leg as she stroked his head.

Joel put his arm around Kat's waist and said to Mary, "So when was the last time you were here in Alpine Grove?"

Mary squinted at him. "In the mid-seventies I think. Perhaps 1975? Downtown looks very much the same, actually."

Joel nodded and glanced over at Kat. She shook her head almost imperceptibly. "So, um, mother, I guess I should ask, why did you decide to come here *now*?"

Mary ran her index finger along the table, looked at it, and made a face. "Shouldn't a mother be able to visit her daughter? I needed a vacation. And I knew you had room. Or I *thought* you had room."

"There's plenty of room." Kat reached over and clutched Joel's other hand. "You can stay in one of the bedrooms downstairs. I've been using it as an office." She looked up at Joel, who had an odd, pained expression on his face. She let go of his hand and heard him exhale. "Oops. Sorry. I forgot you're broken. That probably hurt. Could you get the suitcase?" She pointed at his arm. "Maybe with your other hand?"

Joel nodded and moved toward the door. Kat heard the door close and turned back to her mother. "So um, is there anything you want to do while you're here? Sorry the weather stinks. Everyone says that in fall it can get rainy here."

"Well, it's certainly not like I want to go off into the wilderness camping. I will just visit with you."

Kat closed her eyes for a long second. What was she going to do? "Okay. Well, um, I guess it looks like Joel is reheating some soup he made the other day. It's really good."

"He certainly doesn't talk much does he? Or shave. Men in Alpine Grove tend to be somewhat disreputable. Like that detestable man Abigail married. Where exactly did you dig this fellow up?"

Kat clenched her fists, digging her fingernails into her palms in an effort to will herself not to shout. "He's not disreputable, mother. He's an engineer and we've been together for a while. Can we *please* not get into this now? He's coming right back with your luggage."

"Humph." Mary settled her hands in her lap and gave Kat a fixed glare. "I do want to talk to you about this person, Katherine."

Kat waved her arms in surrender. "Fine. Whatever."

The front door slammed and the parade of dogs followed Joel and a giant suitcase down the stairs. Kat sighed. If Joel were smart, he'd just go into his office, close the door, and not come out until her mother left.

~

After an extremely uncomfortable dinner filled with a few inane discussions about the weather punctuated with drawn-out silences, Mary retired to the downstairs bedroom. After making up the bed for her, Kat practically ran back up the stairs to retreat to her own space. Joel was lying on the bed fully clothed, with his eyes closed, holding his arm across his chest.

Kat walked over, looked down into his face, and stroked his beard with her fingertips. He opened his eyes, smiled at her, and took her hand. "You look like a woman who wants to crawl under the covers and not come out for a very long time."

"You know me so well." Kat crawled onto the bed and curled up into a fetal ball next to him. "I'm so sorry about this. I know you already know that my mother and I don't get along. But I apologize that you're going to have to witness it first-hand. It's unpleasant. She has a unique ability to say things that make me want to scream."

"It will be okay. She can't stay here forever."

"And tomorrow Roxy arrives. That will be just fantastic. Hey, look Mother dear, it's another dog! Guess what? It sheds too! And this one has a warped sense of humor about hiding and destroying the house."

Joel rearranged himself to sit up straighter on the bed. He put his hand under her chin and tilted her face toward the light. "Are you crying?"

Kat snorfled and moved her head, snuggling her face back down into his shirt. "No."

"Yes you are. Is your mother really getting to you that much? You lived with the woman for years. Is something else going on?"

"I don't want to talk about it. Can we just go to sleep?"

"All right. It has been a long evening." Joel disentangled himself from Kat and got off the bed. He headed for the bathroom and closed the door.

Kat gripped the bedspread and squeezed her eyes shut, trying not to think about the brown bag from the drug store she'd hidden deep in the back of the bathroom vanity.

Very early the next morning, Kat opened her eyes at the sound of crashing noises downstairs, followed by a sharp bark from Linus. *Uh-oh*. What was her mother doing to her office? What might she *find* in her office? Kat leaped out of bed and dragged on a pair of jeans.

Joel rolled over and looked at her. "What was that noise?"

"I'm going to go investigate. It's possible my mother is snooping."

"She snoops loudly."

"You should have heard her when she was trying to find my diary when I was thirteen."

Joel snuggled back down into the covers. "Glad I missed it. I'll just stay here."

"Good plan."

Kat crossed the living room and was joined by Linus, who was standing at the top of the stairs. "Hey, Big Guy. Did she wake you up?" Linus wagged and started down the stairs. Kat followed him and stood in the doorway of her office, aka the guest bedroom. Her mother was on her hands and knees, looking under the bed. Kat put her hands on her hips. "What are you doing?"

Mary looked up from the bed. "I'm rearranging, dear. I had trouble sleeping. It's too quiet here. The flow of this room is all wrong. I can't move around in here with all this clutter. I went to move that floor lamp so I could see better and then I saw what was under the lamp. How can you live like this? Don't you own a vacuum cleaner? And good heavens, what are you wearing?"

Kat looked down at herself. "My night shirt. And jeans."

"What if someone saw you like this? What if you have an accident and the paramedics see you wearing that? And you're not wearing makeup. Don't you ever comb your hair?"

"Mother, I just woke up. *You* woke me up. And the only one who is going to see me at this hour is Joel. He doesn't care. Only you care."

"Well, of course he doesn't care. Consider the source. He hardly looks respectable himself."

Kat put her hands over her face. "It's way too early to have this conversation. I'm going back upstairs. We have a dog arriving this morning."

"A dog? Another one?"

"I told you that I'm boarding dogs. We're building a kennel in the spring."

Mary got up, brushed off her slacks, and sat down on the bed. She picked a clump of fur off the bedspread and placed it in the garbage can. "Why is a dog coming here now?"

"I told the owner the dog could stay here. There are two other dogs coming soon, as well. They'll stay in the outbuilding. Joel still needs to fix the door for that, though." Which would be difficult if his arm was still messed up. It was beyond time to talk to him about that again.

"I see. You keep saying *we*. Is this Joel person staying here permanently?"

"As far as I know. Why don't you ask him?" Kat turned and stomped up the stairs back to her bedroom, followed by Linus.

Joel had gotten dressed and was sitting on the bed, putting on his shoes. "I didn't get a chance to tell you last night, but I'm going to take the chain saw into town to Frank's Repair.

I think it needs work. It's running kind of rough." He stood up and reached into the closet for a flannel shirt.

Kat walked over and wrapped her arms around him. "I'll miss you. Please come back soon. Don't leave me here alone."

He peeled her arms off his body and gave her a kiss. "I'm just dropping of a chain saw, not fleeing to Borneo. Don't worry."

After Joel left, Kat took a shower. She could hear her mother continuing her redecorating and snooping project downstairs. That meant Kat had the bathroom all to herself, at least for the time being. She rummaged around in the back of the vanity and pulled the test out of the bag. She leaned against the counter and unfolded the paper with the long list of instructions. As she went through the steps, she thought about the unappreciated technical writer who must have had to write the directions. Maybe she even had to try them out. Did she have to sit around waiting with a stopwatch in some sterile office ladies' room? "Hi Georgette, don't mind me. I'm testing to see if my directions are correct." Ugh. Kat didn't miss being a tech writer one little bit.

A loud rapping on the door startled Kat from her flashbacks of cubicle life. Mary said, "Are you okay in there? What are you doing? You're not sick, are you?"

"Mother! Could I please have a little privacy here?"

"You've been in there for a long time. Are you okay? I'm your mother. You can tell me."

Kat stared down at the plastic wand, which was indicating nothing conclusive so far. "I'm fine. Go away."

"Do you expect me to go outside? I need to use the facilities, dear."

Kat looked at her watch. Eight minutes to go. She shoved the stick and packaging back into the brown paper bag and jammed it into the little plastic garbage can that sat under the sink. Clutching the can to her chest, she opened the door and marched out. "Fine. All yours."

Mary narrowed her eyes. "What are you up to?"

"I'm emptying the trash for you. Because I know you like that kind of thing. This is me being tidy." Kat scampered off to her bedroom and slammed the door. She leaned against the door and slid down to the floor. Six more minutes to go.

Chapter 6

Performances

As Tracy navigated The Turd around the potholes along Kat's driveway, she pondered the day ahead. Considering the gloomy weather and gunmetal-gray clouds, she was feeling remarkably upbeat. Maybe it was because against all odds, the old car had decided to participate in the transportation program. Although it was probably stupid to go to this meeting and impersonate an artist, a part of her was looking forward to it. She had acted in a few school plays over the years; it could be fun to play dress up and pretend to be a hot-shot designer for an afternoon. She'd never see any of these people again, anyway—might as well really work it with an over-the-top performance.

Tracy parked under a tree, got out of the car, and was greeted with utter silence. No dogs were around and the birds weren't feeling enough joy about the weather to say anything either. It was awfully early. Even Roxy didn't seem to want to bark, for a change. Maybe she should make sure Kat was awake before she got Roxy out of the car.

Tracy walked up the steps and knocked on the weathered wood door. A thin older woman with light-brown hair opened it. Daunted by the woman's penetrating and unfriendly look, Tracy shifted her stance and put her hands in the pockets of her jeans. "Um, uh, is Kat here?" Tracy hadn't felt this uncomfortable since she was a third-grader asking if her friend Lisa could come out to play. It was strange.

The woman frowned and stepped aside. "Yes. You must be the person with the dog. Please come in."

A door in the house closed somewhere and Kat walked into the entryway with an unusually somber expression on her face. "Hi Tracy. This is my mother, Mary Stevens. Let's go outside and get Roxy."

Tracy nodded. "Okay." The tension oozing from Kat was palpable. Yikes. What the heck was going on here? The last time she was here Kat was cheerful, surrounded by happy cavorting dogs. Today it was like the clouds had enveloped the whole place in a shroud of murky bleakness.

Kat helped Tracy unload the crate from the back of the car. They set it on the ground and Tracy shut the door. "So where's Joel?"

"He's in town. Could you grab the other end of the crate? We can bring it inside first, then come back for Roxy."

Tracy obliged and the two women hauled the crate up the steps and into the house, where Mary was sitting at the table clutching a mug in front of her with both hands. She glowered at them again and Tracy was eager to get back outside. That woman was seriously unfriendly.

Back at the car, Tracy clipped a leash on Roxy, took her out, and placed her on the ground. She handed the leash to Kat. "So I hope it's still okay for Roxy to stay."

Kat looked down at Roxy, who was busy sniffing the ground around her feet. "It's fine. I'll do a better job of paying attention to her this time. And as you saw, my mother is here, so there's another person to keep an eye on her too."

"Okay. Well, I'll be back tomorrow to get her. So it's really just over night." Tracy smiled in an effort to lighten the mood. Kat looked so unhappy. Should she ask? Maybe it was none of her business. "I know you don't know me very well, but is everything okay?"

Kat looked back up at her. "I'm fine. Just stuff on my mind, I guess. And I have a house guest." A corner of her mouth turned up. "Isn't there some saying about house guests being like fish or something?"

"Yeah, they start to stink."

Kat smiled for real this time. "Exactly."

Tracy impulsively reached out gave Kat a hug, since she looked like she needed one. "Thank you again for letting Roxy stay. I'll see you tomorrow!"

Tracy got into the car and fired up The Turd, which after a few tries decided to sputter back to life. *Come on baby, just one more trip to the big city. You can do it.* After the weird vibe at Kat's house, she was ready to hit the open road. At least her parents weren't unpleasant and sour like Kat's mother. In fact, Tracy's mom was pretty much the ultimate Earth Mother who took care of everybody. Growing up, all of Tracy's friends thought her mom was the coolest mom *ever*.

At her mom's gift store, even the employees called Bea "mom." They loved Bea and most of them had worked at the store for more than a decade. Pretty much everyone else in Alpine Grove loved her too, since for years Bea Sullivan had donated to every sport team, charitable auction, and fundraiser in town. Even though Tracy had endured a couple of huge fights with her father and he thought she was a flake, Tracy knew he did love her in his cranky, grumbling old dude kind of way.

Tracy slowed down and stopped at the Alpine Grove traffic light. Larry Lowell was standing at his big plate-glass office window, looking out at the street. She looked at him and he suddenly straightened and waved enthusiastically back at her. He looked like he might hyperventilate. Tracy looked away from him, up at the traffic light. There was no one around. Why was it red? Did the stupid thing break again? The Turd coughed, sputtered, and stalled out. The ancient station wagon was not fond of bad weather. There were clouds today and it was getting colder. Someday she was really going to have to get a new car—this was getting ridiculous. It used to be that the decrepit automobile didn't like snow. Then it didn't like rain. Now it couldn't even cope with clouds. Sheesh.

Tracy looked over and saw Larry turning the door handle to come outside. She cranked the key hard in the ignition. *Go! I mean it, you giant hunk of scrap metal. Just start!* The car made a horrible screech and belched as it resurrected itself. Tracy revved the engine, trying to keep it alive. The light changed and as she let off the clutch, the car lurched gracelessly forward through the intersection. Tracy looked over her shoulder and saw Larry standing on the sidewalk, looking crestfallen.

After the guy had gotten her fired, Tracy wasn't feeling terribly sympathetic. It was beyond time to get out of town.

～

Kat walked into the house with Roxy in her arms. "You have to be good this time, Roxy. I know you have teeth, but please don't bite my mother. No matter how much you may want to, biting is really considered poor form."

She opened the door and put Roxy down. Roxy started toward the kitchen and Kat pulled back on the leash. "I think you and the kitchen need to spend some time apart." She walked over to the table and handed the leash to Mary. "This is Roxy. She's a dachshund who has an unhealthy obsession with kitchenware. I need to do an errand. Could you watch her for about an hour? Make sure she doesn't get into the cabinets. She's really sweet. Just keep her on the leash, so she doesn't get lost. If you go downstairs, please be sure to carry her. She's only got three legs. The other dogs are downstairs napping, so they should all be fine. I'll be right back."

Mary looked at the leash in her hand, then down at the dog, who wagged her long feathery tail. "What do you mean the cabinets? Where are you going?"

"I'll be back in a little while." She crouched down to pet Roxy. "You be good, you hear?"

Kat grabbed the keys to her Toyota and jammed them into her pocket along with another key. She flew down the stairs and ran across the driveway toward her car. Rather than letting the car warm up like she usually did, she gunned it and hauled down the driveway, oblivious to the damage the potholes were committing on the Toyota's suspension. Instead of heading toward town, she turned and took one of the back roads that headed north of Alpine Grove.

Making her way down a grassy, narrow single-track driveway, she arrived at Joel's old cabin, which he affectionately referred to as The Shack. It had been quite a while since she'd been there, but the place looked exactly the same, nestled in its small clearing surrounded by huge old cedar trees. She parked the car and took the key out of her pocket.

Feeling guilty and a little like a criminal for sneaking around a house that wasn't hers, Kat unlocked the door, opened it, and looked around. The Shack was a simple log cabin comprised of a single open space with a loft. The small kitchen area was located under the loft and the only walls in the place surrounded a tiny bathroom. The interior still smelled a little like smoke because Joel's prior girlfriend had almost burned it down. No amount of cleaning seemed to completely eliminate the crispy wood campfire smell that pervaded the small cabin.

Kat walked over to the old mission-style sofa, lifted the receiver off the cradle of the phone on the end table, and dialed Maria's number. "Hey, do you have a minute?"

"Girlfriend! Why are you calling me at work so early in the morning? You know Mark is going to be harassing me for his morning coffee soon. The man is cranky if he doesn't get his caffeine. It's not pretty." Although Maria was looking for a new job, for the time being she was trying to play nice with her boss, Mark.

"I know. But I need to talk to you. My mother is visiting."

"I'm sorry, but I missed something here. When did she show up? Time with Little Mary Sunshine never improves your mood."

Kat twisted the phone cord around her finger. "Nope. And she's even less fun than usual too. It's been less than 24 hours and she hates Joel already. I left her with Roxy."

Maria giggled. "The tiny destruct-o dog? That serves her right. Wait, if you're not there, where are you?"

"I'm at The Shack. I took the key."

"You illicitly broke into the engineer's place? Why? I mean, I do like that little cabin, after my love-nest rendezvous there, but you have your own phone and your own house that doesn't smell like smoke."

"I know. I needed a private phone without my mother nearby. The Shack is definitely private. I took the test. And I need to talk to you, because now I'm confused."

"You did? What do you mean? What did it say?"

"I'm not sure. I think I did it wrong or something. I mean, I read the directions and I thought I followed the instructions. But there are supposed to be lines. One or two lines. Not none. What does that mean? That I have no hormones at all? That I'm dead? *What?*"

There was a clunk and Kat could hear Maria snarling at Mark about the status of his morning coffee. Maria came back on the line. "Sorry. I'm back. Mark needed a little reminder that he is capable of getting his own beverages. Anyway. I'm not sure. I've never heard of that. You really dare to be different, girlfriend."

The front door opened and Kat jumped up off the sofa with a small shriek. Joel stood in the doorway, and he looked annoyed to see her in his house. Kat pressed the receiver to her chest and could feel the vibration of Maria's voice yelling at her through the line. She smiled at him feebly. "Hi."

"What are you doing here?"

Kat put the receiver to her ear. "I'll have to call you back."

"Engineer alert?"

"Yes. Gotta go." Kat slapped the phone receiver on the cradle and walked over to Joel. "I needed to use the phone."

He crossed his arms across his chest. "You have a phone."

Kat walked around him and shut the door. "I know. But I needed to talk to Maria without my mother around."

"What was so important that it couldn't wait until later? Don't you have a dog coming today?"

Kat walked over to the sofa and sat down. She leaned forward, clasping her hands together between her knees. "Roxy is already there. I, uh, left her with my mother."

"So you could break into The Shack?"

"Well, not technically." Kat leaned back and pulled the key out of her pocket. She held it up so he could see it. "It was just sitting there. I figured you wouldn't mind."

Joel sat down next to her, took one of her hands in both of his, and looked into her eyes. "What is going on with you?"

Kat bowed her head and shook it so her long hair fell in front of her face. "Nothing. I'm fine."

"Why don't I believe you?" He reached over and wiped a tear off her cheek. "You don't seem fine."

Kat collapsed in his lap and burst into the full festival of quasi-hysterical snotty sobbing that had been building up for days. He was being so sweet, she couldn't stand it anymore. "I...I took a test. And I don't know what it *means*."

Joel gently took her by the shoulders and pushed her upright again. "What are you talking about?"

"The stick! It's supposed to have lines. One line means no and two means yes. But I don't have any lines. What does that mean?" She put her hands over her face and sobbed into her palms.

He pulled her hands away. "I'm not exactly an expert on these things, but are you talking about a home pregnancy test?"

Kat looked into his green eyes, which were filled with concern and sympathy. "*Yes*! I didn't want to tell you if it's nothing. It's probably nothing." She hiccupped and snuffled.

"So you really think you're pregnant?" Although the expression on his face remained ostensibly calm, a range of emotions flickered in his eyes. If Kat had to guess, she'd say surprise, shock, confusion, and maybe fear.

"I'm not sure. I don't keep very good track of these things."

"You don't know? Don't you have a calendar or something?"

Kat sniffed again and wiped her nose on her sleeve. Crying was so gross. "Do you remember what you were doing twenty-eight days ago?"

He shook his head.

"Me neither! We've been so careful. I probably just lost track. Or I'm late. But what if I am pregnant? I have no idea how you even feel about kids. I don't know how *I* feel about kids!"

Joel tucked a strand of tousled dark hair back behind her ear. "To be honest, I'm not sure. I've never really put much thought into it, since it was never an issue. It was one of those "maybe someday" things. But if I were going to have children with anyone, I'd want it to be you."

Kat wrapped her arms around him and sobbed uncontrollably into his chest. He put his arm around her and stroked her hair until she was completely cried out. All the stress and crying left Kat feeling drained, shaky, and headachy. She slowly lifted her head and looked into his eyes again. "Wow, I'm so sorry about that. I think I'm done now. Thanks for being, well, you. I love you."

He ran his fingertips behind her ear and through her hair, pushing it out of her face and behind her shoulder. "I love you back. Do you feel better? You know, you're going to have to rescue Roxy from your mother at some point."

Kat jerked back away from him. "I totally forgot! I hope they haven't killed each other. Two strong-willed, opinionated alpha females together. This could be bad."

Joel stood up and stretched his arms over his head. "So are you ready to go home?"

"Okay." She sniffed and wiped her eyes one last time. "By the way, now you know why I was here. Why were *you* here? I thought you went to town."

He grinned. "Dropping off the chain saw didn't take long. You're not the only one who wanted to get away from your mother."

Kat laughed weakly. "She has that effect on people. I think she scared Tracy. I felt a little bad for her."

"Your mother *is* kind of scary."

"I know. Maybe we could come back here again. Every time I've been to The Shack, it was because someone was staying here. I've never even seen the loft."

"That's the bedroom."

Kat hugged him again. "I know."

"I guess you *are* feeling better." He bent down to give her a kiss and then looked into her eyes. "It will be okay, you know."

"I know."

～

Kat followed Joel back to the house and parked her Toyota next to his truck. She got out of the car and Joel walked over and stood next to her. They looked up at the house, which was shrouded in a heavy drizzly cloud. The mist clung to their skin like a clammy veil. Kat turned to face him. "Could it possibly be any more dreary today?"

"You haven't lived here in the spring yet, have you?" Joel ran his fingertip along her jaw and cupped her chin with his hand, tilting her head up to look at him. "So you're going to tell me if you do another test or your situation changes, right?"

"Yes. I think I've successfully proved that bottling up my emotions and keeping things from you leads to a meltdown of epic proportions."

"I think it's better if I stay in the loop." He kissed her and looked at her questioningly. "So are you ready to go inside? I'm starting to feel like a mushroom out here."

"If we have to."

He took her hand and they walked up the steps together. Kat opened the door and was greeted by the sound of outraged barking. She looked at Joel. "I think the furry crew is miffed at us."

Kat started down the stairs and recognized another noise beyond the hysterical barking. She stopped in the doorway to her office. Mary had neatly stacked all of Kat's books on one side of the desk and placed a sewing machine on the other side. Roxy was sitting on the bed, surrounded by a wall of pillows that had apparently been collected from multiple locations throughout the house. The dog actually looked quite content in her cushy enclosure and wagged happily at Kat.

Mary paused in her sewing and turned in the chair. "Hello. You're back. That was certainly longer than an hour. What happened to you? You look terrible."

"Thank you." Kat sat on the bed and reached over the pillow wall to pet Roxy. "My hair doesn't appreciate this misty weather. What are you doing?"

"Finishing these quilts." Mary pulled the cloth out of the sewing machine and held up a blue-and-white star quilt. "Isn't it lovely? The whole thing is pieced, and even quilted already. All it needs is the edges to be finished. I found it in that little room across the hall."

"Wow, you have been busy. I haven't been able to face that pile of boxes yet. Cleaning out these two downstairs bedrooms wore me out. When I got here, they both looked like that storage room. It was scary. Was the sewing machine in the room too?"

"Yes! And it works wonderfully. I plugged it in and just started sewing. It all functions perfectly."

Kat examined the ancient black Singer. "I think I remember Abigail using this. It sounds exactly the same as it did then."

Mary turned back to the machine. "So where were you?"

"I had to go somewhere. I'm going to take the dogs for a walk now. Thanks for keeping an eye on Roxy. I think she likes your pillow fort."

"Well, I certainly couldn't sew with a dog attached to me." A corner of Mary's mouth turned up. "She is being a very good girl."

"Yeah, watch out. That's right when she turns into the Evil Demon Dachshund."

Mary paused in her fabric ministrations. "Oh, your loud friend called. She wants you to call her back."

"You mean Maria?"

"Yes. The loud woman. She sounds a bit put out with you. I think the words she used were 'you'd better' call her back. But she included an unflattering expletive about you as well, which I won't repeat because I don't think words like that should be used in polite company."

"I can imagine." Kat picked up the dog and put her down on the floor. "Come on Roxy, it's time to go walkies."

The dogs all crowded together in the hall as Kat put Tessa's backpack on her and attached the dog's leash to Linus. She had discovered that the only way to successfully walk Tessa and tire her out was to weigh her down with a pack and attach her to Linus, so the big dog could do the walking. He outweighed Kat by almost a hundred pounds and could keep the hyperactive golden retriever from running off. The arrangement worked out well for everyone. Tessa and Linus wagged happily, excited about going for their walk. Kat leashed up Chelsey and held her leash along with Roxy's.

Joel stepped out of his office, leaned on the doorjamb, and surveyed the commotion. "It looks like the convoy is ready to roll."

"Wanna come?"

He glanced toward Kat's office, where the sound of the sewing machine was winding back up to full motorized-power whirring. "Sure."

Kat opened the back door and all of the dogs shot out toward the forest trail. Tessa and Linus ran out first and Lady and Lori followed, playing and chasing each other through the trees. Roxy and Chelsey strolled alongside Kat and Joel as they walked through the sodden brown leaves and pine needles that coated the ground. The vibrant green of the pine trees was muted by a cloak of cold fog that hovered over the forest.

Kat reached out to take his hand. "So how's your arm?"

Joel looked down at his free hand as he flexed his fingers and then made a fist. "Much better. It doesn't hurt when I move my hand anymore. Now it's just my forearm that has a dull ache."

"Does that mean you can do things like use tools?"

"Among other things."

Kat squeezed his hand. "I'm glad you're just about fully functional again. It's getting cold and I'm hoping you'll have time to fix up the door of the Tessa Hut before Swoosie and Rosa get here." The Tessa Hut was a somewhat dilapidated outbuilding that had a chain-link enclosure inside, but only a marginally functional door. Although it had been used to house Tessa and other dogs, it probably wasn't usable in the winter without significant improvements to the door.

"Yeah, it's on my list. I should be able to get started on that soon."

Kat stopped and waited for Roxy to complete a complicated sniffing ritual near a particularly interesting shrub. "There's one other thing."

"Did something else fall apart while I was gone?"

"Other than me, no. But I was thinking that it might be good if you maybe cut your hair." At the expression on his face, she raised both of her hands in front of her. "I know. I wasn't lying when I said I like the long hair. And the beard. There's a lot to be said for no razor stubble. I really do enjoy the softer-faced you. And your hair is so wavy and sexy. I wish my hair was that good. Men always have such great hair."

Joel grinned. "I suppose. Until they have no hair. Is there a point here?"

"Would you be willing to shave and get a haircut? I think it might help matters with my mom. She's sort of prickly about stuff like that."

"Prickly?"

"Um. Critical? Nasty? Mean? You know how I'm kind of insecure about what I look like? Well, now you know why."

Joel nodded. "Okay. I get it. If you think it would help, I'll go over to Joe's barber shop after we get back. Maybe your mother will like the clean-cut me better."

"Probably not, but it couldn't hurt. And if nothing else, Tracy won't be worried about you going native for a while."

"Hey, I told you. I've still got all my real teeth. And I even floss regularly!"

Kat wrapped her arms around him. "I'm sure your dentist is very proud of you."

~

Traffic was good and Tracy got to Shelby's apartment without any more unfortunate stalling incidents. It was a relief to park The Turd at the curb and slam the tin-can-like door in disgusted finality. She had plenty of time before Rob got there to make herself look like a professional, instead of a hick who had just rolled down off the mountain.

The interview suit was easily the nicest article of clothing Tracy had ever purchased. It was a gorgeous blue that matched her eyes and fit her perfectly. She put her blonde hair up in a French twist and spent far more time on her makeup than usual.

Billy Bob decided to hang out in the bathroom with her and supervise. He sat on the toilet until he fell asleep and rolled off with an ungraceful thud onto the tile. Sometimes it wasn't easy being an oversize cat. He stood up, looked around, and sauntered off, trying to pretend nothing mortifying had just happened.

Later, Tracy stood in front of the full-length mirror, stretched out a leg, turned her ankle, and admired her handiwork. Thanks to her matching blue pumps, her legs looked fantastic. Realistically, she didn't ever look much better than this. Rob couldn't accuse her of not trying to look the part, anyway. Perhaps today she'd adopt the persona of Annette, a fabulous artiste from a chi-chi LA neighborhood who lived in a loft with huge windows that let in perfect light so she could create important paintings that gallery owners fell all over themselves to sell. What would Annette say about the design of the Alpine Grove web site?

Tracy was interrupted from her artistic fantasies by a knock at the door. She sashayed over, opened the door, and leaned seductively on the entrance with her arm coiling up the side of the doorway. "Hi, Rob."

Rob's eyes widened as he took in the view. "Uh, eh, wow. Hi."

Tracy giggled, put her arm down, and waved him inside. "Come on in. Try not to drool on the floor. Shelby wouldn't appreciate that."

Rob walked by her, put down his briefcase, and turned to face her. "You look...fantastic. I mean really, really good."

"Thank you. And I hope you're going to be more eloquent at this meeting." She bent to grab her bag off the sofa, noting his admiring glance. Men were so predictable. But it was nice to know he appreciated her efforts. She held up the bag. "I brought a whole lot of photographs. I hadn't looked at them too closely in a long time, since they've been hanging in my mom's store forever. But it turns out my father was a fairly good amateur photographer. Even though I've seen these places a million times, some of the photos are really gorgeous."

Rob covered his mouth with his fist and coughed. "That's great. I knew you'd have some pictures." He sucked discreetly on a lozenge. "It's such a beautiful area—you'd just have to take photographs."

"I suppose." Tracy tilted her head. "Are you feeling okay? You're not sick, are you?"

"No. Not really. I think I just have the beginnings of a cold. It's no big deal. Probably just the smog getting to me."

"Before we head out to lunch, can I make a suggestion?"

Rob swished the lozenge around in his mouth and nodded. "What?"

"How about we do something about your hair? It's sort of, well, everywhere. Did you comb it?"

He looked a little irked as he ran his fingers through his wavy brown hair. "Yes. I always do. Every morning. But this week, I didn't have time to get around to getting a haircut. When my hair gets past a certain point, it starts to have a mind of its own."

Tracy studied him. "That's obvious." It looked like Shaggy had been zapped with a stun gun. She said evenly, "I have some hair junk that might help calm it down."

"I'm not going to smell like a girl, am I?"

"No. It's supposed to be unscented. The scented stuff tends to be too interesting to animals, which can be a problem if you're a vet tech."

"You're a vet tech? You never told me that."

"Well, I'm a veterinary assistant, actually. I'm not certified. Now you know that I'm a woman of mystery and intrigue who also spends a lot of time covered with dog hair." She took his hand. "Come with me."

He followed her into the bathroom, sat as directed on the dainty wire chair in front of the makeup mirror, and took off his glasses. Tracy squirted some gel onto her hands and ran it through his hair. Even if his hair was out of control, at least it was soft. He managed to sigh only once as she worked over his hair. Tracy turned to the sink and washed her hands. "There. All better."

Rob leaned closer to the mirror and touched his hair. "Well, I guess it looks better. But yuck, I can't wait to wash my hair."

"It's one afternoon. Do you think I like wearing these heels?"

"No." He looked down at her legs and then back up at her face and grinned. "But they make you look hot."

She tapped him lightly on the shoulder with her index finger. "Oh pshaw. You'll give me a swelled head. Let's go eat, so you can show me all those geeky diagrams."

Rob smiled at her reflection in the mirror. "You're gonna love it. This site could be so cool!"

"Whatever. Let's go."

After lunch and going over Rob's web site diagrams, which he referred to as "wire frames," Tracy was more than ready to get the meeting over and done with. It was time to earn her five hundred bucks and get back to her real life.

On the way to the meeting, Tracy determined that she was completely in love with Rob's car. It was a newer Honda Prelude with every possible option. Power everything. And even a moon roof. The seats were plush, the stereo worked, and it didn't stall out in intersections. There really was something to be said for modern technology.

Tracy snuggled up to the upholstery. Maybe he wouldn't mind if she just hung out in his car for a while after the meeting. As she watched him shift gears, she so wanted to drive the car. Really fast down a winding road out in the country somewhere. With the moon roof open and the wind in her hair. In Alpine Grove, the Farm to Market Road would be just the place to really open it up.

She laughed and Rob took his eyes away from the road to glance at her. "What's so funny?"

"This car is wonderful. Can't we just drive around instead of going to the meeting?"

He patted the steering wheel. "Yeah, I got it not too long ago. It's not one of the brand-new ones, but I like this body style better and it was more affordable. But no. We're going to the meeting."

Tracy crossed her arms in front of her and made a pouty face. "Okay, fine. It was worth a shot."

Rob parked and got out of the car. Tracy ran her hand across the sleek lines of the Honda's roof. "I love this car. I want this car."

Rob bent down to grab his briefcase from behind the seat. He stood and looked over the roof of the car at her. "I'm sure she loves you too. Are you ready?" He pointed to a tall steel-and-glass building. "The office is over there in the Walsh Building."

"I think the car would love me more if I got to drive it.

"Let's just get through this meeting first. Then we'll talk."

~

Tracy and Rob took the elevator up to the eleventh floor. They were directed to a conference room that had floor-to-ceiling glass windows that looked out over the street. An easel with a pad of oversize paper sheets was in the corner.

Tracy sat down and fiddled with the handle of her bag. The huge gleaming mahogany conference table was intimidating. It probably cost more than everything she owned combined. Rob sat next to her and started lining up his charts and pencils, much as he had done in class. He certainly was organized. Good thing he didn't know about the level of disarray in her apartment. The poor guy would probably have a coronary.

A tall gray-haired man with a crew-cut and military bearing walked into the room. Tracy and Rob stood up. Rob shook his hand and introduced Tracy to Ben Walsh, the owner of the firm. The older man smiled at her politely. "You look somewhat familiar. Have we met before?"

Tracy gave him her most dazzling smile and said she didn't think so; however, she was pretty sure she'd seated him at the Italian restaurant. It would be seriously embarrassing if he figured that out. Maybe because he was seeing her out of context, he wouldn't remember that in her real life she was a hostess. Or had been before she was fired.

Several other people came in and sat down. Ben introduced them as members of the marketing committee.

Tracy mentally forced herself to embrace her imaginary Annette persona and not to be nervous about the fact that there were way more people in the room than she had expected. She thought the presentation was going to be for just one guy, not a *committee*. But Annette wouldn't care. She would relish the challenge because she was a brilliant artiste with legions of adoring fans.

Rob spread out his diagrams on the table and started explaining how the databases would drive the web site and display information about Alpine Grove. Along with the real estate information, he planned on including a classified section and business listings, which could be updated easily using online forms.

After Rob had regaled them with nerdy stuff for a while, Tracy could sense the audience's attention waning. Plus, Rob seemed to be losing his voice, which was distracting. At the restaurant, if customers started looking anxious or unhappy, they referred to it as a "bread-stick situation." Back in the kitchen, shouts of "bread sticks on table two *stat*" meant "feed those people some bread sticks *now* before the mood turns ugly." Tracy didn't have bread sticks, but clearly something had to be done here. They were losing them.

Rob paused to cough and Tracy stood up. She pulled the many photos of Alpine Grove from her bag and spread them out on the table. "Although the technology is interesting, I'm sure you all want to know what we envision the site will actually look like. Here are some sample photos." She handed a particularly glorious photo of a sunset over the lake to Ben. He held up the image for the others to see. "This is right near my house!"

Tracy smiled. "That's near Gray's Point on the lake. It's a lovely spot."

"Yes. I own the house at the end of the peninsula."

"Are you the one who restored the old house? It's gorgeous now! That place was fenced off and boarded up for years. It was so sad, since it was such a beautiful Victorian. When I was in high school, we would boat to the beach, have a bonfire, and tell ghost stories about Miriam Gray."

Ben laughed warmly. "Yes, everyone told me I was buying a haunted house."

"So have you seen Miriam?" Tracy gestured toward the photo. "She used to like to sit in the branches of that huge tree near the beach. The story was that she was waiting for her lover to return, but there was a storm and his fishing boat sank in the lake."

"You certainly know your Alpine Grove history."

"I lived there for a long time." Tracy picked up another photo. "As Rob pointed out earlier, we want the web site to show off the beauty of the location. But what's equally important is that the site needs to be easy to use."

Tracy paused to move the flip chart easel and pad closer to the table. "A lot of designers get so wrapped up in the cool graphics that they create a web site that takes forever to load and is impossible for anyone to actually use. A site this large needs to be extremely well organized with clear navigation. What you want is a site that is so easy that even my mom could figure it out."

Ben's mouth curved in a smile. "I'm sure your mother is a smart lady."

"Oh she is. But she's not a big fan of computers or technology. And she's really busy. She owns the gift store in

Alpine Grove and loves pretty things. So the goal is to use the design to catch her eye and direct her, so she knows exactly what to do."

Ben waved his hand to interrupt. "Wait, your mom owns Bea Haven Gifts? I love that place! She's a nice lady too."

"Well, I think so. But she is my mom, so I'm biased." She turned and sketched a quick design of her ideas for the home page on the pad. "Design is all about balance and contrast. For example, here we would pull highlight colors out of the photos. We take those colors and use them for the text to direct people to the various areas of the site. The contrasting color stands out, but because it's also part of the photo, it unifies the design, making it more pleasing to the eye."

Rob cleared his throat and croaked, "I know it might sound like common sense, but you've probably all seen web sites that just didn't work. We want to avoid that."

Tracy said. "Exactly. When you have a large web site like this one, you need to create a visual hierarchy that shows what's important, so people can tell where to go to get the information they need. When people are looking at the real estate pages, for example, what are the first things they want to know? What a place looks like. Where it is. How much it costs. Then who to contact to learn more."

Tracy went on to describe the color scheme for the site and the overall look of the various sections. As she drew her presentation to a close, everyone was smiling.

Ben said, "This has been very insightful and I like your ideas. The marketing committee and I have some more firms to interview and I'll be in touch."

Rob and Tracy thanked everyone, and as the attendees filed out, they began collecting their materials. Tracy scooped up her photographs and paused to look at one of her father. She hadn't really examined it closely before, but Dad was standing next to an incredibly ornately hand painted car. She'd always assumed it belonged to someone else in the commune. But maybe not. It looked suspiciously like a Subaru station wagon. Did someone actually paint over the car with brown paint to turn it into The Turd? She needed to remember to ask her father about that the next time she saw him.

Rob nudged her. "Something wrong? We should probably get going."

"Nope. I just noticed something about this picture. Never mind."

They walked to the elevator and stood staring up at the descending numbers. Rob popped a throat lozenge into his mouth and turned to look at her. "I thought you weren't a web designer? How do you know all that stuff about usability?"

"I went to the library. One of the librarians there at the Alpine Grove library is a total researching machine. She found all kinds of great stuff and made copies for me." Tracy grinned at him. "I'm a quick study, I guess."

"Well, it worked. I think they liked it!"

Tracy glanced at him. "Yeah. You'll have to let me know what happens. Do you have my check?"

"No. But you were amazing. You totally earned the money. How about I take you out to dinner tonight to celebrate? I'll bring the check with me then. I'd like to go home and wash my hair."

Tracy chuckled. "Okay. I want to get out of these shoes too. Where are you taking me?"

"How about a Japanese restaurant? Then you won't have to wear shoes at all."

"Works for me!"

~

Later, Tracy had changed into one of Shelby's colorful floppy skirts and comfy flats. Once again, Shelby was off tutoring some undergrad somewhere. The two women had an open-closet policy, so Tracy knew her friend wouldn't mind that she had run off with one of her favorite skirts. It was nice to be comfortable again and Tracy was looking forward to more free food. She had to admit Rob had been nice about feeding her frequently. Being a guest instead of an employee at a restaurant was a refreshing change. It made her feel like she was an adult again instead of an indentured servant.

Billy Bob stretched out on the rug, indicating that he was ready for a tummy rub. He reached out a paw toward Tracy and meowed loudly. Tracy bent down to oblige. "Okay, fine."

There was a knock at the door and Tracy gave the large cat one final pat. "Sorry, buddy, you're on your own until Shelby returns." Billy Bob stood up and sauntered off in disgust.

Tracy opened the door, where Rob stood with a bouquet of flowers. He waved and whispered, "Thank you for everything you did at the meeting. I have big news too!"

"Come on in." Tracy took the flowers and waved toward the apartment. "Thank you. I see your hair has returned to full force. But I think there's even less left of your voice than before. You really are a germ. Are you sure you want to go out?"

"Yes. Other than speaking more softly than usual, I feel fine. I think some Japanese tea will help. This week I was up on a roof doing an installation and it was really rainy and cold."

"Are you sure you're okay to drive? Because I'd be happy to drive your car."

He grinned and rasped. "Nice try."

"It never hurts to ask."

As Rob had promised, the restaurant was a traditional Japanese place with little compartments next to the door, where people placed their shoes. It had sunken tables and a clean, minimalist design. After removing and stowing their shoes, Tracy and Rob settled in to their table on the floor and ordered a pot of tea.

Tracy handed Rob a menu. "So what's this big news?"

"I got a call from Ben. He already wants to talk to us again."

"What do you mean us?"

Rob cleared his throat, took big gulp of hot tea, and winced. "Ben said he wants to talk to us again. But not here. He's going to be at his house in Alpine Grove for a couple of weeks. I guess it's some sort of a working vacation or retreat or something. I don't know. I figured that would be great, because it would be easy for you to attend."

Tracy looked down into her little round white porcelain teacup. "Another meeting? I'm not sure about that. I thought you wanted to hire a real web designer."

"Well, I don't have the contract yet. He said he doesn't want to wait on this project, so he wants to meet with us again there."

"So what am I supposed to do at this meeting?" Tracy waved her menu at him. "I pretty much said everything I learned from the stuff the librarian gave me. I'm out of material."

Rob said in a more normal voice. "He wants us to bring some complete mock-ups of sample pages and a quote for what it will cost."

Tracy dropped the menu on the table and leaned back in her chair. "You mean *comps*? Are you saying you want me to design this? I don't even have a computer. Are you nuts?"

"Comps?"

"Comprehensive layouts. Designers give them to clients to show the design. They are a lot of work."

Rob interlaced his long fingers around the teacup and studied it. The backs of his large hands were weathered and chapped. Looking back up at her, he said, "We can work on it together. I'll take some time off of work and come up to Alpine Grove. I have a lot of calculations to do to figure out the scope of work and the money part of it anyway. I have tons of vacation time that I haven't used and all this rainy weather has been horrible for installing satellite systems." He frowned. "To tell the truth, I could really use a break."

Tracy said, "I have to work, you know. I can't afford to take a vacation."

Rob took a sip of tea. "I know. I'll bring my computer and stay at a hotel or something. We can work on it after hours. You are so good at the Photoshop stuff and you know what the wire frame layouts look like. All you have to do is take those and make them pretty."

"They were boxes that said things like *menu goes here*." Tracy waved her hand at imaginary wire frames. "How am I supposed to make *that* pretty?"

"It's no big deal. Just do what you said in the meeting with color and stuff. It will be great!"

Tracy poured some more tea into her cup. "You say *great* a lot. I think you're seriously overestimating the greatness of this situation. You really need to get a new adjective."

A waitress in an elaborately embroidered kelly green silk kimono appeared, and Rob asked Tracy, "Are you ready to order?"

"Yes. I want the agedashi tofu and vegetable tempura."

Rob peered over his menu. "No sushi for you?"

"I spent too many years being the one stuck cleaning the fish my father caught at the lake. No raw fish for me, thanks."

Rob ordered and after the waitress left, he turned back to Tracy. "It's not like you'll have to code the site. It doesn't have to work. All we need are pictures of web pages for this meeting. I know you can draw pictures."

"Code? What do you mean code?"

"I mean you don't have to write the HTML code that runs the site. That's what I'd do. And only after I get the contract." Rob looked down at the teacup he held in his hands again. "Except, this site is going to be so big, I'd probably have to hire another coder too. I don't think I can do it all myself. That's part of the money stuff I have to figure out."

"HTML? What? Now you're *speaking* in code. Nerd code. I have no idea what you're even talking about."

"HTML stands for hypertext markup language."

Tracy smirked. "Oh yeah, that clears everything right up."

"It's the language you use to create web pages."

Tracy crossed her forearms and rested them on the table. Leaning forward, she said, "I don't know about computer languages and all that stuff. I'm a vet tech. You said you were hiring a designer. Why don't you just do that?"

"Because Ben Walsh loves you. He went on and on about you and your ideas." Rob's shoulders slumped. "And if you want to get picky, I can't afford to pay a pro designer until I get the contract. Well, *if* I get the contract. That $500 I gave you was a substantial portion of my budget."

Tracy cocked her head. "Well you certainly didn't plan that out too well. So what you're saying is that I'm supposed to do all this work for you for free? And then when you get the contract, you just kick me to the curb. No thanks."

"Well, maybe you could work on design stuff after I get the contract too." Rob swirled the tea in his teacup and looked at her. "There's going to be a lot of work to do. Scanning and editing all those photos. And other images, like ads. I don't know. I haven't really gotten that far. Financially, it's all a bit of a risk for me to bid on this job. But it will be worth it, if I don't have to crawl around on rooftops in the rain anymore. I'm dreading winter."

"You and me both." Tracy fiddled with a chopstick, spinning it in her fingers. "Winter in Alpine Grove is lovely in a picture-postcard kind of way. But I hate the cold. I'd rather be lying on a beach in the Caribbean."

"Maybe you can give me a reasonable hourly rate because you don't have professional web design experience? But you'd learn a lot too." He smiled and leaned forward. "You'd be able to put the work experience on your resume."

"My resume? That's a joke." Tracy sighed. "But I do need a job. What's a fair rate? I work at a tiny vet clinic in a small town and I'm basically starving." She had all those revolting boxes of ramen noodles to prove it.

Rob threw out a number and Tracy's eyes widened as her brain moved into power calculation mode. She straightened in her chair. "So how many hours are we talking about here?"

"I don't know. Maybe 20 hours to get the mock ups done? Then the meeting will be a couple of hours I guess. I'll keep track."

Tracy put her chopstick back down on the table next to the other one. "You're really sure you want me to do this? I'm not a computer person, you know." That was putting it nicely.

"I know. You just don't have much experience. You can learn it like you did in the class. But you *are* an art person."

"An art person who really needs money."

Rob sipped his tea. "If that's the way you want to put it, yes, I suppose so."

Chapter 7

Cooties & Hunters

As Tracy limped The Turd up the mountain road back toward Alpine Grove, she tried to imagine she was driving the Prelude instead. The weather was gray and dreary again, which was making the tired old car cranky. It backfired and slowed to twenty-five miles per hour, which effectively destroyed the feeble illusion of driving bliss that Tracy was attempting to conjure up. Real life had an unpleasant habit of intruding on her fantasies.

An obnoxious booming *ooo-gaaa* horn sound came from behind her on the road. Tracy looked in her rearview mirror and spotted Bud Fowler's truck following her. He leaned his grizzled bald head out the window and shouted, "Come on Tracy! Put that thang in gear wouldja?"

Tracy waved her hand out the window indicating he should go around. Bud honked at her again. She glared at the rearview mirror. *Just go around, Bud.* But no, he honked again. She slowed The Turd down to a crawl, which made the car happy, but given the expression on Bud's face, seemed to infuriate him. He spit some brown fluid out the window. Yuck. Tracy had seen Bud's car around town and noticed that there were streaks of brown that had dribbled down the side of the truck door. Why did men chew tobacco? It was disgusting.

Bud leaned out the window again. "Outta my way, sweetheart. I gotta git home or the wife is gonna kill me." He revved the engine of the old truck for emphasis.

As Tracy approached a pull-out on the road, she slowed the car to a stop and let Bud go by. He waved out the window as he accelerated. The Turd's idle started to sputter even more than usual and Tracy jammed the car into first gear and popped the clutch. "Don't you dare crap out on me here!" With a lurch, the car moved back onto the road. Tracy floored it, trying to will the car to at least accelerate up to the speed limit. But the geriatric machine had other plans and it was not to be. Tracy frowned as she grudgingly accepted the second-gear lumbering. It was slow going, but at least the car was still moving, which was better than walking home.

After the interminably slow ride up the hill, Tracy finally arrived at her apartment. She waved to her mom through the window of the gift store and Bea smiled back at her warmly. At least Mom was glad to see her. She went up the stairs to her apartment and opened the door. An array of unpleasant odors assaulted her senses. Had Roxy hunted down something when she wasn't looking? Although dachshunds were originally bred to hunt badgers, Roxy wasn't picky. If she had found a rodent in here somewhere, she might have hidden it before Tracy took her to Kat's place. Tracy gazed across the sea of clutter in the small apartment. It wasn't like there weren't a lot of places to hide a partially masticated rodent body.

Tracy put down her suitcase and started making an effort to pick up the items on the floor and put them away. As she unearthed a path through the room, she sniffed repeatedly, trying to isolate where the noxious odors were emanating from. The smell of decomposing food seemed to be stronger as she approached the kitchen. Tracy got a garbage bag out of a cabinet and dealt with the detritus of past meals. That helped tone down some of the olfactory ills, but there was still an underlying aroma of something dead.

She walked over to the laundry pile in the corner and noticed a few of her t-shirts had been scattered, like someone had been digging. Tracy hadn't had a chance to do her laundry at her parents' house or the laundromat lately. The laundromat was no fun and it was easy to think up excuses not to go. But like most dachshunds, Roxy loved to dig. Maybe Tracy had put off laundry day a little too long this time. She grabbed another garbage bag and started throwing the dirty clothes into it, one by one. And there at the bottom of the pile, she found the body. *Thanks Roxy.*

After disposing of the expired rodent in the dumpster behind the store and washing her hands three or four times, Tracy called Kat, who said it was fine to pick up Roxy any time. Now that the floor was visible again, Tracy had certainly done enough cleaning for one day, anyway.

The Turd was less than enthusiastic about starting again, but Tracy finally got it going and wound her way out to the sticks. As the car clunked down Kat's driveway, she hoped everything had gone okay. Kat had made it sound like all was well on the phone, but Tracy wasn't looking forward to seeing Kat's mother again, since mother and daughter obviously didn't get along.

Tracy parked the car under a tree, where it belched out some smoke and convulsed a few times before finally settling into silence. Maybe it was time for a tune-up.

Joel emerged from an outbuilding and waved at her. "Hi, Tracy. I'm sure you know this, but your car seems to have a problem."

Tracy's eyes widened as she appraised his appearance. Joel had gotten a haircut and shaved. Holy moly, he was good-looking again. Given that she hadn't had a date in a while, it was difficult not to stare. Or swoon. When he smiled, he was incredibly cute. His forest-green eyes made her want to start down some R-rated mental pathways. Oops. Kat's boyfriend. Don't go there.

He raised his eyebrows. "Are you okay?"

Tracy nodded. "I'm fine." Working all the time was really putting a crimp in her social life.

Joel motioned toward the house. "Roxy is inside with Kat. I'm sure she'll be glad to see you."

"Thanks." Tracy turned toward the steps and looked back over her shoulder. Joel was bending down to pick up some lumber. Nice. She tripped over a root and caught herself before she crash-landed on the ground. Wow, she really needed to get out more.

She knocked on the door. Kat opened it and Roxy was standing next to her, barking furiously. Tracy bent down to collect her little dog in her arms. "How's my brave defender? I found the gift you left for me in my laundry. That really wasn't necessary." Roxy wagged, squirmed, and tried to lick her face.

Kat waved toward the house. "Come on in. Do you want something to drink or anything?"

"No, I'm fine. Was Roxy good?"

"Yes. No problems."

Tracy looked down the stairwell. Kat's mother was coming up the stairs. "Hi, Mrs. Stevens. It's nice to see you again."

Mary grimaced. Maybe it was her version of a smile. "Hello. It appears Roxy is pleased you have returned."

Tracy put Roxy on the ground. The dog circled her happily, obviously ready to head back home. "Yes. Thank you for taking care of her."

"I think you should be more careful about her diet." Mary frowned. "Small dogs like Roxy are prone to gaining weight."

"Actually, I work at the vet clinic here in town, so I know all about that." Tracy looked at Kat, who was standing with her hands clasped in front of her, a resigned expression on her face. "The fat dog chat is one of Dr. C's favorite speeches. She talks to owners about the risks of obesity a lot."

"Hmmph." Mary scowled. "I'm just worried about the dog's health."

Kat said, "I'm going to go ask Joel to get the crate for us."

Tracy turned and picked up her dog again. "I'll put Roxy in the car."

The two women and Roxy hurriedly went outside. Tracy busied herself ensconcing Roxy in the back seat of the car while Kat walked over to the outbuilding to talk to Joel. Tracy slammed the car door, stood up, and saw Joel say something to Kat, stroke her cheek, and kiss her tenderly. So much for R-rated fantasies. Sure, she knew he was taken, but he was *really* taken. They were like teenagers in an after-school special or something. Ugh. Why was it that when she was utterly dateless, everyone else in the world was in love?

Kat and Joel walked hand in hand, back toward Tracy. Kat stopped next to Tracy as Joel continued on up the steps to the house. Kat shook her head. "I'm really sorry about my mother. She can be sort of opinionated."

Tracy waved toward the backseat of the car. "So can Roxy."

"I think they're best friends now; it's sort of cute. I had to go out...somewhere...and my mother made Roxy a pillow fort."

"Really?"

"She was worried Roxy might fall off the bed and hurt herself."

"Aww, that's adorable." Tracy smiled. "She really did take good care of her."

The door opened and Joel came outside with the crate. He stowed it in the back of the car and stood next to Kat. He pointed at The Turd and said to Tracy, "You really should get your car looked at. I'm guessing that at a minimum, it needs new spark plugs."

Tracy paused as she opened the driver's side door. "Oh, it needs way more than that. And it's cloudy today. This car is old and sensitive to weather like an old guy with rheumatism in his knees. Unless I get a new car, you won't have to worry about seeing me this winter because I'll be walking everywhere."

$\sim$

Kat sat on the front steps of the house next to Joel and watched as Tracy's car sputtered down the driveway. "What is wrong with that thing? I didn't think she was going to get it started again."

"The possibilities are numerous and probably expensive. I'm impressed she got it going. For a minute, I thought we were going to end up with another house guest."

"She and the car seem to have an understanding, particularly about meteorological conditions."

He tilted his head back and looked up at the dreary gray sky. "Talk about a fair-weather friend."

Kat poked him in the ribs. "Very funny. So are you coming inside? It's almost dark. I know I asked about the door, but you really don't have to work on the Tessa Hut all day. Aren't you cold? It's so damp out here."

"I've got gloves. And there are advantages to being outside. For one thing, your mother is inside. Have you found out when she's leaving yet?"

"No. Maybe we can delicately inquire at dinner. She seems pretty settled in, though." Mary had a way of moving into a space and taking it over. Like a virus.

"Yeah, I noticed. That's what I'm worried about. Her big suitcase weighs about four-hundred pounds. Have you heard anything from your family at home?"

"Not a peep. Would you say anything if she went on an extended vacation?" Kat's sisters had probably been partying hard since Mary left.

"Good point."

Kat stood up and turned to go inside. "Coming?"

"I'll be there in a minute. I need to go put stuff away before it gets dark and I can't find it anymore."

"Don't leave me in there alone for too long."

"She's *your* mother."

"Don't remind me."

Joel strolled off toward the Tessa Hut. Kat sighed and continued up the stairs. She went inside and dealt with the pet-feeding program, much to the joy and delight of all the canine and feline residents.

Mary stood in the doorway of Kat's office and watched as Kat herded all the dogs back downstairs for their post-dinner nap. "You seem to have quite a system for that."

"Yes. Usually the dogs spend more time upstairs, but I know how you feel about fur in your food."

"I think I made that quite clear last night."

"Yes. So they'll be down here." Kat turned to go back up the stairs and held the gate at the bottom open for her mother. "I need to figure out what we're having for dinner."

Mary walked through the gate and marched up the steps. Kat closed it and followed her. The same question kept repeating in her mind like a loop: when was her mother leaving?

Joel came in the front door and almost ran into Mary at the top of the stairs. "Oops. Sorry."

"You're so tall and gangly. Men are always in the way."

Joel arched a single eyebrow at Kat. She shook her head minutely and said to Mary, "It looks like you're almost done with the quilts."

"Yes. I need you to get some dowels for me so I can hang them up. You have nothing on the walls here. Tomorrow I am going to look through more of the boxes in that little room."

Joel said, "I can pick up some dowels at the hardware store tomorrow. I have to go there anyway to get some supplies for the door."

Mary turned to glare up at his face, but didn't reply.

Kat said. "Looking through the boxes might be interesting. By the way, there's a box of photographs in the bedroom closet. You might enjoy looking through those too."

Mary turned and gave Kat a sharp look. "I certainly don't think so."

After Mary turned away from her, Kat crossed her eyes, contorted her face, and stuck out her tongue at Joel, who smirked in response. What the heck? "Oh-kaaay. So what do you have planned for tomorrow, Mother? I actually need to use my computer in my office because I have an article deadline coming up. I'm sorry to infringe on your space, but I really need to work on the article."

Mary sat down at the table. "Weren't you listening? I told you. I am going to clean out that bedroom. You can move that machine."

Kat and Joel busied themselves chopping vegetables for dinner while Mary leafed through an old magazine that was sitting on the table. She put it down and the slick paper hit the table with a loud slap. "Do you really read about computers? How tedious. Isn't there anything else to read here?"

Kat turned from the cutting board and leaned back on the counter. "I have some novels, but they aren't the kind of stuff you read."

"I certainly do not read that trash you do."

"You could go to the library. For a small town, it's got a great selection."

"I don't think so." Mary folded her hands in her lap. "I want to talk to you. Alone. Perhaps tomorrow you could stay here instead of disappearing."

Joel whacked the cutting board with the knife extra loudly and Kat looked at him to make sure he still had all of his digits. She said to her mother, "I'm not going anywhere, but I do have to write that article."

After they sat down to dinner, Mary looked at the plate. "Is this Chinese food? She poked at something with her fork. "What is that loathsome-looking white thing?"

Kat paused and put down her chopsticks. "It's just rice and veggies with tofu. I'm a vegetarian, remember?"

"Tofu? How revolting."

"Feel free to eat around it. Tofu rarely contaminates the other parts of the meal with evil cooties."

Mary frowned, poked at an offending block, and shoved it to the side of the plate. "Perhaps you can feed it to the dogs."

Joel smiled. "I'm sure they'd like that. They think bean curd is great stuff."

Mary shifted her gaze toward him. "I want to talk to you too."

Kat picked up her chopsticks and pushed some veggies around. She knew that tone. This was going to go downhill fast. "I have ice cream for dessert if anyone wants it."

Mary ignored Kat's comment and turned to Joel. "How did you meet my daughter?"

Joel looked momentarily taken aback then replied evenly, "My sister Cindy was hired to walk the dogs here after Abigail died. The first time I met Kat, I was with my sister who was having trouble with her car."

"And then you figured you could just move in here and freeload?"

Kat covered her mouth with her hand and watched as Joel's expression shifted to what his sister termed, "Spock face." When he was extremely annoyed he tended to take on an eerie calm instead of flying off the handle as Kat was likely to do. More than once she had been in awe of his level of control.

Joel put down his chopsticks and leaned forward slightly toward Mary and said quietly, "There was quite a bit more to it than that."

Mary scowled. "I can only imagine."

"I doubt you can."

Kat stood up quickly. "Wow. This sure has been fun. Mother, maybe we could talk about this later?"

Joel grabbed his plate and left the table. "If you'll excuse me, I have some work to do."

After Joel went downstairs to his office, Kat turned to her mother. "You really know how to clear a room. No wonder we stopped eating together when I was growing up."

Later, Kat had fallen asleep reading in bed when she was awakened by Joel crawling in next to her. He pushed her hair aside and nuzzled the back of her neck. She rolled over, put her arms around his neck, and kissed him. "Welcome. I guess you're not mad anymore?"

He whispered in her ear, "I wasn't mad at *you*."

"You didn't miss much. I did dishes and my mother gave me the evil eye for a while, which seemed to make her feel better."

"Did you explain how we got together?"

"Yes. But she was not impressed with the story. She is convinced you are a scuzzy freeloader after my vast fortune."

Joel tickled her waist with both hands. "Yup. That's me. I'm a gold digger."

Kat squeaked and tried to stifle her laughter as she squirmed away from him. "Cut that out! I already have cramps."

He stopped tickling, flattened his palms against her ribs, and looked into her eyes. "Really?"

"Yes." She hugged him. "As Maria would say, Aunt Flo has arrived at the station."

"Maria has a way with words. I think I'll pick up a calendar when I go to town tomorrow."

Kat giggled and kissed him. "Good idea."

~

Tracy spent the rest of her weekend doing laundry. Time with the other citizens of Alpine Grove who did not have their own laundry facilities tended to make her cranky as she reacquainted herself with the nuances of laundromat etiquette. On the other hand, Roxy had fewer places to bury her little lifeless gifts now. And having a big stack of clean underwear in her dresser drawer gave Tracy a sense of security. All was right with the world. Plus, she could stop hand-washing panties in the sink for a while.

Monday morning, Tracy arrived at the vet clinic a little early. The morning routine went more quickly when all her clothes were clean and either in the dresser or the closet. Tracy stood at the front desk and looked over the schedule to see what she'd missed. It was looking like an easy day. A few pets getting dropped off for neutering and some basic appointments for annual exams and shots. Easy-peasy. Relieved that there didn't appear to be anything unusual ahead of her today, Tracy busied herself cleaning kennels and getting everything set up for Dr. Cassidy.

The vet arrived a few minutes later and unlocked the front door of the clinic. People started dropping off animals and the day revved up to full steam. The phone rang and Tracy ran to the front desk to answer it. "Alpine Grove Veterinary Clinic."

A rich, deep voice on the other end of the line said, "Is this the vet?"

Why did people always ask that? "Yes, this is the Alpine Grove Veterinary Clinic. May I help you?"

"My buddy and I were out in the woods and his dog hurt himself. The dog—Max—he's bleeding and we need to bring him in. It's bad. Where are you?"

"We're in downtown Alpine Grove." Tracy gave the man directions and got Dr. C on the line, so she could give him advice about caring for the dog on the way to the clinic. After the vet hung up the phone, Tracy said, "So much for your easy morning."

Dr. Cassidy put her hands in her lab coat pockets and sighed. "I know. 'Tis the season for hunting-dog accidents."

Later, two men outfitted in camouflage gear came in with a blue-tick coonhound. A huskily built man with light-brown hair was carrying the large dappled black-and-white dog, which had floppy black ears and a big bandage wrapped around a rear leg. Both the dog and the man were filthy and looked extremely distressed. The second man was taller with black hair and brilliant blue eyes that looked almost electric, set off by the dirt smudges on his face. Tracy wrinkled her nose at the stench that followed them in through the door. It was a grotesque olfactory cocktail made up of campfire smoke, male sweat, and the nasty animal urine hunters doused themselves with to confuse whatever they were hunting.

Tracy directed the group to the exam room and restrained the dog on the table while Dr. Cassidy took a look at the injury. The invisible stink cloud the men had carried into the small room with them reminded Tracy of Pig Pen in the *Peanuts* comic strip. Sure, Pig Pen was always surrounded by a dirt cloud, but neither Charlie Brown nor anyone else ever seemed to mention how Pig Pen must have *smelled*. Tracy had a pretty good idea now.

The dog whimpered as the vet carefully removed the bandage. She gave the dog a shot and looked up at the men. "So can you tell me what happened to Max here?"

At the sight of the wound, the shorter man gulped audibly. His face was pale and he looked queasy. Tracy nodded at the taller man. "Um. You might want to have Mr. Collins sit down outside."

The tall man looked over at his friend. "C'mon, Fred. Maybe it would be good if you waited in the lobby. I'll tell them what happened."

"The bathroom is around the corner," Tracy volunteered as they left the room.

Dr. C gave Tracy a knowing smile. "Good call."

"I'm getting better at recognizing the barfers."

"It's a gift."

A few minutes later, the tall man returned to the room. Now that the dog was lightly sedated, Tracy was able to relax and get a better look at the man. On the phone she'd learned that the owner's name was Fred Collins, but she hadn't caught this guy's name. He did look oddly familiar though. She readjusted her hold on the dog and said, "Is your friend okay?"

"Yeah. It's not like he faints at the sight of blood or anything."

Tracy looked up at him over Max's prone body. "I hope not, if you guys were out hunting."

The man put his hands in his pockets. "Yeah. Good point. It's just Fred loves that dog. He's spent hours and hours training Max, ever since the dog was just a little pup. Is Max going to be okay?"

Dr. Cassidy looked up from her examination of the dog's leg. "It looks like he landed on a tree branch. There's a pretty serious laceration here. The puncture wound is fairly deep, so I'd like to do surgery to make sure I remove all the pieces of wood and dirt, so the leg won't get infected. Then I can stitch Max up. He should be as good as new after he heals."

Tracy stood up straighter and readjusted her hold on the dog to see if he was still inclined to move around. "Your friend will need to sign the surgery consent form." With one hand still on Max's drowsy body, Tracy reached over and grabbed a piece of paper out of a file folder. "Could you take this out to him? If he doesn't want to come in here, just tell him what Dr. C said and get him to sign it."

The man nodded, took the paper from her, and left. Tracy turned to Dr. Cassidy. "Do you know that guy?"

Still bent over, focused on poking at the dog's leg, her brown curls moved from side to side. "Nope. What did he say his name is?"

"He didn't. The owner is Fred Something-or-other. I think I've met the tall guy before."

"Maybe he was a customer at the restaurant?" The vet straightened and grinned at her. "Presumably he would have been less grubby then. And smelled better."

"It looks like Max is on the high road to sleepy-land. Should I go out and tell them to come back later? What time?"

Dr. Cassidy looked at the clock on the wall. "Yes, I'm fine here for the moment. Tell them to come back at three thirty. We'll have to rearrange some stuff to fit Max in."

Tracy went out to the lobby, where the men were talking to each other. They both were exuding anxiety, so Tracy went for the most reassuring smile she could muster. "Max should be fine, but surgery is going to take a while, so you guys can come back later. He should be ready to go at three thirty or so."

Fred handed the piece of paper back to Tracy. "Here's the form. Please, take good care of Max. I feel so bad about this. He's such a good dog. Don't let anything happen to him."

"We'll do our best. Dr. Cassidy is an excellent vet."

The tall man put his hand on Fred's shoulder. "Hey buddy, why don't you go on out to the rig. I'll meet you in a second. I think the hunting trip is over, so we should go break down camp. Maybe check into a hotel or something?"

"Yeah. I'm starving too. We missed breakfast."

"I'll be out in a minute."

With a look of relief, Fred walked out of the clinic. The other man turned back to Tracy. "I'm sorry, I didn't get a chance to introduce myself." He held out his hand. "I'm Todd Delaney and you look really familiar. Have you lived in Alpine Grove for a while?"

Tracy shook his hand slowly. "Yes! That's why I know you. I'm Tracy Sullivan. We went to school together. You moved away right before ninth grade. It's so good to see you. How have you been?"

"Doing well. Okay, today wasn't so good. But I can't believe you still live here. You look fantastic."

Tracy felt the color rise to her cheeks. His eyes truly were the most remarkable shade of blue. And now that she had a chance to evaluate more closely, it was obvious that under all that dirt and grime, he was incredibly good looking. "Thank you. So what have you been up to for the last however-many years?"

"The usual. School. College. Job. You know."

Tracy laughed. "Yeah, me too."

"Does your mom still own the gift store?"

"Yes. You should stop by and say 'hi.' She'd love to see you!"

"I'll be sure to do that, but right now we need to get back to the campsite before a bear discovers that we left it alone."

"Okay. See you later."

He grinned. "I'm looking forward to it."

As Tracy watched him leave the building, her heart rate started to settle back down to normal. Todd Delaney! She'd had such a crush on him and had probably drawn a thousand little hearts that said T.S. + T.D. on her junior high school notebooks. He was even her first kiss. Chaste and kind of icky in a dorky junior-high kind of way, but still. When she'd found out his family was moving away, she'd cried for hours.

~

Max made it through surgery and by the time the afternoon rolled around, he was starting to howl about being stuck in his stainless-steel prison. Tracy couldn't wait for three thirty to arrive. An unhappy coonhound could make a powerful amount of noise when he set his mind to it.

Fred and Todd walked through the door at precisely three thirty. They both obviously had spent some serious time hosing themselves down and Tracy tried not to gasp when she saw Todd. Grubby he was sort of attractive, but when he was all squeaky clean, he was downright gorgeous. If it wouldn't have been humiliating, she would have fanned herself with her hands. The cute, but kind of gawky ninth-grader had evolved into a complete hottie. He had the whole dark Irish thing going for him, along with an incredible build and those astonishing blue eyes.

Tracy walked over to the desk. "Hi Todd. Hi Frank. Max is going to be mighty glad to see you." A howl arose from the back room to emphasize her point. "See what I mean?"

Frank leaned on the desk. "It sounds like he's feeling better. God, that's such a relief." His eyes misted. "When he was bleeding, well, I just thought..."

Tracy put her hand over his. "It's okay. He's fine. Let me go get him."

Dr. Cassidy followed Tracy and Max out of the surgery area. The vet was holding a large semi-circular piece of plastic. "Hi guys. Max is doing great, but you'll need to be really careful about him trying to rip out his stitches. At this point, he still might be a little groggy, but once he's back to himself and the wound starts to bother him, he's going to want to lick and chew on it." She curved the plastic into a circle. "This is an Elizabethan collar or E-collar." She handed it to Frank. "You just connect it together with the little tabs and put it over Max's head. If he's like every other dog in the world, he will hate it and give you dirty looks. But it's necessary. We really don't want infection to set in. I've put a little drain in his leg, which you should check regularly.

Make sure to wipe it a few times a day, and if the area around the tube starts to look red or angry, call us. I've also given you some pain medication for him, which will help take the edge off. And this bottle has antibiotics. Make sure you give him all of them as directed, even if it seems like he's feeling better."

Tracy handed Max's leash to Frank, who paled again at the sight of the huge bandage and the tube sticking out of the dog's leg. "Okay. I'll make sure he behaves himself. It's gonna be a more low-key vacation now anyway, since we can't go hunting. We'll probably spend a lot of time hanging out and watching football."

Dr. Cassidy smiled sympathetically. "I'm sure he'll like that."

Frank handed the leash to Todd. "Keep an eye on him while I pay." Todd took the leash, sat down in one of the chairs, and stroked the smooth fur on Max's head.

After settling the bill, the two men left. Todd hadn't said much of anything to Tracy, which was disappointing. After his dazzling smile earlier, she'd had some rather enjoyable fantasies about seeing him again. What had he been doing all these years? He was well-dressed, so he probably had some high-paying job. And he was living somewhere other than Alpine Grove. Maybe that's why he didn't say anything. Because she obviously hadn't gone anywhere. Why would he want to go out with a lowly vet assistant who never made it out of Alpine Grove? In an effort to not dwell on that whole depressing train of thought, she sat at the desk and busied herself with the final accounting for the day.

She was startled from her calculations when the bells on the front door jingled again. Todd walked in and flashed her his patented smile. "Hi again. Frank's waiting for me, but I wanted to come back here and see if you'd let me take you to dinner tonight. I know it's last-minute, and you probably have plans already. But I thought I'd give it a shot, anyway. I'd love to catch up."

Tracy wondered if he could hear her heart pounding in her chest. "Yes...yes. That would be great. I'd love to!"

"Okay. It looks like there's a nice Italian restaurant on the main drag. You want to meet me there? Would seven work?"

"Sure. That would be great." It was so annoying that there were no other decent places to eat in this town. Dining at the place she'd been fired from was likely to be unpleasant and possibly mortifying in any number of ways. But there weren't any other options. Maybe, with any luck, Jerry would be gone for the night. He usually didn't do Mondays. That was something, anyway. And she might have a chance to say 'hi' to Lou. She missed the gruff old chef. Plus, he made the most fantastic lasagna in the known universe. She missed that too.

Todd left again and Tracy was left to her thoughts. He hadn't asked if she was involved. She could be married with six children, for all he knew. Okay maybe not six, unless she had really been an over-achiever on the parenting front. But why did he assume she wasn't involved? She looked down at her hand. If she were married, she would be wearing a ring. Little did he know that there was no way she'd subject a fine diamond to all the cleaning chemicals and potentially disgusting things she had to clean up here.

She gathered the papers together and said goodbye to Dr. C. She had to get home quickly and deal with Roxy before her big date. Unbelievable! An actual date with a gorgeous guy who had all his teeth. Yippee!

Chapter 8

Trout

Tracy walked into the Italian restaurant and found Todd leaning on the podium chatting with the new hostess, who appeared to be a recent Cedar County High graduate. Apparently Jerry had found himself a younger, cuter hostess. Nice. "Hi Todd."

He turned to her. "You look pretty tonight. Sherry says our table is ready."

Tracy nodded at the hostess. "Thanks. Aren't you Glen Harris's daughter?"

Sherry turned to look behind her as she walked them to a table. "Yes, my dad knows Jerry. That's how I got the job. I'm still trying to figure stuff out though."

Tracy sat down in a chair "You spell your name with a 'y' don't you?"

"Yeah, like the liquor, but Jerry wants me to change it, so it ends with an i." She leaned over to Tracy to hand her a menu and whispered confidentially. "Isn't that a little weird?"

Tracy took the menu gently and said under her breath, "Get used to it."

Todd tipped his menu toward Tracy. "Did you work here in high school or something?"

"Not in high school. I worked at the marina in the summers. It was a blast hanging out with the summer people and I got a great tan."

Todd leaned forward. "You sure seem to know everyone."

"You would too, if you had stayed here in town. Eventually, you know everybody." And they all knew you too, whether you want them to or not. Time to change the subject. "So did you and Fred find a place to stay?"

"Fred is out at the Enchanted Moose. They take pets, but they only had one room available. There's no way I'm staying in the same room with that guy. He snores like a freight train. Camping is okay, since I bring my own tent. But cooped up with him in a little room would not be much of a vacation. So I'm at the H12 here in town."

"It has a convenient location." That was its primary selling point. Probably its only selling point.

A waitress walked up to the table. "My name is Jenny and I'll be your waitress. Hello Tracy." The woman smirked in her typical snide way. "Long time, no see."

Tracy plastered a fake smile on her face for Todd's benefit. "Hi Jenny. Why don't you tell us what the specials are tonight?"

Jenny looked momentarily flustered and reached into her smock for her pad. She read off the list from her pad. "What would you like?"

"I'd like the lasagna. With a side salad and balsamic vinegar dressing on the side."

Jenny sneered at her. "Nice choice. And you, sir?"

Todd ordered and Jenny stalked off to the kitchen. He turned back to Tracy. "I guess you know her too? And you aren't best friends."

"Yes. And no, definitely not." Not in this lifetime.

Todd looked around the room. "So do you know *everyone* in this restaurant?"

Tracy unfolded her napkin and put it in her lap. "Well, quite a few of them. The summer people are mostly gone, so it's just locals."

Todd glanced over at a thin man in a brown suit. "Okay, who is that guy?"

"That's Larry Lowell. He's a lawyer. You might have met his parents, since they own the hardware store in town." As Tracy had predicted, Larry had returned. Look out, Sherry.

"Who is the sad guy in the corner?"

"That's Ron." Tracy fidgeted with her napkin. "His wife just had gall bladder surgery and she's in the hospital recuperating. She's fine, but she probably told him to go get a decent meal. She's a little bossy like that."

"How about that couple?"

Tracy peered beyond Todd's shoulder to a table behind him. "That's the guy who cheated on the librarian. I forget his name, but he doesn't live here. The blonde woman is the daughter of some rich guy who owns a manufacturing company and has a vacation house south of here."

Todd opened his mouth to say something, when an older woman ran up to the table. "Tracy, it's so good to see you!"

"Hi Mrs. Zelenski. How is Martin doing?"

The woman gave Tracy a hug around her shoulders and kissed her cheek. "That enema Dr. Cassidy gave him worked just great and he's pooping like a champ!"

"That's good news." Tracy could feel the flush rising on her face. "Give Martin a pat for me."

"I made an appointment for his shots, so see I'll you soon my dear. Have a lovely dinner!"

Todd chuckled. "I really hope Martin is a dog."

Tracy giggled. "Yes, Martin had a little digestive problem. But it's better now."

"So I gathered."

Tracy had an enjoyable time reminiscing with Todd about being a kid in Alpine Grove. They both had spent summers at the lake and had a number of the same teachers in school.

Todd tilted his wine glass at her. "So whatever happened to Mr. Lewis? He had more hair gel than any other man I've ever seen. And those huge horn-rimmed glasses." He laughed conspiratorially and said, "Remember the huge wad of keys with the retractable key chain?"

Tracy grinned. "Yeah. He was Mr. Word Problem. You buy six bushels of apples and the trains are going two-hundred miles an hour, blah, blah, blah. I'm thinking put the apples on the track and let the train run over them. Problem solved. I think he got a teaching job somewhere else. You have to figure there are opportunities to teach Algebra in the big city too."

"I suppose."

"So tell me about life after Alpine Grove. I heard you moved to Los Angeles. I was just there visiting my friend Shelby and taking a class. What area did you live in?"

Todd looked down into his glass as he swirled the burgundy liquid around. "I went to high school in the Valley."

"So you were a Valley Guy? Like, totally, you know, wow."

Irritation flashed in his blue eyes, but he smiled. "Yes, I suppose."

Oops. Maybe he didn't like LA. New topic. "So what do you do now when you're not out hunting with Fred?"

"I work for an oil company. So I travel a lot to Alaska and Texas."

"That sounds interesting. I'd like to be able to do more traveling." A better automobile would certainly help. "I've heard Alaska is beautiful. I'd love to see the glaciers."

He frowned at his wine glass. "I don't get to do much sightseeing. I do a lot of maintenance and troubleshooting of hydraulic systems. I spend a lot of time on the rigs."

Tracy twisted the napkin in her lap. "Well, to me it all sounds like an exciting adventure far away from here."

"It pays the bills."

The mood of the conversation deteriorated to the point that Tracy started to wish her imaginary electronic "shut-up zapper" really existed. She couldn't say anything right and she got the distinct impression that Todd didn't want to talk about his current life. Tracy wrung her napkin in her lap and made another effort to move back to safer subjects. "So did you get a chance to say 'hi' to my mom?"

His expression brightened. "Yes. She remembered me! And the store looks almost exactly the same. She's probably selling different stuff I guess, but it still seems the same, you know?"

Tracy gestured toward the street. "Yeah, that's my mom. She loves everybody, so the store always has a 'come on in and look around a while' feel to it."

By the time dinner was over, Tracy had run out of Alpine Grove anecdotes. Todd paid the bill and they went outside, where the wind had picked up and a flurry of leaves were cavorting along the sidewalk. He put his arm around her shoulders to shield her from the wind. "I'm kind of glad I'm not out in the woods right now. It's getting cold!"

She looked up into his deep blue eyes. "Do you want to go somewhere else? The same dive bars still lurk down the street if you want to get a glimpse of some more local color."

Todd smiled. "No thanks. Do you want to come back to my room for a drink?"

Tracy's back stiffened and she mentally cautioned herself not to do something dumb. "Um, well, I have to work tomorrow, so I probably shouldn't." No matter how cute he may be. "I live right down the street. We can walk down there and then say good night. I really do have to get up early. The vet clinic opens at eight and I have to get there at seven thirty to set up."

Todd nodded. "All right. Maybe I can see you again, though."

"Sure, that would be great. It's been fun catching up."

In front of her mom's store, at the doorway leading up to her apartment, Tracy stopped. "This is me."

"You live in your mother's gift store?"

"Actually, upstairs above it. There's an apartment."

Todd looked surprised. And not in an "I'm impressed" way. More like a "you're a loser" way. Tracy took one of his hands in hers. "Thank you for dinner. I had a great time."

Todd suddenly let go of her hand, reached out, and grabbed her around the waist, pulling her to him. "Would you like me to come upstairs?"

Tracy shifted in his arms. Sure, she hadn't had a date in long time, but this felt way too uncomfortable. "Maybe another time. My place is kind of a mess." That was an understatement. He bent down and kissed her, triggering an unwelcome flashback to eighth grade. Maybe she was doing something wrong. She tried to readjust her head. What was he doing? It felt like she was kissing a trout. Was she really *this* out of practice? How pathetic.

He released his hold on her and a corner of his mouth turned up. "I'll give you a call."

"Okay. Thanks again for dinner. I had a great time."

Tracy turned, slowly unlocked the door to the stairway up to her apartment, and watched as he strolled away. The traffic light was off for the day and flashing, which cast an eerie red glow on the blustery street. He certainly was handsome and obviously successful at whatever he did for the oil company. Maybe he really would call tomorrow. Or maybe he'd already written her off as a small-town loser.

~

As Tracy walked into her apartment, the strident yapping of her angry dachshund surrounded her. "Hi Roxy. I know I interrupted your evening routine, but I actually had a date." Roxy paused, seeming to contemplate this news for a moment, but then resumed her angry diatribe.

Tracy waved her hands at the dog. "Quiet, Roxy! Let me check my messages, then we can go for a walk. You're not gonna like it, though. It's getting cold out there."

Tracy pressed the button on her answering machine and heard Rob's deep voice tell her that he hadn't made it to Alpine Grove today, but would be there tomorrow afternoon. She looked down at Roxy. "I'm sure glad he didn't show today. I forgot about it when the whole prospect of actually going out with a hot guy came up." She grabbed the leash, bent down, and clipped it on the dog. "Okay little dog, let's go."

Roxy eagerly rushed to the door and Tracy picked her up for the journey down the stairs. They exited the stairwell and Tracy put the dog down on the sidewalk. A big gust of wind whipped at the small dog's fur and Roxy looked up at Tracy in dismay.

Tracy moved forward, dragging the dog behind her. "I told you that you wouldn't like it." Roxy ran to a patch of grass, relieved herself, and turned back toward the gift store. Tracy followed the dog back to the doorway to the stairs. "You sure get a lot more efficient when the weather turns."

The next day at the vet clinic was mercifully free of emergencies. Tracy was relieved to finally get the "easy" day that was supposed to have happened on Monday. At the end of the day, Tracy was doing the final accounting and looked up when Rob walked through the door. She pointed at his head. "Hey, you got a haircut." The shorter hair lowered the *Scooby-Doo* factor somewhat. Shaggy's hairstyle really wasn't a good look for anybody. Rob's hair was still sort of all over the place, but at least now there was less of it.

He leaned on the desk. "I can take a hint. And I never want to subject my hair to that nasty junk you put in it ever again."

"You're not going to forgive me for that, are you?"

"I'll get over it. Are you ready to leave? We have a lot of work to do. Do you have any sketches I can look at yet?"

Tracy shook her head. The idea hadn't even occurred to her. "I was busy. There was an urgent laundry situation and then an emergency here yesterday, so I had to work late. Are you staying at the H12?"

He rested his elbows on the counter. "Yes. It's really kind of a dump, isn't it?"

"I didn't say it was nice. I said it was convenient. There's a difference."

"That's true." He turned and waved toward the greater Alpine Grove area. "It's great that I can walk everywhere. I did some window shopping on my walk down here to the clinic. It was fun. And everyone is so friendly, which is such a change from LA. In the city, everyone walks around like they're wearing blinders. Here people smile and talk to you. I met a lawyer standing outside his office and we had a nice chat."

"Oh, that was Larry Lowell. He likes to get away from his desk and stand around watching the world go by. But hey, don't knock anonymity. Here, it can take forever to get through the line at the grocery store. And then you'll meet someone you know in the parking lot. But if you really want to get to know people, go to the post office. That's where the real action is."

Rob laughed. "You seem to have this place figured out. I should get you to write the copy for the web site too."

"I'm not much of a writer, but I have lived here for a long time." She paused. "Actually, I do know a writer who lives here, if you need one."

"I'm starting to think you know everybody."

Tracy put her notebook away and closed the drawer. "Sometimes it feels like it. I have some stuff to finish up here and then I need to walk my dog. Can I meet you in about an hour?"

"That sounds great. I'm in Room 2 at the H12. I think I'll stop by the gift store on my way back. Isn't that the store your mom owns?"

"Yup. Say 'hi' to Bea for me."

After tending to Roxy, Tracy walked up to the H12 and found Rob's room. The H12 was one of those motels that never seemed to change. It had looked pretty much the same for as long as Tracy could remember. Periodically, it would sport a new paint job and the owners would remodel the rooms somewhat, but the basic configuration remained. So no matter what cosmetic changes were made to it, the place always had a somewhat retro fifties motor-lodge feel to it.

Tracy knocked and strolled into the room when Rob opened the door. "Wow, I haven't been here in a long time. This brings back memories."

"What? Prom night?"

Tracy put her hands on her hips in mock indignation. "I beg your pardon. I was not that kind of girl." Okay maybe she was, but not at the H12. Yuck. "It looks like you've got yourself a serious nerd set up going. I can't believe you hauled all this computer stuff up here."

Rob surveyed the room, which was outfitted with a folding table loaded down with a computer, a printer, and a large monitor. "I'm used to dragging around computer boxes. That's your workstation. I have a laptop over here." He pointed to a small computer on the desk.

"You have a laptop? Those things cost a fortune."

"Actually, it's the one I use for work. Don't tell. But I'm just going to be calculating costs and writing up the quote. You get to use my good computer that has Photoshop on it."

A knot formed in Tracy's stomach. "Maybe we should go get something to eat. There's a little cafe right around the corner."

Rob's brows pulled together. "We really need to get started on this. We've only got a few days to figure out what this whole huge site is going to look like. I set up the meeting for Sunday, since it's your day off. And I already lost a day getting here, because I had to do an emergency network installation yesterday."

"There are networking emergencies?"

"Yes. The company couldn't communicate with the home office, so they were freaking out. When people lose money, it's an emergency. The boss wouldn't let me go until I fixed it."

"Yeah, like I said, we had an emergency at the vet clinic too, if that makes you feel better."

Rob looked horrified. "No, it doesn't. Was an animal hurt? What happened?"

"A dog had a run-in with a large tree branch. This type of thing happens a lot in hunting season."

"Is the dog okay? That sounds bad."

Tracy smiled at his expression. "Max is going to be fine. But he has to wear an E-collar, so now he's a conehead. That's probably making him cranky."

"I think your emergency trumps mine. Still, all this means that we're behind schedule. We need to get to work."

Tracy glanced over at the computer. "It can wait until after we eat, right? I'm starving."

"I suppose so. But then we really need to get started."

"Whatever you say."

～

Rob insisted that they get their meals from the cafe to go, so they could work. Tracy capitulated unwillingly and carried her little white bag of food back to the motel. After they got inside, she put down the bag, kicked off her shoes, and flopped down on her stomach on one of the beds. She waved her stockinged feet back and forth. "My feet are killing me. All that time standing on the hard floor at the clinic wears me out."

Rob turned on the computer and monitor on the table. "Maybe you should get some new shoes."

"I have some shoe inserts, but they're kind of worn out." She rolled over on her back with her feet hanging off the end of the bed. "I'm tired."

Rob grabbed her bag of food from the table and handed it to her. "Eat something. You'll feel better. Then we can get to work."

Tracy took the bag from him and sat up cross-legged. "Okay. Thanks for feeding me again." She took a huge bite from her sandwich and chewed ravenously.

Rob sat down at the desk and flipped the switch on the laptop. "You have to be one of the hungriest women I have ever met. Don't you ever eat?"

"It's hard to get a free moment at the clinic. I buy frozen food when it goes on sale. When I get a chance, I pop one into the microwave. A lot of times it's when Dr. C is busy doing surgery and I can monitor the anesthesia machine while I eat."

Rob frowned. "You eat while she's cutting up dogs and cats?"

"By then I'm usually starving. If I don't eat, I get a headache."

With a look of distaste, Rob took a bite of his sandwich and put it down. He walked over to the table with the large computer and monitor, bent over the keyboard, and poked at some keys. "This is all ready to go."

Tracy flopped back down on her back. "I think Jon and Annabelle finally got new beds in here. This one is actually comfortable. I'm just going to digest for a minute." She put her hands behind her head and closed her eyes.

Rob said sharply, "What are you doing?"

Tracy opened her eyes. "I told you, I'm resting. What's your problem?"

"Is there something you're not telling me?" Rob walked over and sat down on the edge of the bed. "We need to get started. If you're going to back out on me, now would be a really good time to let me know. Because I've got to make a whole lot of calls, if that's what's going to happen."

Tracy sat up. "No. I'm just waiting for creative inspiration."

"You'd be a lot more prepared for that blast of inspiration if you actually sat at the computer. Why are you avoiding it?"

"I'm not!" Tracy frowned and snatched her bag of food. She bounced off the bed and walked over to the computer. "See—this is me going and sitting down. Fine. Don't be such a taskmaster. I'm getting there. Can't a woman relax a little after a long day?"

Rob sat down at the desk, grabbed his sandwich, took a bite, and stared at the laptop screen. He gathered some printouts and got up to hand them to her. "Here are the pages you need to do designs for, with the dimensions. You remember how to set up the file in Photoshop, right?"

"Yes." *Not really.* Tracy snatched the papers from his hand. "No problem." She turned to the screen and clicked the software icon. A blank white screen appeared in front of her. "Okay, then. Look, it's Alpine Grove in a blizzard!"

Rob turned in his chair. "What?"

"I'm done. We're doing the winter white-out edition!"

"That's not funny." Rob turned back to his screen.

"You really have no sense of humor at all, do you?"

He scowled at the laptop. "My sense of humor will return after I get some work done. I have to figure out how I'm going to do this quote. Let me know if you need help with anything."

"Fine." Tracy clicked and clicked, looking for the elusive screen that would let her change the size of the page. It had to be here somewhere. She took another bite of sandwich and glared at the monitor. Stupid computer. It was hiding it. She hunched over the desk. This was like a scavenger hunt, except programmers were doing the hiding and it wasn't fun.

At last she found the right place and typed in the correct page dimensions. After clicking the *OK* button, she threw up her arms and leaped up out of her chair. "Yay me!"

Rob turned and looked at her. "Everything okay?"

"My snowstorm is the right size now!" At his dour expression, she sat down again. "Never mind. Working."

"Maybe you should save the file." He pointed at the computer. "By the way, I scanned a bunch of your photographs for you to start with. They're in the folder named *photos.*"

"How creative." She smirked. "You could have called it Fabulous Bygone Days in Small-Town America."

"Folder names aren't supposed to be creative. You name them something obvious so you can find them again."

"Gee, you're just a thrill a minute. Wanna go out and get some dessert? We could stop by the Italian place and grab something decadent. The chef, Lou, makes a tiramisu to die for."

"Maybe after you get something on that screen beyond a snowstorm." He turned in the chair and leaned his arms on the chair back. "I know you can do it."

Tracy sighed. She wasn't so sure. "Okay. But only because I want tiramisu."

Rob ignored her, turned back to the computer, and began pounding the keys on his little laptop keyboard with what some might have regarded as excessive force.

An hour later, Tracy had created the beginnings of a page. She saved the file and leaned back in the chair. It was horrible. She hated it. Why was she even trying? She didn't know what she was doing with this stuff. Looking at this page, people would certainly not be rushing to their phone to book a vacation in lovely Alpine Grove. They'd be running fast in the other direction. And she'd be leading the way. Yuck. She shut the program, stood up, and stretched her arms toward the ceiling. "I need to go tend to my dog before she stages another revolt in my kitchen."

Rob reluctantly turned his focus away from the screen and hurriedly pressed some keys. "Already? We just got started."

"I've had enough for one night. And I have to get up early."

He wagged his index finger at her. "You just want dessert again, don't you?"

"No. I'm going home."

"Do you want me to walk you down to your place?"

"This is Alpine Grove. I think I can make my way through the vast crowds of late-night revelers all by myself."

He shrugged. "Okay. Well, I'll see you tomorrow, then."

"Fine." Tracy gathered up her things and left the room. This was going to be a very long week.

~

The next day, after an exhausting amount of work at the clinic and an afternoon that included many complicated and heart-rending pet-related issues, Tracy knocked on the door of Rob's room at the H12. She was dreading opening the file she had worked on the day before. How to make a bad day worse: look at your crummy design and visualize yet another professional failure. Her father was right. Nobody ever made any money as an artist. The words *starving* and *artist* went together for a reason.

Rob opened the door and smiled in welcome. "Hi there! Ready to make more art?"

Tracy wandered into the room and sat on the bed. "I guess. I'm tired." She flopped backward and splayed her arms out onto the bed. "Sometimes people are horrible. And I hate that animals get sick."

Rob leaned over the bed and peered down at her. "Bad day?"

"Yeah. I don't know how Dr. C can make these life-or-death decisions every day. Today there was a tiny kitten that this guy was threatening to drown in a river if we didn't take it in." She propped herself up on her elbows and looked at him. "I don't suppose you'd like to adopt a tiny cat, would you?" She flopped back on the bed. "I mean, jeez, we're a vet clinic, not an animal shelter. What is wrong with people? Then later we had to tell this guy his dog was sick. Really sick. I hate that. I mean the dog is old, and the owner knows his dog is sick...the owners—they always know when something's really wrong. But it's just...so...hard." She covered her eyes with her arm. Why was she telling Rob all of this? What was wrong with her? Couldn't she ever just shut up?

A tear slipped down her cheek and fell onto the mattress. She wiped it away hurriedly and looked over at him. He had a distressed look on his face, as if he wanted to run away. "I'm sorry," she said. "This isn't your problem. I love animals, but sometimes I hate having a job that can make me cry. Usually I go home and hug Roxy, eat a lot of ice cream, and zone out on TV reruns. I did hug Roxy before I came here, anyway. I also told her she needs to never get sick and live to be the oldest doxie in recorded history."

Rob took a deep breath, removed his glasses, and put them on the nightstand. He rubbed his eyes and sat down on the edge of the bed. Taking one of her hands in his, he said, "I'm so sorry. That does sound like a really bad day. I wish we had more time to work on this, so you could go veg out."

Tracy rolled over on her side. She considered the concerned look on his face. He was being so nice, even though he probably thought she was a flaky basket case. "Have I mentioned that I hate deadlines?"

He squeezed her hand. "I figured that out all by myself."

She pulled her hand out of his, pushed herself back up to a sitting position, and glanced over at the computer. "Oh yippee, you turned it on for me."

"I wanted to take a look at what you were working on yesterday."

Tracy scowled at the evil machine and put her face in her palms. "Ugh. I hate what I did. It's awful." She lifted her head and her expression brightened. "I know the ice cream place is closed for the season, but maybe we can get some of that tiramisu."

"I was hoping we could talk about the page. I have a couple of ideas."

"Do we have to? She hugged her knees and put her forehead down on them. "It's terrible. I knew you'd hate it."

Rob reached over and took her hand again. "I don't hate it. But nothing is perfect on the first try. That's what the Delete key is for. Can't we talk about it?"

She lifted her head and turned to look at him. "What's the point? I should just go home." She moved to get up off the bed.

He gripped her hand more tightly so she wouldn't get up. When she turned, he looked into her eyes. "Yesterday, I asked you why you're avoiding this, and you said you're not. But you are. What's wrong?"

Tracy's shoulders slumped. "What if it really stinks and everybody hates it? I'm not really a web designer. I mean, who are we kidding here?"

Rob let go of her hand and moved toward the top of the bed so he could lean on the headboard. "What you're saying is that if you don't ever design something, then no one will hate it. Nothing bad will happen, right?

She shrugged noncommittally. "I guess."

"I agree that doing something creative is a risk. But you must have taken risks before. Done something you've never done before?"

"Yes. Usually I screw it up. Like when I left college. Twice." Tracy slumped down and rolled over on her stomach. "I wanted to be a vet, but I couldn't handle the math requirements. I dropped out. But then I went back and took some other classes, including some art classes. But I washed out again." She traced the ugly pattern on the well-worn bedspread with her index finger. "My father said he wasn't paying for me to be a screw-up, as he called it, and I came back here."

Rob looked down and picked at a loose thread on the bedspread. "So you view that as a failure?"

"Yes." Tracy crossed her feet at the ankles and swung them back and forth over her back. "My father reminds me periodically about how much he spent on my lack of education, just in case I might forget."

"But now you work at a vet clinic. You must have learned something."

Tracy sat up and crossed her legs. She leaned forward and smiled. "Actually, that's why I got hired. Dr. C loved that I knew so much about anatomy already."

"Sometimes good things come about in ways you don't expect. But you don't know unless you go out and do something. Every choice you make has pros and cons."

She wrapped her arms around her knees again. "Give me a break. What's the pro of me flaking out on you?"

Rob looked up. "Well, it's great for you. You can continue with what's familiar, doing what you've always done." He waved toward the door. "You can go home, eat ice cream, and hang out with your dog."

Tracy grinned. "That sounds good to me."

"But you'll never know if you could do something else. Maybe you wouldn't have to work at a job that makes your feet hurt and sometimes makes you cry. Maybe you could be a web designer. Do something that lets you use the incredible artistic gifts you have."

She said in a quiet voice, "You think I have gifts?"

He nodded. "Yes. You do. Our teacher thought so too. Weren't you listening?"

"She probably had to say that."

Rob made a wry face as he continued to pick at the thread. "Um, you may have noticed she didn't say it to *me*."

"Oh yeah."

Rob tugged and finally ripped the errant thread off the bedspread. "Like I said, this whole project is risky for me too. But I don't want to install networks forever."

Tracy poked at his leg playfully with her index finger. "Yeah, but you're not like me. You're a diligent buckle-down kind of guy. Dudley Do Right has nothing on you."

He looked up and his eyes met hers. "It's not often I'm compared to a Canadian Mountie who rides horses backwards. I'm not sure if I should be flattered or insulted."

"It was a compliment." Tracy poked at his leg again. "You'd totally rescue a damsel in distress."

"I appreciate your confidence in my ability to uphold justice, if not my equestrian skills."

Tracy giggled and flopped back on the bed next to him, putting her hand on his thigh and patting it amiably. "If I were tied to railroad tracks, you'd totally be there."

Rob removed her hand from his leg and slumped down on the bed, so he was almost nose to nose with her. "Maybe we should get to work now."

At the intense look in his hazel eyes, she started and moved away quickly. Up close, Rob's eyes were extraordinary —a deep amber color with gold flecks throughout the iris. "I think you're right. I'll shut up now." She scuttled off the bed and sat down in front of the computer. "If you need me, I'll be over here. Working."

Chapter 9

Scientific Experiments

Tracy worked late with Rob at the H12. They didn't say much, but she made some progress on her designs. By the time she went home, she was worn out from the long, draining day. She pressed the button on her answering machine and was surprised to discover that Todd had left a message. A little glimmer of excitement fluttered through her exhaustion at the thought of seeing him again. After giving Roxy a brief outing, Tracy was asleep almost as soon as her head hit the pillow. Her alarm went off at what seemed like an obscenely early hour and she dragged herself off to the clinic.

When Dr. Cassidy came in, Tracy had gotten most things set up, but was still working on cleaning out kennels. The veterinarian came into the room and Tracy turned to face her. "I know. I'm late getting stuff set up. Sorry!"

The vet put her hand on Tracy's shoulder. "We got a cancellation, so you have a little more time. Are you okay? I know yesterday was rough."

Tracy leaned back against the rows of metal cages. "Yeah. Then I had to work on the web site stuff with Rob. Sorry if I'm kind of spaced out."

The vet busied herself laying out her surgical implements. "How's that going?"

"I don't know. Rob is being nice, but I think he's figured out I'm a flake."

Dr. Cassidy looked up. "You're not flaky when you're here."

"Here, animals could get hurt or die. Or I could get bitten if I screw up. I couldn't stand hurting an animal, and dodging personal pain is a great motivator. But this thing is just a web site, not life, death, or physical harm. He thinks I'm avoiding working on it. Like I'm afraid to take a risk or something because I'm afraid people will hate it. So I goof off and procrastinate."

The vet nodded her head. "I could see that."

"I thought you said I wasn't a flake."

"You have said you want to do a number of things, but then you back off. Like the art class. You almost didn't go. But I saw some of your paintings at your place when I had to pick you up that time. You're really talented. But the paintings I saw aren't done. It seems like you find reasons not to finish them."

The bells on the front door jingled and Tracy looked toward the lobby. "Oops. Somebody is here. Guess it's time to get started." As she hustled to greet the client, she was still thinking about what Dr. C had said. Did she really do that?

The last appointment of the day was late and Tracy rushed out of the clinic when it was over. She decided to walk straight over to the H12, so Rob wouldn't think she was ditching him. Plus, she was going to have to leave early to meet Todd, which Rob probably wasn't going to appreciate either. The good news was that after her little crisis of confidence last night, she'd made progress and was actually looking forward to working on her designs today.

She knocked on the door of Room 2 and Rob opened the door and waved her into the room. "I was starting to wonder what became of you."

Tracy walked through the door. "I'm sorry. This guy was late for his appointment and the dog was not exactly excited about going to the vet. It took a while to get them out of there. I came here first to let you know, but I really have to go walk my dog now."

"Do you want company? I could use a break."

"Okay. After staring at this stuff all day, your brain has probably melted."

"I think I'll live." He went inside, grabbed the room key, and locked the door. "Let's go. You seem to walk everywhere. How far away do you live?"

"My place is above the gift store. Most of the buildings along the main drag have offices or apartments above them."

They walked across the H12 parking lot and down to the street. At the slam of a door, Tracy looked behind her. Todd was exiting room number six. It would probably be awkward if Rob and Todd met each other. Best not to go there. Tracy picked up her pace. She looked over her shoulder again. Todd wasn't alone. Hmm. Interesting. Who was that woman?

Rob matched her increase in speed. "Wow, you can really move when you want to."

"Like you said, I walk a lot. And Roxy hates it when I'm late." She wrapped her arms around her torso. "I need to grab a warmer jacket too. I've been resisting breaking out the winter wear. I'm not ready to deal with the cold yet."

Rob shuffled through some leaves. "Oh come on, fall here is incredible. I love this weather. It's all crisp and bright.

Even though the trees have just about dropped all their leaves, there are so many pine trees, it's still green."

"You wouldn't be so enthusiastic if you had to trudge through the snow for the next five or six months." She rubbed her hands together and turned toward the door to the stairs up to her apartment. "Here it is. That sound you hear is angry dachshund."

Rob laughed. "I figured." He followed her up the stairs and into her apartment. Roxy's barking evolved into a paroxysm of deafening canine hysteria.

Tracy kicked aside some magazines and grabbed the dog off the floor. "Quiet, Roxy. That's enough." The little dog growled in her arms.

Rob looked around and walked toward the painting that was sitting on her easel. He stumbled slightly over the box of paints. "Oops, sorry."

"I haven't found a home for that. I trip on it all the time." Roxy growled for emphasis. "Roxy, stop that!"

"This is a really good start. You should finish it."

"You sound like Dr. C. She said the same thing to me earlier today." She bent her head to peer at Roxy's face. "Have you got yourself under control, little dog?"

Rob turned back to her. "I guess your dog isn't particularly friendly, is she?"

"It depends. She tends to hate men." Usually only men she was dating. Roxy was selective that way. Who knew what her problem was now? Good thing she hadn't let Todd up here.

"I'll try not to take it personally."

Tracy clipped on the leash and put the dog back on the floor. "Can you behave?" Roxy started toward Rob and launched into another barking episode to let him know exactly what she thought of him. Tracy picked the dog up again. "Okay, that's not going to work. Let's get going."

Rob left and waited at the bottom of the stairs while Tracy locked up. She followed with Roxy in her arms. He said, "So does that dog ever walk on her own?"

Tracy put Roxy down and the dog immediately started motoring down the sidewalk. "Yes. She's quite mobile when she wants to be. She's only got three legs and dachshunds can develop back problems too, so I never let her run up and down the stairs."

The humans walked together in silence while Roxy sniffed all her favorite spots for any new information that might have transpired since she'd been out this morning.

Tracy wondered what Rob was thinking about. He usually wasn't this quiet. Maybe after seeing her painting, he was having doubts. She couldn't remember the last time she'd actually finished a painting. Maybe he was coming to some obvious conclusions. He already knew she wasn't exactly a workaholic. And he was going to be really irritated that she had to leave early tonight. But there was no way she wasn't going to miss out on another date with Todd. Not to mention she was curious who he was with at the H12. Even the idea of starting something with Todd was stupid, given that he lived so far away, but she still wanted to see those gorgeous blue eyes again.

Tracy turned around, pulling Roxy back in the opposite direction. "Okay little dog, you've done what you came here to do. Let's go home." Roxy wagged her tail and started pulling on the leash, back toward the apartment.

Rob looked down at Roxy. "She certainly is a determined little thing."

"Roxy likes being in charge. Usually she is, so it works out well for her." Tracy turned to look at him. His eyes were downcast, watching Roxy's short legs propel her forward. Behind the glasses, that man had some seriously long eyelashes. It would take six tubes of mascara to get her eyelashes to look that thick. Life was so unfair.

They stopped at the doorway and Tracy unlocked the door. "Okay, so I have to tell you something you're not going to like."

Rob followed her up the stairs. "Thanks for warning me."

Tracy ensconced Roxy in the apartment and locked up. "So, I have a...uh...an appointment tonight, so I have to bail out early."

Rob touched her forearm quickly. "Is everything okay? This isn't about the dog yesterday or anything, is it?"

"I'm fine. I just have to meet someone."

"You mean a date?"

"Sort of. I'm meeting a guy who used to live here a long time ago." Rob didn't have to look so surprised. She could have a date. It wasn't the most impossible thing in the world to think she might have a social life, was it?

He removed his glasses and pinched the bridge of his nose. "We really should talk about that one page you weren't happy with, though."

"I know. I did some stuff last night that I like better. I think I'm starting to get the hang of the program again."

They crossed the parking lot and went back into Room 2. The computers were still sitting there, waiting. Nothing had changed. But today, Tracy sat down and turned on the machine. She turned in her chair to look at Rob. "Okay, so tell me your ideas on the hideous design."

Rob pulled a chair over to her table. They went through the page and Tracy wrote notes on the motel notepad. Then they discussed how the ideas could be used in other areas of the site.

Tracy glanced over at the clock radio next to the bed. "Is that really what time it is?"

Rob looked at his watch. "Yes, the clock is right."

"I've got to go." She looked down at herself. "I was going to go change my clothes first. Oh well, I guess this is it." She gathered up her coat. "Sorry!"

Rob nodded. "I'll see you tomorrow. We need to figure out how we can finish this up. We've only got two days."

"I know. I know. But I really have gotta go now."

~

Tracy ran down the street to the cafe where she and Todd were meeting for coffee and dessert. She opened the door and the wind caught it with a whoosh, so everyone at the small tables looked up at her. Her tenth-grade English teacher was sitting closest to the door. "Hi Mrs. Plunkett. Sorry about that."

Todd waved from across the room and she sat down across from him. "I'm so sorry I'm late. Thanks for waiting."

He flashed her a charming smile, revealing his perfect white teeth, and she was reminded again of how handsome he was. Yowza. He gestured toward the cafe. "No problem. It was nice to just sit and relax for a few minutes."

"How are Fred and Max doing?"

"They're good. We're all taking off tomorrow. After lots of time in front of the TV, I think those two are well rested. And they've cleaned the store out of junk food."

"Did you watch football, too?"

"Yeah, and I did some other stuff. Who is that guy you're hanging around with? I didn't realize you were seeing someone."

Tracy bit her lip and shook her head. "I'm not. That's Rob. I met him at a class and we're working on a project together."

"So he's not a boyfriend? That's good. I was hoping we could spend some time getting to know each other better."

"Do you want to go somewhere? Not much is open at this hour. This cafe is about to close, so we should probably get moving. Betsy is going to want to start shutting down here soon."

"We could go somewhere for a drink."

"Yeah, I suppose. Where? The 311 bar is pretty disgusting."

"I bought some beer. We could go to my room."

Tracy looked at him sharply. "What?"

Todd rested his elbow on the table and leaned toward her. "We could have some fun. All work and no play isn't good, right?"

She looked into his blue eyes. "Actually, most people seem to think I don't work hard enough."

"Jobs where you're on your feet are tough. Physically, I mean. I know how that is. It's good to relax and unwind."

Tracy looked over at the menu on the wall. The first item was chicken. Was he *really* suggesting that she sleep with him? After the trout kiss? She was stupid, but not *that* stupid. Time to change the subject. "So when I was walking with Rob I saw you with a woman at the H12. Who was that?"

Todd squinted at the window toward the street. "Oh, just an old friend."

"Someone who lives here? She didn't look familiar to me."

"Oh come on, you don't know everyone."

Tracy offered up her most sickly sweet, syrupy smile. "No. Just everyone who has a pet, eats out, boats, or buys gifts. So there might be some demographic I'm missing. But I'm not sure what that might be."

Todd looked out the window again. "Whatever. How about the Mystic Moon place? Maybe we could have a drink there? I could use a drink. It's the last night of my vacation and I want to have a good time."

"All right, that would be okay. Although I don't think it's a lot better than the 311."

"Do they still have beer?"

"Yes, the last time I checked. It's a bar."

"Good enough for me." He grabbed his coffee cup and got up out of his chair. "Let's go."

Tracy gathered up her things. This was probably a bad idea. It wasn't just that she couldn't talk to him. He actually was more of a jerk than she thought. But it was his last night here and it wouldn't kill her to keep him company for old-time's sake. She had been desperately in love with him in eight grade, after all. "Okay. I'm coming."

They walked down the street to a bar that had a sign above it made of old wooden letters that spelled "Mystic Moon Soloan."

Todd tilted his head to gaze up at the sign. "They still haven't fixed it?"

"The Soloan is part of local lore now. At this point, if they changed it to say *saloon* there would probably be a local uprising or something."

She opened the heavy wooden door and walked inside. The paneled walls were dark from years of cigarette smoke. The regulars were hunkered up to the bar, their grumpy expressions reflected in the mirrored beer signs scattered across the walls. The *thwack* of pool balls crashing into each other occasionally punctuated the general low noise of conversation.

Tracy sat down on one of the empty stools at the bar. "Hey, Fred. How's Charlie doing?"

Fred the bartender looked like a refugee from a Harley Davidson rummage sale. His leather vest covered a prodigious gut and he sported a leather bandanna on his cleanly shaved head. Even though he looked like a criminal, Tracy knew that he was a nice guy with a huge soft spot for his miniature poodle Charlie. Fred grinned at Tracy, showing off the gaping hole where one of his front teeth used to be. "Charlie is doing great. So how's my favorite artist?"

Tracy picked up a cardboard beer coaster and twirled it on the bar. "Actually doing some art for a change." She waved at Todd, who had settled on the stool next to her. "This is Todd. He went to school here before he bailed out to go to the big city."

Todd nodded. "Beers for both of us."

Fred grabbed some glasses and busied himself at the tap. Tracy turned to look at Todd. "I suppose you never came here when you lived in Alpine Grove before."

"No I was too young, but I dragged my mother out of here a few times right before we left."

"Really?"

Todd scraped at the wooden bar with his fingernail. "I don't want to talk about it."

Fred placed their beers in front of them and smiled at Tracy. "Give Dr. C my regards."

Tracy wrapped both hands around the tall pilsner glass. "Will do. Give Charlie a big hug for me. He's a sweetheart."

Todd took a long drink from his beer, draining half the glass. "Ah, that's better." He turned to Tracy. "You even know the guys in the dive bars. You sure get around. So who's Charlie? One of your past flings?"

"No. Charlie is a poodle. Like I said, if people have pets, odds are good I'll meet them eventually. Fred has a sweet little poodle named Charlie who had an ear infection."

Todd snorted. "You're telling me that guy has a poodle? Yeah, right. Nice story. You just don't want to admit to whatever really happened."

Tracy plunked her beer glass down on the bar and a few drops splashed out. Now he was really over the line. "What are you getting at? Do you think I'm the resident Alpine Grove slut or something?"

Todd raised his palms in front of him. "Hey, I'm just saying. Small towns like this are boring. Maybe you've had more fun than you're letting on. You sure know everybody. Really well. You wouldn't be the first woman I've met who was looking for a little action on all those cold winter nights."

Tracy got up off her stool. "I don't know what happened to you, but I'm not going to sit here and listen to it anymore. I'm outta here."

Fred walked up to them and leaned over the bar. "Everything okay here, Tracy?"

"I'm fine, Fred. Thanks for asking. But I've gotta go." She reached into her purse and pulled out a few bills. "This should cover it." It better, because it was all she had. "Don't forget about Charlie's shots, Fred. I think your appointment is next Wednesday, but you might want to call the clinic and check." She turned to Todd. "Have a nice trip back to wherever you come from. 'Bye."

Tracy turned away from the bar as Fred's deep baritone rose behind her. She looked over her shoulder. Fred was leaning over the bar toward Todd, which made Todd seem tiny by comparison. Sometimes it was good to know massive human beings. Bigfoot had nothing on Fred. Although to be fair, Bigfoot probably didn't own a poodle either.

～

The next day, Tracy managed to get out of the vet clinic on time and walk Roxy before heading over to the H12. She knocked on door number two and tried not to gasp when she saw Rob. "What did you do? You look different." And *so* much better.

"Come on in." He stepped aside. "I got another haircut."

She walked in and circled him to view his hair from all angles. "Somebody sure did something right." The Shaggy look was gone. It was a miracle.

"I was taking a walk at lunchtime and I explored one of the side streets. There's a little barber shop over there."

"Yeah, that's Joe's."

Rob ran his fingers through his hair. "Joe and another guy were sitting outside in chairs and they said hello to me. So I stopped and talked to them."

Tracy sat down on the edge of the bed, kicked off her shoes, and crossed her legs. "Yeah, Joe is a nice guy. I went to school with his daughter. Was Joe hanging out with George?"

Rob nodded. "Yeah, that was his name."

"I figured. George used to go there every week for a haircut. Mostly he just went to hang out and talk with Joe. Then he went bald and had no excuse to go to the shop anymore. But he couldn't give up the routine, so now that he's retired, he walks over there every day and they just sit and yak during Joe's lunch hour. If it's nice out, they sit outside. George is a character. He cracks me up."

"George kept saying that Joe needed to fix my hair. They got into a whole debate about it. There was a lot of analysis and it got a little embarrassing, since I was standing right there. I let Joe cut my hair, just so they'd stop talking about it. I guess my hair is like some kid's named Neil."

Tracy slapped her hand on the bed and laughed. "Neil's hair was like yours? That's hysterical. I never would have known. Neil had great hair!"

"I guess you know Neil? According to local barbershop legend, his great hair is only thanks to Joe."

Tracy leaned forward and put her elbows on her knees. "I didn't know that. But Joe is said to be a magician with scissors. And yes, I knew Neil. I went out with him in high school. In fact, he helped me get my car running, which was quite an accomplishment. I think he got an A in auto shop because of me."

Rob sat down at the desk and took off his glasses. "So what happened to Neil?"

Tracy picked at a piece of antique food that was stuck to her jeans. These pants may not have participated in the big laundry event. Oops. "Well Neil did have great hair, but he wasn't the greatest boyfriend. We agreed to go our separate ways after high school. He joined the Air Force and now lives somewhere out East with his wife and kids. I still have the car, though. It got me to LA." Barely.

"Wow, it still runs? That's impressive. I don't like working on old cars. That's why I got a newer one."

"It's a miracle the thing moves, really. You have no idea. I'm not very good about regular automotive maintenance. There's a reason I want to drive your car. I have this twisted desire to find out about the advancements in automotive technology over the last twenty or thirty years."

Rob chuckled. "Maybe we can talk about that after we get through the meeting. I think it's time for a status report. Since you got here late and left early yesterday, I'm not sure we're going to get everything done."

"I finished the four screens we talked about the other day."

"How about the other sixteen?"

Tracy looked down at her hands. "Okay, maybe we're a little behind schedule."

Rob got up and sat next to her on the bed. "I hope that was a really good date, because it's starting to look like we aren't going to be even close to ready for the meeting on Sunday."

Tracy threw up her hands in frustration. "No, actually it was horrible! You see this amazing-looking guy and your mind goes to all these fantastical places about what it might be like to kiss him. And then it's a trout."

"A trout? Like a fish?"

"Yes. Do you know how disgusting it is to kiss a fish?"

Rob leaned away from her. "Uh, no. Do you?"

"There was a fishing trip and a dare." She waved both hands in front of her. "Never mind. Let's not go there. That's not the point! I mean he's this gorgeous guy. Totally hot! But then, yuck. Maybe it's me. I mean it's been a long time." Tracy shook her head. "Maybe I'm just so out of practice I forgot what to do. And then, after all that, he seemed to think I was the town slut."

Rob raised his eyebrows. "I assume you're not, but what do I know?"

Tracy glared at him. "I'm *so* not! Do you know how long it been since I've even had a date?"

"No."

"All I do is work! I have no life."

"You found time for Trout Dude."

"Yeah, and look how well that turned out." She looked down at the ugly bedspread. "I am so pathetic. I don't even know how to kiss a guy anymore."

Rob put his index finger under her chin and gently turned her head so she was looking at him. His eyes had turned a stunning amber color and the gold flecks were catching the light, so they looked like tiny sparks. Tracy's heart pounded in her chest. He leaned to kiss her and said in a soft voice, "This is purely for scientific purposes." His lips skimmed hers and Tracy reached up and ran her hands through his new, improved wavy brown hair. Soft. Nice. As the kiss deepened, her thoughts evaporated into a sea of sensation. With no trout anywhere.

Tracy reluctantly released her hold on him and opened her eyes. "Wow. I love science. I may have almost flunked it, but I have a new appreciation now."

He gave her a warm smile. "Yes. I think we've learned that you haven't forgotten much of anything."

Tracy let out a long breath. "I guess so." Zoinks. That was incredible.

Rob moved to get up. "So, are you ready to work?"

"No. But I'll get over it." Although any semblance of concentration had now gone right out the window.

He went back to the desk, put his glasses back on, and ruffled through some papers. He leaned over and handed them over to her. "Here's what we're looking at."

"Spreadsheets? You're showing me spreadsheets? You are a real buzz kill, you know that?"

"Just trying to return your focus to the task at hand." He sat down next to her on the bed again and pointed at the page. "This shows the pages and the estimates."

"That's what you'd charge?" She looked at the numbers then at him, trying not to think about how close he was and how much she wanted to kiss him again. "Are you kidding me?"

"Nope. I told you the site would cost a lot. There's a lot of work involved. I've finished figuring out the quote. Is there any way I can help you get these sample page layouts done?"

Tracy hunched over the papers, holding them with both hands. "Those are some big numbers. Whoa. Okay. Let me think for a second." She readjusted herself, putting one foot up on the bed to try to put a little more space between herself and Rob, so she could concentrate. She rested her elbow on her knee and faced him. "Here's why I'm so slow. I spend a whole lot of time clicking around looking for stuff because I don't know the software very well. It also takes me forever to put in all the text for menus and that stuff, since I can't type. When I was in college, Shelby typed some of my papers because she can type like 120 words a minute or something ridiculous like that. Maybe we could do the same type of thing here. Kind of an assembly line. You do the boring filling with color and typing stuff. I'll do any drawing stuff."

Rob looked thoughtful for a moment. "That makes sense. Is there any way you can take tomorrow off from the clinic? Even if you could leave early, it would help."

"No, it's really too late to try and dump my shift on Gail."

He pulled off his glasses and rubbed his face with his hand. He looked back up at her. "I'm not sure what to do, then."

Tracy jumped off the bed and turned around to face him. "Nope. We're going to do this thing! We've still got tomorrow. This is like college. We need to pull an all-nighter. I'm on it. I'll call Kat and see if she can take Roxy while we deal with finishing this and the meeting too. No more distractions."

She looked into his face and noted that the intense look was in his remarkable hazel eyes again. Okay, there might be one distraction.

He smiled. "I like your enthusiasm. And by the way, just so you know, I hate trout."

"Me too."

Chapter 10

Lost & Found

After Tracy made her calls, she and Rob walked to Tracy's apartment to collect Roxy for her journey out to Kat's place. Rob carried the crate downstairs for Tracy and placed it next to The Turd, which was parked in the lot behind the gift store. "This is your car?"

"Yes. Like I said, you really don't want to subject your lovely automobile to the road out to Kat's place. The Turd is beyond the point where even the most vicious pothole could do anything to it."

Rob laughed. "You call your car The Turd?"

"My father named it. But it fits."

Rob peered through the filthy windows at the torn brown Naugahyde interior. "Are you sure it's safe to drive?"

"I'm not dead yet." She opened the rear door. "Just throw the crate in here."

Rob obliged while Tracy stowed Roxy in the back seat. After an enormous amount of outrage and hysteria at the apartment, the little dog had finally calmed down, so that now she was downright composed. Tracy slammed the door. "Maybe Roxy is finally getting used to you."

"That's good news for my eardrums."

They got in and Tracy started up the car. It coughed itself awake, spewed a plume of exhaust, and sputtered a few times to emphasize that it was cold outside. "Come on baby, you can do it." She turned to Rob, "It needs to warm up."

"Along with lots of encouragement."

"That too." She turned and smiled at him as she ground the car into gear. The Turd lurched into motion. "All *right*! We're mobile."

Later as they bumped down the driveway to Kat's house, Rob looked back at Roxy. "Your dog copes with the bad roads remarkably well. It's a good thing she doesn't get carsick, because this would do it."

"She's spent a lot of time riding around on bumpy dirt roads. I guess she's used to it."

The car slammed into a deep crater and Rob placed his hand on the dashboard to brace himself against more impacts. "I'm so glad you volunteered your car."

Tracy turned to him. "Told ya."

The forest canopy opened up and the house came into view, and Tracy pulled up in front of it. Rob got out of the car and looked up at the massive cedar trees that towered above the house. "It's beautiful here. Look at the size of those trees."

"Yeah, growing up, I always wanted a place like this. The woods around here are so peaceful. When you sit outside in the summer, you hear birds singing and bugs buzzing. In the winter, it's just this envelope of silence. A lot of people never get to experience forests like these."

"You're really lucky to have grown up here."

"I suppose. Most of the time I don't think about it, I guess. It's just home."

The front door opened and Kat walked down the steps, followed by Linus. When the big dog saw Rob, he leaped around Kat and bounded up to greet the new human. Rob looked momentarily startled, but put out his hand so Linus could sniff it. "That may be the largest dog I've ever seen."

Kat pointed at the dog. "His name is Linus. And he's a sweetheart."

Tracy nodded. "He is. And at work, he's famous because he barfed all over Dr. C. It was a spectacular performance."

Rob bent to ruffle the fur on Linus's neck. "Aww, you didn't do that, did you?"

"Yes, he did." Kat said. "The full Technicolor yawn. But it wasn't his fault. He was poisoned. It's kind of a long story."

Tracy turned to Kat. "Kat, this is Rob. Rob, Kat. Feel free to say 'hi' while I get Roxy out of the car."

Rob and Kat smiled politely at each other, but didn't say anything. Tracy removed Roxy and put her on the ground. The dog immediately went over to Linus and sniffed a paw. Linus looked down at the small dog with a worried expression and wagged his tail feebly.

Kat walked over to Roxy, picked her up, and stroked the silky fur on her head. "Hi Roxy. Yes, it's me again. And yes, my mother is still here. You're probably the only one who is happy about that."

Tracy handed the leash to Kat and then went to remove the crate from the back of the car. "Thanks for taking her again on short notice. I'll see you late Sunday afternoon."

"We'll be here. You can just leave the crate there." Kat motioned toward the steps up to the house. "I'll get Joel to bring it inside later."

Tracy went around to the driver's side and she and Rob got into the car. She looked at him. "Be glad you didn't meet Kat's mother. Kat is nice, but her mother is seriously unpleasant."

Rob said, "Instead, I got to meet the cool dog. He was great. I'd love to have a big lovable dog like Linus, but I travel too much."

Tracy put the key in the ignition and turned to him. "Hey, if we get this contract, you can become a homebody and get your dream canine. Lots of dogs need homes, you know."

"I'll keep that in mind."

Tracy went through the starting and begging routine and successfully convinced The Turd to move. They bumped their way down the driveway back toward town. It was time to get to work.

~

Kat brought Roxy into the house and put her on the floor. "Okay Roxy, I know it's part of your heritage, but don't forget that we have the 'no burrowing into the house' rule." Roxy wagged her tail, looking pleased that Kat had remembered her achievements.

Mary came up the stairs and looked down at Roxy. "Oh, the little dog is back."

"Yes, Roxy is going to be here until Sunday afternoon. If you'd like to be her caretaker, that would be helpful, since I have to finish my article today and hand it in."

"No, I can't. I have things to do."

Kat nodded. It had been worth a try. Her mother was on some type of mission and was not letting anyone in on what it was. Joel and Mary had moved into a largely silent detente. Kat just tried to stay out of the way. Her mother obviously was intent on finding something in this house, but she refused to say what it was. At this point, Kat was tired of asking. The good news was that Mary was a cleaning machine. The house was probably cleaner than it had been in thirty years. Maria wouldn't be able to refer to it as Chez Stinky anymore.

After the weather had improved and he'd gotten his chain saw back, Joel spent most of his time out in the forest cutting firewood. At this rate, they'd probably end up with fifteen cords of wood. At dark, he returned to the house dirty and exhausted, so he took a shower and retired to his office. Presumably he ate at some point, but Kat didn't know when. She had barely seen him in the last few days, except when he was asleep. It had been a long, lonely week.

Fortunately, before Joel had disappeared into the depths of the forest, he had moved Kat's computer upstairs for her. If he hadn't, she wouldn't have had a prayer of finishing her article. All that was left was one more editing pass and she could hand it in.

She sat down at the table in front of her computer and looped Roxy's leash under a chair leg. "Sorry, but you're not going anywhere. And your favorite caretaker has ditched you for the time being." Roxy wagged once and curled up at Kat's feet, settling in for her morning nap. Kat finished her article and sent it off to the editor. She stood up and stretched. Roxy did the same and Kat looked down at the dachshund. "We have learned that you don't like the long walks. I'm definitely not carrying you through the forest again. So you are getting your own special walk first."

Kat picked up Roxy and took her out to the front yard. After about ten minutes of wandering, Roxy indicated she'd had enough of the great outdoors. They went back inside. Now it was time to muster everyone else for the big walkie.

Kat picked up Roxy and carried her down the stairs to the hallway where the other dogs were enjoying their morning naps. Mary was still attacking boxes in the room formerly known as Kat's office.

Kat walked to the doorway, followed by a parade of yawning canines. Her mother was sitting on the floor, rummaging through boxes in the bottom of the closet. She clearly had not found the object of her massive quest yet, and she didn't look pleased about it.

Kat put Roxy on the floor and knocked lightly on the door jamb. "I took Roxy out separately since she can't handle the long walk, but the other dogs really need some exercise. All that bad weather made them a little squirrelly. We haven't reached canine equilibrium yet."

Mary sat back on her heels and wiped her hands on her apron. "I noticed."

"Could you watch Roxy while I take everyone for a long walk? Maybe you could keep her in here again on the bed? That worked out okay before and she seemed happy."

Mary sighed dramatically. "Fine. If you must do that, I'll take care of her."

"Okay, we'll be back in a little while." Maybe a long while.

Kat picked up Roxy and placed her on the bed. Having successfully handed off her charge, Kat got the other dogs ready for the walk amid great enthusiasm, cavorting, and expressions of canine joy. Maybe she'd go for a really extra-long walk. Everyone seemed enthusiastic about the idea of getting out of the house.

She opened the back door and Linus and Tessa charged out. Lori leaped around them, performing great feats of border-collie acrobatics. Kat and Chelsey followed along more sedately to the trail that went into the forest.

It was a crisp, sparkly fall day. The air was cool and the wind sighed through the trees. As her feet crunched through the twigs and brown fallen leaves, Kat smiled up at the brilliant blue sky. The article was off into the Internet ether and all was right with the world. Well, except for her mother still being there. A member of a flock of Canada geese flying overhead honked for emphasis.

Kat felt her muscles relax as she walked along the trail, absorbing all the sights, sounds, and smells of the forest. After so much rain, it was good to feel sun on her face again. When the weather finally decided to behave, it was often stunningly beautiful and Kat wanted to drink it all in.

She looked down at Chelsey, who was happily toddling along, her tail waving behind her. "Are we going to have a house guest forever?" Chelsey looked up with worried eyes. "I know. You're right. This can't continue. But you and I are the same as far as our deep dislike of confrontation. I hate starting something that's going to make my mother angry, but I can't have her rummaging through my house indefinitely. For one thing, I think Joel will move out. And none of us want that, do we?" Although Chelsey looked sympathetic, she didn't seem to have any wisdom to impart. "Yeah, I know. It's my fault this has gone on so long." Chelsey's ears cocked and she turned her head, looking ahead on the trail, where the dogs were now playing with Lady, who had emerged from an opening in the forest.

Joel came down the hillside, stopped on the trail next to the group of dogs, and put down his chain saw. "I see you all decided to go farther afield than usual."

Kat scampered up to him with Chelsey leading the way. "Fancy meeting you here." She wrapped her arms around his waist and hugged him hard. "It's so good to see you. Even if you are coated in Kevlar."

He returned the hug. "You see me every day."

"Not lately. I just made a promise to Chelsey that I will talk to my mother today. Now I'm promising you too. I've been a wimp, avoiding what will undoubtedly turn into a huge, horrible fight. She obviously hasn't found whatever mysterious thing she's looking for. But it's *our* house. She needs to go."

Joel released her and looked down into her face. "Way to be forceful."

"It all sounds good, but I haven't done anything yet. I could still chicken out. I left Roxy with her."

He removed the hard hat and ran his fingers through his hair. "That's a start. I guess our small yappy guest has returned?"

"Yes. Tracy was with some guy named Rob. I guess it's the guy she's working with. He's kind of cute, in a way."

"Oh really?"

"Well, not to-die-for handsome like Jan's boyfriend. Or like you."

He grinned. "Nice save."

Kat waved toward the trail. "You and Lady seem to be on the high road home. Are you done?"

"No. But the chain saw ran out of gas and I forgot to bring the gas can with me this morning."

Kat took his hand. "We'll escort you home."

"It's always nice to have an entourage."

~

Kat opened the back door to the house and the dogs rushed into the hallway in a great furry flurry, followed by Joel. Kat bent down to remove the harnesses from Linus and Tessa.

Mary ran out of the bedroom and up to Kat. "You have to do something! I can't find the dachshund!"

Kat stood, glanced at Joel and looked back at her mother. "I thought you were going to make her another pillow fort."

Mary frowned and waved in the general direction of the room. "I did and she was happy for a while, but you were gone so long. She started trying to break out. I thought she might hurt herself if she tried to jump off the bed. She was being so good, so I just put her on the floor, so she could walk around a little."

Kat clenched the harness in her hands. Uh-oh. "I told you that she has a little problem with disappearing. She's small, but she has a warped sense of humor."

Mary waved her hands in exasperation. "You have to do something. I've been looking everywhere."

Kat looked over at Joel. "We'll help you look. Where did you last see her?"

Mary turned and walked back into the bedroom. "We were right in here. I was working on organizing the shelves. She was right beside me. Then I looked around and she was gone."

Kat said, "Well, I don't think she does stairs. Tracy and I carry her everywhere. So she's probably down here somewhere. You didn't open the door and go outside, right?"

Mary shook her head. "No. I haven't."

Joel said, "I'll get a flashlight. Kat, maybe you could start pulling stuff out of the closet."

Mary wailed, "I just got it all cleaned up and organized!"

Joel looked at her but said nothing, and then turned and left the room. Kat crouched down on the floor and looked under the bed. No eyes peered back at her. But it was remarkably free of dust under there. How bizarre. She crawled over to the closet, looking under the furniture as she crossed the room. She sat in front of the sliding door and began removing the boxes from the floor, in case Roxy was hiding behind something. "Come on Roxy. Not again. This is *not* cute. Really. I mean it."

Mary sat on the bed with her hands folded. "I can't believe this. She was *right* there."

Kat removed a few more boxes. While her mother was preoccupied, it might be a good time to get this conversation over with. "I know you won't tell me what you're looking for Mother, but clearly you haven't found it. Don't you have things to do back at home?"

Mary straightened. "Are you saying I've been a bother?"

Kat stopped moving boxes, sat back on her heels, and put her hands on her thighs. "You hate my boyfriend, you hate my dogs, and the cats are afraid of you. No one has seen them in days. And to top it off, we can't even stand to eat together. Why are you here?"

"I thought Abigail had something of mine and I wanted it back."

Kat leaned back on the bedroom wall with her legs out in front of her and gazed up at her mother. "What is it? I spent a lot of time cleaning this place when I first moved in. If it's canned goods, you're out of luck. I threw those away."

"What? No. That's disgusting. Anything canned would be spoiled by now."

"You have no idea."

Now Kevlar-free, Joel walked back into the room with a flashlight and his toolbox. He crouched down next to Kat to shine the light on the closet floor. "Did you see anything?"

Kat turned and peered into the closet. "Nope."

"Hear anything?"

"Nope."

Joel sat on the floor and pulled out some more boxes. "This built-in thing is attached, so at least she can't be behind that."

Kat tapped on the wood. "Do you think she could get behind the drawers?"

"I don't think so, but I didn't think she could get behind a cabinet either."

Kat sighed. "Roxy is very creative."

Mary said from behind them. "Why do you think she's in there? She could be anywhere!"

Kat said, "Because the door to Joel's office was closed and there's no place she can go in the hall. Unless you were digging in the storage closets again, that leaves this room. Roxy likes to get into small spaces. It's her thing."

Mary said quietly. "No, I already went through those closets the other day. What can I do? I feel terrible."

Joel raised one eyebrow at Kat and moved a few more boxes. Kat said, "It's okay, Mother. Joel will find her. He always does."

He touched Kat's arm. "Maybe you could pull those drawers out?"

Kat stood up. The built-in cabinet in the closet had three shelves and four drawers below them. Starting at the top, she pulled out the drawers and stacked them on the floor. The contents of the drawers were organized into neat little piles. Her mother had been busy. But no dog appeared.

Joel got on his hands and knees and crawled into the closet. He shined the light in the corner under the row of shelves that ran up the side. "There's a hole back here." He laid down on his stomach and shined the light into the hole to get a closer look.

Kat sat back down on the floor with a thump and put her face in her hands. "Oh no."

Joel started thumping his knuckles along the drywall at the back of the closet and was rewarded with a small *yip*.

Kat dropped her hands and bowed her head. "What is *wrong* with this animal?"

Mary stood up and walked over to the closet to peer inside over Joel and Kat. "Is she really in there? It's okay, Roxy. I'm so sorry!"

Joel backed himself out of the closet and sat next to Kat. He rummaged around in his toolbox and then looked at her. "Do you think you can convince Roxy to come out? If not, I have to shred another wall, you know."

"I know. I think I have bad karma."

He pulled a small saw out of the toolbox. "I think the walls have bad karma. If we live here long enough, eventually I'll have to cut holes in all of them."

Kat moved around Joel, crawled into the closet, and laid on her stomach. She held a dog treat into the hole. "Come on Roxy. Lookie, it's a treat! Don't you want it? Come out and I'll give it to you."

There was a lot of scrabbling and whining. Roxy seemed to be making an effort to leave and get the treat, but it wasn't working. Kat crawled back out and looked at Joel. "Maybe she's too long to turn around?"

"I guess dachshunds don't do reverse?"

"Apparently, this one doesn't. Maybe because she has three legs? I don't know."

Joel sighed. "Okay. I guess I have to do it." He grabbed the saw and laid on the floor and began cutting the drywall.

Mary had been silently watching the proceedings. Suddenly, she bent down and pulled something out of the empty area where the drawers had been in the built-in cabinet. It was a stack of letters. She clutched the papers to her chest. "Oh my goodness. It's them!" She ran over to the bed and sat down. "Abigail saved them after all. I knew she would." She bent her head and began sobbing quietly.

Kat stood up and walked over to her. "What is that?"

Her mother looked up and wiped a tear off her cheek. "Letters. All the letters I wrote to Abigail. We corresponded for years. I told her all my hopes and dreams when I was a young girl. I miss writing to her so much. I just wanted to see the letters again."

Kat sat down on the bed next to her. "I had no idea. I didn't even think you liked Aunt Abigail."

Mary wiped her eyes with a fingertip. "Oh, she was my favorite aunt. I could tell her anything. But after I had the huge fight with her friend, we only communicated in writing. I just couldn't face her."

Kat put her arm around her mother's shoulder. "I think I told you, I talked to Louise. She feels bad about your argument too. Maybe you should talk to her."

Mary sniffed. "Perhaps I'll write her a letter."

A cracking noise came from the closet and Roxy ran out. Kat jumped off the bed, grabbed the little dog, and sat down on the floor with her, snuggling her in her lap. "Welcome back, Roxy! Here's your treat."

Joel crawled out of the closet and put his tools back into the toolbox. Mary crouched down to pet Roxy. She turned to Joel. "Thank you."

He smiled. "You're welcome. I'm glad Roxy helped you find what you were looking for."

Chapter 11

Not a Mushroom

After they returned from dropping Roxy at Kat's, Rob and Tracy managed to get a few more screens designed before she went home and fell asleep. Her apartment felt quiet and dreary without Roxy's small energetic presence. And she spent way too much time thinking about kissing Rob. Apparently, he had quite a few undiscovered talents. In addition to amazing lips, he was an absurdly fast typist, making Tracy wish she'd taken typing class in high school. She'd heard enough things about the typing teacher, Ms. Hightower, that she'd evaded that particular elective class. Ms. Hightower had always proudly proclaimed that touch-typing was the only way to type and the hunt-and-peck approach was slow. Now Tracy realized just how much slower it really was.

The next day, Tracy got out of the clinic as quickly as she could. She grabbed a few things from her lonely apartment, walked down to the H12, and knocked on the door of Room 2.

Rob opened the door. She walked by, threw her bag onto one of the beds, and handed him her coffeemaker. "Here it is. I hope you got coffee."

Rob took the machine and tilted it to the side to examine it. "Wow, I haven't seen a Mr. Coffee like this one in a long time."

"Think of it as a cherished heirloom from the heyday of the Alpine Grove commune. With vintage harvest gold floral accents."

Rob put the coffeemaker on the dresser. "As opposed to a yard-sale reject?"

Tracy sat down in front of the computer. "Very funny. I'll have you know I found that when I excavated my apartment. My mother had it for years. It probably really did live at the commune."

Rob said, "You're serious? There was a commune?"

"Yes. My parents were card-carrying members. Except I'm sure they didn't have cards. That would have been catering to the Establishment."

Rob sat down at the desk. "Where was it?"

"Out past Kat's place, way out in the woods. It was beautiful. Or it was when I was a kid, anyway."

Rob folded his arms on the back of the chair and grinned. "You were a flower child? How groovy."

Tracy turned on the computer. "Don't knock it until you try it. I had a lot of fun. There were a lot of people there, so it wasn't like I was unsupervised. But I had the opportunity to splash around in creeks, play with goats, and run around in pastures. Stuff that today would be deemed unsafe for a child."

"You could have stepped on a nail or drowned."

"Exactly. But I didn't." She splayed her arms above her head. "I lived to tell the tales. And there are many, but I'm sworn to secrecy."

"Did you take a hippie oath or something?"

She put down her hands and shook her index finger at him. "If I told you that, it wouldn't be a secret, would it? But I do have a hippie name."

"Tracy?"

"No. That's my regular name. I never tell anyone my hippie name. It's another secret."

Rob tilted his head. "That hippie code sure is complex. But I bet your mother would tell me. She likes me." He stood up, crossed over to the computer, and stood next to her chair. Very close. She could feel the warmth of his body next to her. He said, "So where were we? Do you want me to type again?"

Tracy looked up at him. From her vantage point in the chair, he really did have a nice build. Tall, broad shoulders. She already knew those shoulders were muscular. It would be interesting to find out what the rest of him was like under those clothes. Wait. This was ridiculous. When did she start thinking he was cute? Sure, the date with Todd was demoralizing, but she'd kissed Rob exactly once. And now she was acting like a goof in front of him. This was stupid. Sure, he was nice and easy to talk to, but they'd been hanging out for days. What was her problem?

He touched her shoulder. "Is something wrong?"

She stood up quickly. "Nope. I'm fine. Doing great." *Yes. Not fine. Feeling like an idiot.* "Why don't you type first?"

"Okay. Then maybe you can work on those illustrations for a while."

"Sounds good. My mouse will be at the ready."

Tracy pulled over the other chair and told him what colors to use, where to add photos and put in placeholders for her illustrations. Periodically, she'd lean in a little too close and lose focus again. The way Rob's hair curled around his ears made her want to reach out and touch it. And whatever shampoo he was using smelled really good. Mmm.

After about an hour, Rob turned and looked at her. "I need food. Let's switch for a while. You can draw some illustrations and I'll go over to the cafe and get something to eat before they close. Betsy is probably starting to shut down by now."

"You're starting to know the neighborhood better. And the neighbors."

Rob put on his coat and said, "Betsy is really nice. And I've eaten so many meals there, I'm probably helping to put one of her kids through college. I'm actually at the point where I'm looking forward to cooking something myself again."

"You know how to cook?"

"Of course. Doesn't everyone?"

Tracy sat down at the computer. "Sure." *No. Not really.*

Rob left the room and Tracy found an illustration she was supposed to be finishing up and opened the file. She began working and was so deep in concentration that when Rob opened the door, she almost had a heart attack.

Rob put the white bags of food on the desk. "What happened? You look like you're doing the Pledge of Allegiance."

"Nothing." Tracy looked down and realized she had her hand on her chest. "You just startled me."

He looked over her shoulder at the drawing on the monitor. "Wow, that's great. It looks like you're done with that one."

"Yeah. Moving on." He needed to stop getting quite so close to her. "I think I need coffee, though."

She got up and started brewing a batch of coffee. She turned back toward him. "See! The Mr. Coffee may be old, but it still works."

Rob stopped chewing. "Good thing. Because I'm already tired and we've got a long way to go."

Tracy sat down with her sandwich. "I know."

Hours later, Tracy had consumed enough coffee that she was starting to remember why all-nighters were a bad idea. It was almost three in the morning and her mousing hand was starting to shake from all the caffeine. Time to switch to cropping photographs, since drawing was becoming problematic.

She opened the image of her father with the car. "This is so cool! I can really take a look at this old photo by zooming in."

Rob was lying on his side on the bed, looking rumpled. "The magic of zoom. It's not just a kid's TV show."

Tracy turned around in the chair to look at him. "What TV show?"

"You never saw *Zoom*? It was on PBS in the seventies."

"I was at the commune. We didn't do TV. Or electricity." She turned back to the monitor. "I think this car really is The Turd. Check out the art. It's so creative! There are peace signs, happy faces—and even a rabbit."

Rob got up, dragged himself over to the computer, and squinted at the screen. "Uh, is that a hookah? And a caterpillar?"

"Maybe. I think it's an homage to *Alice in Wonderland*."

"Or Jefferson Airplane."

Tracy started humming the tune to "White Rabbit." She clicked a few times to look at different parts of the photograph. "See what happens when you chase rabbits. Check out that mushroom!"

Rob sat down in the other chair next to her and picked up his glasses off the table. "We might not want to have images of stoned wildlife on the web site."

Tracy giggled. "Oh, you're no fun. I'll just modify it a little. Once the photo is small, no one will be able to tell that's a magic mushroom." She zoomed in on the image and began painting. She moved aside so Rob could take a look. "See. I fixed it."

Rob looked at the monitor and burst out laughing. "That does *not* look like a mushroom, Tracy."

"I know. I made it thinner."

Rob threw his glasses on the table and flopped down on the bed laughing uncontrollably. "Yes. Now it looks like. Well. Something else." He caught his breath and waved weakly at the monitor. "Zoom out a little."

Tracy did as instructed and started to laugh. "Oh nooo. And it's sitting right next to the smiley face too. This gives new meaning to the term Mr. Happy. I think this poor guy may have some type of disease, though. That's not a good color. I think it's inflamed." She burst into loud peals of laughter.

Rob sat up and made an effort to try to get himself under control. He cleared his throat and gasped, "Look! It's Freudian Photoshop!" He collapsed back onto the bed, holding his stomach and convulsing with laughter.

"Here, let's add some effects." She made a few passes with the mouse, adding a stone texture. "Look, now it's rock hard!"

Clutching her midsection and laughing, she got up from the chair and gazed at the monitor. Tears were streaming down her cheeks and she said weakly, "This is disturbing on so many levels. That's my father standing next to the car."

Rob said, "Good thing your father's last name is Sullivan and not Johnson." He rolled over and pointed at the monitor. "It's Mr. Johnson and The Turd—famous seventies folk band!"

Tracy fell down on the bed next to Rob in a fit of laughter. She tried to collect herself, but it wasn't working. She looked at Rob's face and saw the twinkle of amusement in his eyes. "Stop that!"

He opened his eyes wide, giving her an innocent look. "I'm not doing anything."

She shoved at his shoulder as she dissolved into another laughing fit. "Yes you are. Cut it out!"

Rob rolled over on his back breathing heavily. "Ugh. My stomach hurts."

"Mine too. I wonder if it's possible to actually die from laughter."

"Only at three in the morning."

Tracy giggled and sat up. "Okay. I'm getting it together again." She stood up and returned to the computer. "This is me getting back to work. What's that command that makes it all go away?"

"Revert."

"Sorry, Mr. Happy, I'm reverting you. No more phallic Photoshop!"

Rob started laughing again and rolled over on his side. "That sounds painful."

Tracy giggled. "I wouldn't know. And stop that."

"Trying." He sat up and made a feeble effort to look serious. "If we don't get the contract, there are a lot of porn sites on the Internet. I bet there's photo retouching work available."

"It seems I have hidden talents."

"I think so." Rob chuckled and rolled over on his back again. He took a deep breath. "Okay. I'm more or less under control now. Really. For sure this time. I think it's probably my turn at the computer, anyway. If I have some more coffee, I'll be fine."

Tracy breathed deeply. "Okay. There are only a few pages to go. I'll just crop this photo. No more mushroom. I promise."

He turned from the coffee pot and grinned at her. "I'm afraid I'm never going to be able to look at fungi the same way."

Tracy nodded. "Or my dad."

~

At around five in the morning, Tracy raised her hands over her head in victory. "It's done! I'm done. So done." She stood up and got out of the chair. She walked over to the bed and shoved Rob's lethargic body. He stirred and looked up at her groggily. She peered down into his face. "Are you alive? Because I'm done."

He groaned and sat up. "Really? Completely? Done, done?"

She pointed at the computer. "Yes. All photos are in place, illustrations are drawn, and empty boxes are filled. The pages are complete."

He reached out, grabbed her around the waist and pulled her down to him for a bear hug. "I can't believe it. You did it!"

Tracy hugged him back. "*We* did it. This was definitely a team effort."

He released her. "I have a splitting headache. Maybe we should get some breakfast."

"Nothing is open yet. Let's walk down to my place. I have some cereal there. And I'd like to spend some time with my toothbrush."

Rob stood up and ran his fingers through his hair. "Good idea. Be right back."

While Rob brushed his teeth, Tracy looked at herself in the mirror above the dresser. She looked like she'd been run over by something. It was not pretty.

She grabbed her coat and they walked out into the cold, quiet morning. A whisper-thin layer of frost coated the leaves on the ground and they sparkled in the lights of the motel parking lot. Getting out in the cold air felt good after being cooped up all night in the motel room. Rob seemed to perk up a little. Tracy turned to him. "Are you feeling better?"

"A little. I still have a headache. And I'm spaced out. I'm not sure if taking a nap before the meeting would make me feel better or worse."

"I don't know about that. I do know that a shower is going to be extremely important to my well-being. Only a couple of hours and this will all be behind us."

He took her hand. "Thanks again for your help. When we started in on this, I didn't realize how much work we'd have to put into it. I thought it would be just that one meeting, not this huge proposal. But I think the design came out really well."

"I hope I can still channel Annette when I'm this tired."

Rob looked at her. "Who is Annette?"

"My made-up fabulous artiste. At the first meeting, I pretended to be Annette. She's a wildly successful brilliant LA artist who sells tons of paintings to high-end galleries across the globe."

"That's interesting. Is Annette your hippie name? It's not very flower-child-like."

"No, Annette is make-believe. She is creative, confident, and wealthy. She is definitely not a vet tech in a tiny town in the middle of nowhere." Tracy sighed. "If you absolutely must know, my hippie name is Rainbow."

He stopped on the sidewalk and pulled her around to face him. "Rainbow? That's great. I can see you as Rainbow. Maybe that's why you're so good with color. If you can't channel Annette, maybe you can channel Rainbow instead."

She shook her head. "Not a good idea. Rainbow is a flake."

Rob pulled her closer to him into a hug. "But a really cute flake."

She put her arms around his neck. "I don't feel very cute right at this particular moment."

He stroked her cheek. "I think you are. But I'm looking forward to you spending that time with your toothbrush."

Tracy giggled. "Sorry. Coffee breath is icky. Walk faster. It's freezing out here."

They got to Tracy's apartment and she dispensed some cereal. Rob sat on the sofa with his feet up on the coffee table. He looked down into the bowl. "I haven't had Cap'n Crunch in a long time. The crunch berries are sort of scary, aren't they?"

"Hey, fruit is important."

Rob waved his spoon at her. "I hate to be the bearer of bad news, but that's not fruit. On a different note, have you thought about putting shelves on that wall? Then you could get some of this stuff off the floor."

"I suppose that would help. It would require money, though, which has been in short supply. Did I mention that the Cap'n was on sale?"

He examined the crunch berry floating in the pinkish milk on his spoon. "I didn't think about the cost. Maybe you could find some cast-off wood and create a couple shelves that way. You know everybody. Someone is probably building something somewhere."

"I'll ask around."

After Rob went back to the H12 to take a shower, Tracy faced the ugly prospect of finding something to wear for the meeting. After possibly the most wonderful shower ever, she stood and stared into her small closet. Shelby was in possession of her only decent suit, and Tracy had worn it to the last meeting anyway. She riffled through the clothes and found a fairly presentable skirt and blouse that would work. This was Alpine Grove. They should be glad she wasn't showing up in jeans and a flannel shirt.

Later, Rob knocked on the door and Tracy let him in. At this point, he was freshly washed and shaved, so he looked significantly less bedraggled than the last time she'd seen him. But definitely still tired. One advantage of glasses was that they could sort of disguise dark circles. Wearing glasses was certainly easier than applying 700 pounds of concealer like she had.

He surveyed her outfit. "You look nice."

"Anything would be an improvement. You ready to go? I'm looking forward to seeing your car again."

"You do seem to have a special attachment to it."

As she locked the door, Tracy turned to him. "Try driving The Turd around for a decade or so and see how you feel."

"Please don't make me think about your car." He chuckled. "If I start laughing again, I'm so tired I may pass out entirely."

She took his hand and swung it back and forth. "Maybe I should drive your car."

"Nice try."

They drove to the house on the lake and got out of the car. Tracy looked up at the building. The original Victorian had been restored and was surrounded by impeccable landscaping, with stone walls that curved around the property like ribbons trailing across the expansive green lawn. A lot of lakefront property was nice, but this place oozed so much opulence that it was hard to believe it existed in Alpine Grove. Tracy turned to Rob. "So this is how the other half lives. I'm thinking he can afford your quote."

The house had a huge ornate wooden door with a metal lion-head door knocker. Rob raised his eyebrows at Tracy and knocked on the door. "Here we go."

She smiled nervously back at him. "We're prepared. No problem."

Ben Walsh opened the door. He was wearing jeans and a flannel shirt. Tracy did a mental eye roll. In Alpine Grove, even the rich people wore the same clothes. Although with the somewhat dashing Sean-Connery thing he had going, Ben looked as if he had walked out of a J.Crew catalog, not like he'd just rolled out of a tent in the woods. Still, she might be a tad overdressed.

Rob shook Ben's hand. "It's good to see you again."

Ben waved them into a huge entry area with an arched mahogany ceiling. "Come on in. Let's go sit down in the library."

Rob took a chair at the huge wooden table and set his laptop case on the floor. Tracy took a chair next to him. The room was lined with rich walnut bookshelves and antique-looking leather-bound books that were undoubtedly worth a fortune.

Ben sat across from them, looking expectant. "Would you like something to drink? Maybe some coffee? I know I dragged you out here a little early, but I have quite a few meetings to get through today."

Tracy looked at Rob. The expression on his face suggested that even the idea of coffee might make him throw up. She said, "No thank you. We've had our coffee this morning." And last night. In extreme quantity.

Rob pulled the quote out of his bag and handed it across the table to Ben. "Here are the numbers. There are black-and-white printouts of the screens, but if it's okay, we'd like to show you our mock-ups on the laptop, so you can see the colors."

Ben nodded. "That would be fine. Have at it." He turned to Tracy. "I've talked to Rob a few times since we met. How have you been? I still think I've met you somewhere before."

Tracy went for her most winning smile. "I don't know about that. But I do know we've put a lot of work into these mock-ups. I hope you like what we've put together for you." No, she was not going to mention being a hostess at the Italian restaurant. Not at the last meeting. And not at this one either.

Rob got the laptop going and went through the information in the quote. Ben had his elbows resting on the table and looked on in a polite and mildly interested way. He was one of those men who was blessed with a great poker face. It undoubtedly helped him a lot in business.

Rob sat down and said, "I'll let Tracy talk about the design elements."

Ben nodded. "Go ahead."

Tracy moved to stand near the laptop. She started with the home page, which had the glorious sunset photo her father had taken at Gray's point. Ben smiled good-naturedly, which made Tracy feel a little better. Although she wasn't quite feeling her Annette-level confidence, she was doing okay. She went through a few more screens. Ben was nodding and it seemed he liked what he saw.

She pressed the key to access the Alpine Grove history page and looked down at the monitor. There was the photo of her father. It was cropped, but she knew the magic mushroom— or non-mushroom—was there. Momentarily flustered, she stammered, "...and this is a photo of Mr. Johnson." She looked at Rob in horror. Behind his glasses, the twinkle in his eyes indicated barely contained hysteria, and although his mouth was firmly shut in a straight line, his shoulders were shaking. Tracy burst out in a peal of laughter and covered her mouth. "I'm so sorry!" Rob took off his glasses and put his head down on his arm on the table, laughing uncontrollably.

Ben looked at one and then the other. "Are you two okay?" He looked more closely at the screen. "Was there a joke? It just looks like a man standing next to an old car."

Tracy sat down and tried to get control of herself. "I'm so sorry. We're just a little tired."

Rob lifted his head and said weakly. "Yes. I'm sorry. It's just a guy and a..." he stopped and laughed again "...a car."

Tracy held her stomach and stood up again. "Okay. I'm fine now. Really. I'm *so* sorry." She paused to take a deep breath. "Here's the last screen. This page talks about the nature trails in the area. This is a photo of one of the hiking trails in autumn. And. Oh. I forgot. There's a picture of a..." She giggled and covered her mouth with her hand again. "A *mushroom*."

Rob raised his head, looked at the screen, and said weakly, "Oh no, Rainbow." He began laughing again quietly, unable to control himself.

Ben stood up and picked up the folder of printouts from the table. "I'm not sure what exactly is so funny, but I have a phone meeting in a few minutes. So if you'll excuse me, I'll let you gather your things. George will see you out."

Tracy sat back down in the chair and dropped her arms to her sides. She turned and shoved Rob, who was still giggling. "What is wrong with you?"

"Me? I'm not the one who called her own father 'Mr. Johnson.'"

Tracy put her forehead down on the cool wood of the tabletop. "Jeez. I totally blew this."

Rob put his arm around her shoulders. "It's not all bad. I haven't laughed this hard in years. Probably ever. So it's not a total loss, Rainbow."

Tracy mumbled. "Don't call me Rainbow."

~

Rob drove back to Alpine Grove and parked in front of the H12. It had been a quiet ride as the adrenaline of the last twenty-four hours drained from Tracy's system. Rob seemed equally subdued. She got out of the car and watched as Rob grabbed the laptop case from behind the seat. They walked to the door of Room 2 and went inside. The small space smelled like old coffee. Paper debris, laundry, and various remnants of past meals were strewn across most of the flat surfaces.

Rob went to the side of the closest bed, put his glasses on the nightstand, and flopped down on the ugly bedspread. He put his arm behind his head and closed his eyes. He said, "I feel really strange."

Tracy crawled up from the bottom of the bed and laid down on her side next to him. "The word you're looking for here is not strange; it's bad." All the coffee and sleep deprivation had made her stomach feel like a large piece of metal had rusted inside her gut. She closed her eyes, hoping it would go away.

Much later, she started awake. Where was she? She raised her head and realized she was still lying next to Rob, in the exact same spot. He was still fast asleep, his thick lashes utterly still as he breathed quietly. She tiptoed to the bathroom and splashed some water on her face, which made her feel better. Then she swished some toothpaste around in her mouth.

That helped even more. She was getting dangerously close to feeling like a human being again.

She walked out of the bathroom, into the room. Rob had propped himself up on one elbow and was gazing bleary-eyed at her. Tracy waved toward the bathroom. "All yours."

He groaned and got up off the bed. "Thanks."

Tracy started making a mild effort to clean up and find some of her things among the rubble from last night. Maybe she should clean out the coffee pot. The poor thing probably hadn't seen this much action since 1985. It had to be exhausted too. She picked up the brown-stained carafe and tilted it. The dregs of burnt coffee slid across the bottom. She set it back on the dresser and turned to watch Rob wander back over to the bed. He sat back down on the end, staring off into space.

Tracy sat next to him. "You look like I feel. I'm so sorry about what happened. It's my fault, I know."

Rob ran his fingers through his hair. "Not really; it's just what happened. Sometimes you get a case of the giggles and you can't stop, you know? Like those gag reels at the end of videos with clips of actors screwing up scenes. It can happen to anyone."

Tracy studied his face. How could anyone be so impossibly reasonable? This was nuts. No one was that mellow. "Are you kidding? I totally screwed up. Why are you being so nice?"

He shrugged. "I guess I'm just a nice guy. We tried."

She wanted to shake him. "How can you not be mad? I'm mad and it's my fault."

Rob gazed intently into her eyes. The color of his eyes had darkened to a deep amber. "Maybe I'm thinking about other things now."

Tracy's heart lurched in her chest. "Um."

He ran his long fingers through the hair at the back of her skull and took her head in both of his hands, pulling her lips to his. The other kiss, while electrifying, had been tame by comparison. A jolt ran through Tracy and she felt as if all of her nerve endings were on fire. She wrapped her arms around him, reveling in the sensations, wanting to get closer. Their bodies entangled, and they rolled off the bed onto the floor.

Tracy mumbled, "Ow," but Rob's long, lean body was on top of her and his hands were busy unbuttoning her blouse, so she forgot about the hardness of the floor in her own quest to find out what was under all those baggy clothes. So far, the answers were enticing and she wanted to learn more. He was all hard planes and angles. And muscles. Lots of muscles. Biceps, triceps. And pectorals. Exceptional pectorals. Latissimus Dorsi. Nice. Obliques. Even nicer. Those boring muscle pictures in anatomy class didn't do justice to Rob's form. It was like his skin had some gravitational field, and she couldn't take her hands off him.

A few minutes later, Tracy regained the presence of mind to come up for air. She sat up. "Wait a minute."

Rob's hands paused in mid-caress. He moved his head away from her and looked into her eyes. "Are you okay?"

Tracy grinned. "Oh, I'm well past okay and cruising toward a much, much better place. But a small corner of my brain just remembered that this is the H12. And we're on the floor."

Rob looked down at the threadbare carpet. "Ick. That's nasty."

They both jumped up simultaneously and crawled back onto the bed. Rob wrapped her in his embrace and kissed her again. He mumbled. "You feel great."

Tracy smiled. "I'm going to buy you a thesaurus for your birthday. Oh, and while I have your attention, there's something else. It's been a long time." She shook her head. "I don't want to talk about how long, but suffice it to say, I don't generally walk around with a box of condoms in my purse."

Rob pushed a strand of blonde hair back from her face. "You've never rented a room at the H12, have you?"

He stroked the nape of her neck with his index finger and delicious chills went down her spine. If he didn't stop that, the last tiny bit of reason she had was going to fly out the window. "No. I've never really been here much at all until now, I guess."

He trailed his fingertip around her neck to the hollow at the base of her throat. "There's a basket on the front counter with a sign that says "Take one...or more than one." Jon and Annabelle are very into safe sex and they encouraged me to grab a handful. I told them I was staying here alone, but they insisted. I didn't want to be rude."

"Interesting. I guess that's because their daughter had a little too much fun here. She had a kid while she was still in high school. When your parents own a motel, well, I guess you can imagine what happens..."

Rob kissed her again hungrily. "I have a really good imagination."

Much later that afternoon, Tracy opened her eyes. She was lying curled up with Rob, her legs tangled up with his. He was sleeping quietly. Apparently he hadn't been quite as tired as she thought, given that they'd depleted the condom stash. They had explored most of the areas of the room, including the other bed and the shower, but not the floor again. A girl had her limits, after all.

She looked at the clock radio. "Is that what time it is?"

Rob opened his eyes. "Didn't we already establish that the clock works?"

"I have to go get Roxy! Kat is going to start to wonder what happened to me. I told her I'd be there hours ago." Tracy disentangled herself from Rob and ran toward the bathroom. "I need to go!"

Rob rolled over on his back, put his hand behind his head, and leaned on the headboard. He was obviously enjoying watching her scurry around the room. "Are you looking for your clothes?"

Tracy sat down on the end of the bed, suddenly exhausted again. "Yeah. Clothes would be good."

"I think your blouse is under the bed. Do you want me to go with you to get Roxy?"

"Okay. We can take my car."

"I wouldn't have it any other way." He sat up in bed and stretched his arms toward the ceiling, one hand holding the opposite wrist. As he arched his back, Tracy marveled at his deltoid muscles. Who would have thought it? He might not like it, but hauling around computer stuff and crawling around on all those ladders did have some advantages.

~

After some slippery fun back in the shower, Tracy and Rob finally left the H12. Tracy had called Kat and apologized profusely. Fortunately, Kat not only wasn't upset, but she seemed to be in a remarkably good mood. She told Tracy she could stop by for Roxy whenever it was convenient.

Rob bent to peer at the side of the old Subaru. "It's hard to believe this is the same car."

Tracy opened the driver's side door and leaned on it. "We now know that The Turd has a colorful past."

After successfully encouraging the car into motion, they headed out of town. It seemed like ages since Tracy had seen Roxy, even though it had only been a couple of days. Staying up all night really messed with the space-time continuum.

They got to Kat's house and found her sitting on the steps outside with Roxy. Both seemed to be enjoying the late-afternoon sun. Kat waved as they approached, stood up, and picked up the dog.

Tracy and Rob got out of the car. Tracy ran over to Kat and took Roxy from her. She snuggled the dog to her chest, "How's my girl?"

Kat said, "Roxy was great. Hold on a sec." She ran up the steps, opened the door, and said something to someone in the house.

Rob walked over to Tracy and looked down at Roxy, who wagged her tail. He stroked the dog's head. "She seems to like it here."

Tracy said, "I think it's now the only place she's ever stayed more than once. It's a miracle."

Kat walked down the steps. "Roxy gets extra-credit points for finding a long-lost item in the house."

"Wow, good girl!" Tracy scratched Roxy's ears and looked at Kat. "So she didn't damage the house this time?"

Kat shook her head. "I didn't say that. Joel had to take out some drywall. But it was okay. Definitely worth it in the long run."

Joel opened the door and came outside with Roxy's crate. "Hi Tracy. Welcome back. How did the meeting go?"

Tracy readjusted her hold on Roxy. "I'm not sure. It was going pretty well, but then—I don't know." She glanced at Rob.

"We'll see." Rob said.

Tracy said, "Joel, this is Rob. He's kind of the technology brain behind the whole web site thing. You guys probably have a lot in common." She looked at Rob again, "Joel's an engineer."

Joel put down the crate and shook hands with Rob. "Hi. Nice to meet you."

"You too. I actually install networks, so Tracy may be overestimating the technology aspect. I'm not officially a web developer. I'm kind of self-taught."

Kat grinned. "That's probably close enough to join the geek brotherhood."

Joel put his arm around Kat's shoulders and looked down into her face. "Geek brotherhood?"

Kat placed her fingertips on her chest and said, "Well, obviously *I* am not a member. It's a brotherhood. Of geeks. I fail on both counts. You probably write your meeting minutes in binary code."

Joel laughed. "I'll never tell."

Tracy put Roxy on the ground, dug around in her purse for her check, and handed it to Kat. "Thanks again for taking Roxy on such short notice. I think Roxy and I will actually be leaving you alone for a while."

"If you need to board her again, it's not a problem." Kat crouched down to pet Roxy. "You behave Roxy. Stay out of walls, cabinets, and other small spaces, okay?"

Rob and Tracy packed up the crate, loaded Roxy into The Turd, and headed back toward town. As they clunked through the potholes, Tracy's thoughts returned to recent events. What was next? Tomorrow she'd be going back to work. After the intensity of the all-nighter, the disastrous meeting, and the still somewhat astonishing festival of lust with Rob, what happened now? She looked over at him. He had his hand against the dashboard in an effort to mitigate the impact of the craters, but the expression on his face seemed contemplative. When did his vacation end anyway? Had he ever said? Maybe he was leaving tonight. Eventually he had to go back to work too. Time to break the silence. Tracy turned to him, "So hey, Joel actually laughed. Who knew that guy had a sense of humor? I know you've never met him before, but he's usually really quiet."

"Don't underestimate the geeks of the world. Sometimes we can surprise you."

Tracy smiled. That was for sure. Never in her wildest dreams did she imagine how sexy Rob would be. Her dreams were nowhere near as creative as he was. She gripped the steering wheel more tightly. "So when do we hear about the contract? Did Ben say anything?"

"He said he had a bunch of meetings today. I think he's here through this week, shutting down the house for winter. Then he goes back to LA."

"But he didn't say when he'd get back to us? He's going to let us know either way, right?"

Rob sighed. "I sure hope so, after all that work."

"Speaking of work, are you going back to work tomorrow? It's kind of late now."

"It's been a busy day." Rob put his hand on her leg, startling her and causing her to gun the car's engine, which whined in protest. "I had planned to take two weeks of vacation. At this point, I've only used one. I know you have to work, but I'd like to see more of you."

Tracy darted a glance at him and grinned. "I'm not sure there's more of me to see than you already have."

"Well, I liked what I saw. I meant I'd like to spend more time with you. Without computers. Or work. But without clothes would be great too." He caressed her thigh and a little jolt of electricity shot up her leg. That could make driving a lot more complicated.

Tracy squirmed in her seat and looked back over her shoulder at Roxy. "Don't listen, Roxy." She glanced away from the road at Rob again. "I think that could be arranged. I have to go back to work tomorrow, but after I get out of there at three and get home, clothing could be optional."

"After spending so much time looking at photographs, I'd like to explore this area. I can do that while you're at work. I picked up all that information about hiking trails. And you said there's a road that would be fun to drive, right? I mean in a car like mine, not this one."

Tracy downshifted to help encourage The Turd to ascend a small incline. "Yes. I so want to drive your car on that road. So, *so* much."

"We'll see. You might be able to convince me during one of those clothing-optional afternoons."

"I can be pretty persuasive, you know."

"I hope so."

⁓

Kat and Joel went back inside the house and were greeted by the sounds of angry canine barking. Kat took Joel's hand, raised it and twirled around, doing a small pirouette under his arm. "Look at this fantastically empty house!"

He pulled her toward him into a hug. "And clean."

"Yes, it's too clean." Kat snuggled her head into his chest and wrapped her arms around his body.

"Don't worry, the dogs will take care of that." Joel kissed the top of her head. "By tomorrow, you won't be able to tell your mother was here at all."

Kat gave him a final hug and released her hold. "Back to our own wild-and-crazy world, where we don't have to wash our dinner plates the nanosecond we finish eating."

Joel walked into the kitchen. "On that note, what's for dinner?"

Kat spread both arms out toward the kitchen. "Anything you want! We still have Twinkies. I couldn't sell those to my mother either. I need to invite Maria to come back up here."

Joel opened the pantry door. "She's not going to want to visit once it starts snowing."

"That won't be for ages, right?"

"Don't be so sure."

Kat peered around Joel's body into the pantry. "Maybe I'll send Maria a care package. Or—even better—I can call it a housewarming gift!"

He turned and tickled her ribs. "Because nothing says welcome to the neighborhood like a case of Twinkies."

Kat scurried away from the tickling and sat down at the table. "I didn't see anything enticing in there. The cupboard is looking a little bare."

"Me neither." Joel closed the pantry door and sat down next to her.

Kat leaned an elbow on the table and rested her chin on her hand. "So what do you think? Are Tracy and Rob having sex? Because I think they are. Tracy looked way more relaxed."

"Have you picked up Maria's ability to determine these things?"

"No. She is the goddess. I'm just guessing. I have no idea how she can tell with such accuracy when people have done the deed. But she's never wrong."

Joel leaned back in his chair and stretched his long legs out under the table. "I'll take your word for it."

Kat tapped one of his feet with her toes. "Hey, maybe we could actually go out somewhere to celebrate our lack of house guest!"

"Okay. Where?"

"Let's go to the Italian place. I've never been there with you. It could be fun."

"Sounds good to me."

Kat jumped out of the chair and ran to the bedroom closet. "I could wear girlie clothes!"

Joel leaned in the doorway, observing while Kat rummaged through her side of the closet. He poked at a loose splinter of wood in the door frame. "Did you find out why your mother wanted those letters so badly?"

Kat paused in her clothing quest and turned to face him. "Sort of. She wrote to Abigail for years."

"I know. She said that."

"I guess she wanted the letters because they more or less chronicle her entire life with my father." Kat walked over to the bed and sat down. "Including the time around when he died. The day my mother arrived here was the anniversary of his death."

Joel walked into the room and sat on the bed next to her. "Well, that explains a lot. You don't really talk about your father much."

"You're telling *me* I don't talk about something. You? Mr. Clam Up and Walk Away? Really?"

He pushed a long lock of dark hair behind her shoulder and took one of her hands in his. "Okay, I know. Pot calling the kettle black and all that. I get it. But I have wondered what happened with him."

"He was always really quiet. I mean, I guess those of us who lived with my mother kind of found our own ways of coping. Mine was to go hide out and read. His was to be very quiet and kind of disappear. It helped that he worked long hours and I hardly ever saw him, except at dinner. And then like I said, at some point we stopped eating together. I think you can guess why. On the weekends, he tended to leave the house to do errands or something. I don't know. Once he told me he went to the library to read history books, which I thought was interesting." Kat looked up into Joel's face. "Anyway, we weren't particularly close, but he always seemed to be such a kind person, you know?"

Joel nodded. "I'm thinking you learned kindness from him."

"Definitely not from my mother. And my grandmother on my mother's side makes my mother seem like Snow White singing to birdies and chipmunks in a Disney film."

"Your mother doesn't seem like a happy person."

Kat looked down at her fingers interlaced with Joel's. "No. She's always been like that. I thought it was just that we're so different. Which we are. But it's not just me. She doesn't seem to like anybody."

He squeezed her hand. "Definitely not me anyway. When did your father die?"

"Three years ago. He had a massive heart attack, and was in a coma for a little while, then my mother had to pull the plug. It was what he would have wanted."

Joel put his arm around her and pulled her close. "Still, that must have been hard."

A tear slid down Kat's cheek. "Yeah, it was kinda rough. He was only in his late fifties too. I know now that we weren't technically even related, but he was my father. And you've met my mother. Overt displays of emotion aren't exactly her thing. She kind of made it seem like nothing had happened and returned to her cleaning."

"Everyone has their own ways of coping."

"I know. And she never said much about Abigail after I found out about my complicated background either." Kat snuggled into his shirt. "I've read about people who find out they're adopted and freak out. They have a big identity crisis, running around shrieking how they don't know who they are anymore. For me, it just explained some things about why I was so different from my parents. But in the long run, nothing changed. My mother is still my mother and my father was my father, you know?"

"Yes. I understand what you mean."

Kat looked up into his eyes. "She didn't show me the letters, but I'm guessing that's where she let out some of her feelings. About falling in love with my father way back when, then life with him, and finally his death. Almost like a diary."

"That would explain why she wanted to find them."

"And why she hated you so vigorously."

Joel cupped her chin with his hand and kissed her. "I thought she hated everyone. And particularly the guys you went out with."

Kat took his hand again. "That's true, but she seemed to have an extra-special venom for you. I think because you tend to be quiet. Perhaps that reminded her too much of my father."

Joel raised an eyebrow, "What?"

"Eww. Don't give me that look. I'm not having some weird daddy issues with you. I can talk to you. Maybe you don't talk to anyone else, but you talk to me. Well, most of the time, anyway." She reached out and tickled his ribs. "Are you going to tell me how you broke a bone?"

He grabbed her hands, pulled them away from his stomach, and held them out to the side. "Maybe later. It's just us and the critters in the house again."

Kat considered the twinkle in his deep green eyes and flopped backward onto the bed, pulling him onto her. A familiar thrill of excitement flashed through her body as he bent to kiss her neck. "I see what you mean. The critters never tell anyone our secrets. Maybe we can go out to eat some other night."

He raised his head and smiled. "We'll find some food here somewhere. Later."

"Yes. Later."

Chapter 12

The Mood of the Room

R ob carried the crate up the stairs to Tracy's apartment while she carried Roxy. She put Roxy on the floor and opened the door. "We're home, Roxy!" The dog ran into the apartment and across the floor to her food bowl. She examined the empty dish and looked up at Tracy in disgust.

Tracy walked to the kitchen and dispensed some dog food. "Fine. Here you go."

Rob put down the crate, sat down on the sofa, and looked around the room. "Where do you sleep?"

"You're sitting on it. It's a fold-out couch, but usually I don't bother, since the hinges are sort of broken."

"Sort of? Isn't something either broken or not?"

"I use an old lock to latch it together. It mostly works." Sometimes. When she could find the lock.

He looked down at the couch. "I see why you were impressed with the beds in the H12. Do you want me to take a look at it?"

Tracy sat down next to him. "You don't have to. It's been this way forever. I'm not worried about it." She put her arms around his neck. "And you seem overdressed."

He pushed her back onto the couch and slid his hands under her shirt and alongside her body, pushing the fabric up. "So do you."

A few minutes later, they fell off the couch onto the floor with a resounding thud. Roxy barked and walked over to the complicated pile of humans to investigate. Tracy sat up and pushed Roxy's nose away. "Go away Roxy. Ouch. That hurt. I'm glad the store is closed. Shoppers probably don't appreciate loud upstairs neighbors. Not to mention my mom. Ugh."

Rob stretched out a leg and rubbed at his hip. "I hate to complain, but you have a furniture problem."

"I know. There isn't any. And what's here is decomposing. It's trying to return to the land." Tracy gripped his arm. "Hey, I just realized something. You owe me money. I could buy a bed! Or at least a new couch."

"I vote for the bed."

"Would you settle for a futon? I need a place to sit and watch TV too. There's not enough space for both a bed and a couch in here."

"I noticed. Where are my pants?"

Tracy pointed to a heap of cloth on the floor. "Over there."

Rob reached over and extracted a piece of paper from a pocket. "I did a spreadsheet of the hours you worked. I was going to show it to you, but I forgot."

"A spreadsheet? Sometimes I wonder about you."

"I wanted to keep track."

Tracy looked at the numbers. "Wow. I can so afford a futon." She smiled. "I'm going to pick up the freebie classified newspaper on my way to work tomorrow and look at furniture ads."

"What if you got a new futon? One that no one else has actually slept on. Or sat on. Or done anything else on."

She scowled. "Maybe. I haven't looked at anything new in a long time. I don't know what it would cost."

Rob wrapped his arms around her and kissed her. "I think it would be worth it." He looked down at the floor. "I feel like I'm sitting in a sandbox. And I think there's a chew toy digging into my—me."

She peered around his body "That's gotta hurt."

Rob stood up and reached for his pants. "It's getting late. I should probably go back to the H12 and clean up the room. We left it kind of a mess."

Tracy stood up and put her arms around him. "I could help."

"Will Roxy be okay here by herself?"

"Sure. A lot of times, she sleeps in her crate at night anyway." Tracy reached for her shirt. "I'll just take her for her bedtime walk first. Then we can leave. She'll never know the difference."

After walking Roxy and stowing her in the crate, Tracy and Rob went down the stairs to the street. As Tracy was locking the downstairs door, a low howl arose from upstairs. She looked at Rob. "I guess this really shows how little I get out. Roxy is in her crate, so she knows I'm leaving for the night." The howling continued rising in pitch and was punctuated by barking and yipping as Roxy worked herself into an exceptional vocal frenzy.

Rob looked at Tracy. "It's hard to believe something that small can make so much noise."

"When it comes to changes in her routine, Roxy likes to express her opinion."

He cupped her face with both hands and kissed her. "I think you need to attend to Roxy. If she keeps that up, someone is going to call whatever law enforcement there is here. I'll see you tomorrow."

Tracy wrapped her arms around him and hugged hard. "This has been such a—I don't even know what kind of day. But I wish you weren't leaving. I'll call around for futon prices at lunch. Promise."

"I'll come by the clinic at three and bring your check."

Tracy released him from the hug and held one of his hands. "See you."

He let go of her hand and began walking down the sidewalk, but Tracy didn't move. As the traffic light flashed red, she stared at his retreating form, pondering the various intricacies of his body that she'd spent quite a lot of time exploring earlier. Halfway down the block, he turned and looked back at her. "Go deal with your dog. I can hear her from here!"

Startled into motion, Tracy waved and turned to unlock the door. She ran up the stairs and opened the door to the apartment. Roxy stood in her crate, completely silent. Tracy walked over to the dog and crouched down in front of her. "You are really putting a damper on my social life, you know."

Since she was already way too awake with frustrated hormones jangling everywhere, Tracy decided to clean up a little. By midnight, almost everything was off the floor, except for big things like the paint box, which didn't really have a place to go. Now that she could see it again, Tracy even swept and mopped the floor.

She looked down at Roxy, who was sleeping happily in her crate. "This is all your fault. I hate cleaning." Tracy swished the brackish water in the bucket with the mop. "Maybe it was a little dirty. But not *sandbox* dirty. I mean, come on. I do have a few standards." Roxy lifted her head and stared at her sleepily. "Okay. Maybe not."

~

The next morning, the alarm rang painfully early. Tracy dragged herself out of bed and managed to get to the clinic on time. Barely. She began cleaning kennels and preparing for the day. Dr. Cassidy walked in and worked on setting up her surgery station.

Tracy pulled some surgery packs out of the autoclave and set them aside. She walked over to the vet. "I saw on the schedule that we have some new appointments in there that weren't there on Saturday. What happened? We're double-booked for a couple of slots and I would really like to leave on time today. Would it be okay if I try to move some stuff around?"

Dr. C looked up. "Yes. Call the ones getting just vaccinations and see if they can reschedule to later in the week. I came in to do an emergency surgery on a cat yesterday and he's coming in again for a follow-up so I can take a look. And then someone else called with a basset who probably has an ear infection. The poor guy sounds really unhappy. Lots of head shaking."

"Okay, I'll get on it."

"You look tired. How was the meeting? Did it go well?"

Tracy shook her head. "I don't know. It's hard to say. I stayed up too late cleaning my apartment, so I'm sort of tired."

"Cleaning? Really?"

"You don't have to look so surprised. I clean. It's not *that* unusual." Yes it was. And it wasn't the only reason she was tired.

After chatting with what seemed like half of the answering machines in Alpine Grove, Tracy managed to communicate with enough people to reschedule several appointments, so when Rob came by at three, she was ready to leave. She waved to him in the lobby, unsnapped her dog-hair-covered scrub jacket, and hung it on a hook.

He leaned on the counter. "So did you call about futons?"

"Yes. I found a great one. And it's on sale!"

"I'm happy to hear that. On another note, it's a beautiful day out there." He held out his keys. "Here you go."

Tracy's eyes widened. "Ohmigod!" She snatched the keys from his hand and ran out the door. She opened the car, crawled into the plush interior, and reached over to unlock the passenger door.

Rob got in the car. "Be nice. This is not The Turd."

"I can be nice." After putting on her seat belt and adjusting the seats and mirrors, she put the car in neutral and turned the key. The car purred to life and idled quietly. "Wow. Just wow." She leaned over to Rob and gave him a kiss. "I'm glad to see you too."

"Thanks for noticing I'm here."

Tracy put the car in gear and drove slowly through Alpine Grove, carefully shifting gears, getting the feel for the clutch and the car's steering. She headed out toward the long rural road that once was used by farmers taking their wares to the marketplace to be sold. The aptly named Farm to Market Road wound around through the hills with lots of fun dips and valleys. For someone who loved to drive, it was the perfect automotive playground.

Rob was right; it was a gorgeous fall day, probably one of the last of the season. The afternoon sun streamed through the trees as Tracy cruised along the deserted pavement. The Honda was just as much fun to drive as she had anticipated. She opened the moon roof and let the air stream through the car.

Rob pointed at a road off to the right. "I went that way earlier. There's a pretty little park back in there. I guess it's a memorial or something."

Tracy nodded. "Yes. Teenagers also go there late at night to drink beer and make out."

"That wasn't in the brochure."

She flashed a grin at him. "It never is."

After an exhilarating drive through the hills, Tracy returned to Alpine Grove, deposited her check at the bank, and parked in front of the furniture store. "Let's buy me a futon!"

Rob got out of the car. "I get to witness a special moment here. You buying *new* furniture."

"Don't get used to it. My financial picture is rarely this good. I might even buy a new box of cereal."

"I think we ate all the Cap'n Crunch."

After spending some time sitting on the new futon to try it out, Tracy paid for it and asked the store to deliver it to her place that evening.

They got back into the car and Rob drove to Tracy's apartment. Tracy reclined in the passenger seat and reached out to stroke the back of his hand on the gear shift. "That was the best drive ever. Thank you."

"You're welcome. I've never seen anyone enjoy driving a car quite so much."

Tracy sighed. "I would love to go on a long multi-state road trip. Maybe even all the way across the country. The farthest I've ever gone was to LA. In The Turd. Which is just sad."

Rob shifted gears and reached over to hold her hand. "Well, I can't argue that The Turd is sad, but I'm sure you'll take a road trip someday."

"With all that extra cash I have lying around? I haven't gone anywhere in years. I haven't had a vacation, unless you count when I was unemployed. Which I don't, because in case you're wondering, unemployment and vacation are definitely not the same thing."

"Today is the first day I have really been on vacation since—well, I'm not sure exactly. I've done a lot of traveling, but traveling for work isn't a lot of fun. Or at least for the type of work I do. Standing on top of a big-box store in North Dakota in January is not an experience I'd like to repeat."

Tracy released Rob's hand so he could shift gears. "Okay, you win the 'most likely to get frostbite' award. What were you doing?"

"Chain stores have to send their sales to the home office. Something in the network was broken and I fixed it."

She stroked the back of his hand again. "Yuck."

"That pretty much sums it up."

They arrived at her apartment and walked up to collect Roxy. The dachshund apparently had not been pleased about the delay in being let out, and most of Tracy's pots and pans were scattered on the floor.

Rob surveyed the array of kitchenware. "I thought you said you cleaned." He pointed at the kitchen. "I think you missed a spot."

Tracy picked up Roxy and clipped on her leash. "Let's go." She turned the dog's head toward her face. "I'm not happy with you, little dog."

After a short walk, they returned to the apartment. Tracy decided to put Roxy in a "time-out" in the crate while she put her pots and pans back in the cabinets. Again.

Rob handed her a saucepan. "It does look a lot better in here. The floor is even clean."

"I couldn't sleep after you left."

He put a frying pan on the counter and took her in his arms. "I missed you."

She looked into his eyes, took off his glasses, and put them on the counter. "I missed you too. After spending so much time together, it just felt strange not being with you all of a sudden."

"I know." He kissed her lips, then her earlobe, and whispered, "I couldn't sleep either. You'll be happy to hear that room 2 at the H12 is a lot cleaner now too."

A knock at the door triggered frantic barking from Roxy and startled Tracy out of her dreamy languor. Rob leaped away from her, looking disturbed. She smiled at his expression. "That sure killed the mood. But it could be the new futon!"

Tracy let in two burly men in blue coveralls who took away the old couch and plunked the new futon down in its place. After they left, Tracy grabbed both of Rob's hands and took a few steps back across the floor, dragging him to the futon. She fell backward onto it, and although he made a valiant effort not to crash-land and crush her, she pulled him down on top of her anyway. "I think we need to try this out. How do you feel about leaving the H12 and staying here?"

He kissed her. "Maybe I'll grab some supplies from the basket in the lobby when I check out."

~

The next morning when Tracy opened her eyes, Rob was lying on his side, propped up on his elbow, with his head resting on his hand. He was looking down into her face and stroking her upper arm with his fingertips. She gave him a drowsy smile. "Are you watching me sleep? That's kind of like watching grass grow, isn't it?"

"You just looked so beautiful and peaceful lying there. I got up earlier and turned off the alarm." He kissed her. "This seemed like a nicer way to wake up."

She put her arms around his neck and kissed him again. "No arguments there. Best morning ever." She looked over at the clock. "I'm not even late for work for a change. But I should get up and take a shower." She snuggled up closer to his body. "Not that I want to leave this cocoon of warmth you've got going here."

"You have the smallest shower I've ever seen."

"I know. I told my mother it's like it was designed for dwarves. Then she called me Grumpy. Ha-ha, Mom."

Rob laughed. "Your mother is great. I was thinking that after you get off work, maybe we should stop by the store and let her know that I'm here, so she doesn't think I'm a crook or something."

Tracy sat up and stretched. "Yeah, you could be the thief who stole my thiry-year-old broken couch."

He pulled her back down to him. "Have I mentioned that I *really* like the new futon?"

She giggled. "Many times."

Later at the vet clinic, Tracy was sitting at the front desk surveying the afternoon appointments in the book. The bells on the door jangled and Kat walked in with a little brown-and-white dog who looked extremely unhappy. The dog's brown eyes were wide and when Kat stopped at the desk, the dog laid down on the floor, trembling.

"Hi Kat. Thanks for letting me reschedule Chelsey for today." Tracy looked down at the book. "So she's getting a rabies shot?"

Kat nodded and crouched down next to the dog. "Yes. I know we're a little early, but I wasn't sure how difficult it would be to get her out of the house." She stroked the dog's head. "It's really no big deal, Chelsey. We'll be in and out in five minutes."

Chelsey didn't look convinced and started crawling toward the closest chair. Kat shook her head at Tracy. "We'll just be waiting over here."

"Okay. Let me go get Dr. C."

Dr. Cassidy came out into the lobby and peered under the chair. "Hi Chelsey. How's it going? You were just a youngster the last time I saw you."

"I know. She needs a rabies shot," Kat said.

"She doesn't bite, does she?"

Kat shook her head. "Not that I know of. She's actually a really sweet dog. A little shy, maybe. I think she just worries a lot."

The vet stood up. "Maybe we can just do the exam and vaccination here. I have to finish something up first, then I'll be right back."

Chelsey scuttled farther back toward the wall. Kat sat down on the floor and looked up at Tracy. "Could you lift the chair up and put it somewhere else? I'll just sit with her down here so she doesn't crawl under some other piece of furniture. She's an amazingly fast crawler."

Tracy sat down on the floor across from Kat and put a hand on Chelsey's back. "The poor thing is shaking like a leaf."

"Yeah, I feel terrible dragging her here. But she needs her shots. My aunt Abigail kept all the vet records for the animals. And when my mom was here, she organized them. Now they're all in folders and in alphabetical and chronological order. I've never been so organized. But I only had one cat before, so it wasn't a big deal."

Tracy looked down at Chelsey. "Yeah, I know what you mean. Organization is not my strong suit."

"So is Rob still around? Did you find out about the web site thing yet?"

"No. We haven't. And he's still here." Tracy could feel the color rising to her cheeks. "He's at my apartment, actually."

Kat smiled. "That doesn't surprise me. He seems like a nice person."

Tracy leaned across the dog's back and whispered, "He is. We've spent all this time together and he's easy to talk to and fun to be around. But he's *so* not my type. I don't know what I'm doing with him. Plus he's leaving in a few days. What is wrong with me? Getting involved with him is stupid, even for me, and I'm not exactly known for my great life choices."

Kat rubbed one of Chelsey's soft ears. "Never argue with matters of the heart. The heart never lies."

"That's kind of profound."

Kat shook her head. "Not really. I read it on a greeting card. But it sounded good. I think it's true though. Falling in love with someone can happen when you aren't expecting it." She shrugged. "Or it did for me anyway."

"That's so sweet. But I'm not in love with Rob." Or was she? She looked down at Chelsey again. "We haven't known each other that long."

"The amount of time doesn't matter."

Tracy stroked the soft reddish fur on Chelsey's back. "Another greeting card?"

"No. That was definitely based on experience."

The two women and Chelsey looked up as Dr. Cassidy walked back into the waiting area. "I'm sorry for the delay. I had to deal with a cat back there." She efficiently did a physical exam to make sure everything looked okay and then held up a syringe. "Tracy, could you hold Chelsey's rear leg for me?"

Tracy complied and two seconds later the shot was done. Chelsey looked around, seemingly curious what the fuss was about while Dr. Cassidy crouched on the floor and gently continued examining her.

The vet stood up, put the syringe on the counter, and sat on the chair. She leaned forward and held up another larger syringe with a tube attached to it. "Kat, would it be okay if I do a blood draw? Chelsey reminds me of some other dogs that exhibited odd behavior, and it was because of a thyroid imbalance."

Kat looked up. "Is that bad? She's okay, right? I mean she seems healthy to me."

"I'd like to do a thyroid test on her. If she has low thyroid hormones, all you'd need to do is give her a little pill every day. Hypothyroidism is extremely treatable. And if that is actually the problem, she might be happier."

"Really? Okay. Yes, that would be great if it would help her." Kat leaned to hug Chelsey. "She always seems so worried about everything."

Dr. Cassidy got down on the floor and asked Tracy to hold Chelsey's front leg. "She might not like this." She gently stuck the needle into the dog's leg and looked for a vein. "Just a little prick, Chelsey." The dog jumped slightly and the vet nodded to Kat. "Scratch the fur on her head to distract her."

Kat complied and Chelsey settled down. The vet pulled the needle out and stood up. "All done here. I have to send this out to a special lab in the Midwest, so it will take a few days to get the results back."

Kat looked up. "Thanks for doing all this out in the lobby on the floor. I know that's a little weird." She patted the dog's back. "But so is Chelsey."

The vet tucked the vial of blood into her lab coat pocket. "Sometimes it's easier."

After Kat and Chelsey left, Tracy thought about what Kat had said. Was she really falling for Rob? It seemed so utterly ridiculous. But he also was by far the most kind-hearted and understanding man she'd ever met. He seemed to just take her foibles in stride in a way no one else ever had. Not to mention that he had talents that went way beyond networking. The thought of last night's futon fun gave her a little thrill. She looked at the clock. Only forty-five more minutes and she could leave.

~

Kat and Chelsey returned to the house amid a tremendous amount of canine excitement. All of the other dogs wanted to find out where Chelsey had been, so there was a lot of sniffing to determine what exactly the little dog had been up to while she was gone. Having had enough of the nosy interrogation, Chelsey retired to her spot under the table for some post-traumatic nap time.

Joel walked out of his office and bent to peer under the table. "How's the small weird one?"

"She's fine." Kat walked over and gave him a kiss. "The vet thinks she might have a thyroid problem, so I agreed to an expensive blood test that they're sending to some special lab. If we could do something to make her happier, it would be worth it."

"While you were gone, Maria called."

"Really? Is she okay?"

Joel leaned on the table edge. "I'm not entirely clear on what happened. She was...emotional, I guess you'd say. But I did get two things from the conversation. One: she quit her job.

Kat squeezed her eyes shut. "Oh no, that can't be good. What else did she say?"

"Two: she wants to visit. I said it was fine. So she's leaving right now. When she called, she was packed and heading out the door."

"I can't believe she finally quit. I hope she's okay." Kat put her arms around Joel's waist. "I'm sorry we're getting another house guest so soon."

"After your mother, any other house guest pales by comparison." He leaned back to look into her face. "I just have one request: please get Maria to either eat the Twinkies or take them away."

Kat stood on her tiptoes to kiss him. "I will. Thanks. Maybe I'll just go to the store before she gets here and buy the necessary wine for her visit. If I let her go with me, you know what will happen."

"You're significantly better about buying actual food at the grocery store than she is."

"I know. Please keep an eye on Chelsey for me. I'll be back in a little while."

Later, Kat and Joel were quietly working in their offices, when all of the dogs leaped up from their naps and started barking furiously. Kat ran out of her office and up the stairs. "Quiet, you guys!"

She opened the door and saw Maria standing on the landing with a wild-eyed look on her face. When she saw Kat, her expression softened, she opened her arms wide, and shouted, "Girlfriend!"

Kat hugged her friend hard. "Come on in."

Maria walked into the entryway, threw down her bag, and kicked off her pumps. She pointed at Kat. "You need to start pouring. The Whine and Wine begins now!"

Kat laughed. "I can't believe you drove all this way for a glass of wine."

Maria put her hand on her hip. "Oh, I'm having more than one glass, girlfriend. This is the whine to end all whines.

The grapes are gonna quiver on their vines." She paused. "Hey, all that driving turned me into a poet."

Kat walked to the kitchen, got out two glasses, and pulled the wine from the pantry. "Feel free to have a seat. I'm on it."

Maria sat down at the table. There was a great commotion in the downstairs hallway, and then all of the dogs came thundering up the stairs. They gathered around Maria, and Linus put his muzzle in her lap. Maria rested her hand on his head. "Hello, Mr. Gigantic Head. You realize that your nose probably weighs forty pounds all by itself, right? You're gonna put my legs to sleep."

Kat held the two glasses in front of her and gestured with them toward the living room, "Go on, you guys. Go lie down."

All the dogs scattered to locations around the room as Joel walked into the kitchen. "Hi Maria."

"Hey. What's up in the land of engineering?"

"Same old geek stuff. You don't want to know."

Maria waved a hand dismissively. "You know it. I really don't."

Kat said, "You have your wine now. Tell me what happened. Joel said you quit. I can't believe it. After all this time, did you really finally do it?"

Maria sat back in her chair, cradling her wine glass in both hands. "Yes. As you know, I have not been what you might call *satisfied* with my employment situation for a while."

Joel sat down at the table next to Kat. "So we've heard."

Kat nodded. "The twelve versions of your resume that you sent me were a clue. Oh, and you work for Mark, who is completely insane. That was an issue for me too when I worked there, as you may recall."

Maria leaned forward and tilted the rim of her glass toward Kat. "The problem is that when you mix technology with crazy, you end up with a seriously evil brew. You're on the high road to bat-guano-level, wack-a-doo nut-ball."

"Technology?" Joel said.

"Yes. Now, you know that I am an open-minded, modern woman." Maria flipped a wayward brunette curl off her face. "And I see the value of a cell phone. I understand why they are a fine thing. Really, I do. There could be emergencies. Doctors have cell phones because they're on call. That's good. If I'm being rushed to the emergency room, I want a sexy doctor to drop everything when he gets a call to come and resuscitate me."

Kat said, "What does a doctor or a cell phone have to do with anything?"

Maria held up her hand and raised her index finger. "First, I'd like to meet a hot doctor. I'm just putting that out there." She raised her middle finger. "Two, I do not need a cell phone so that I can be on call for every stupid idea my boss has. Mark forced a cell phone on me, so he could call me at any hour, day or night, twenty-four hours a day, seven days a week. And while I have this particular finger raised, I'd like to point out that it is not directed at you, but it *was* directed at Mark. Among other things. When I quit."

"Thanks. I feel better," Kat said. "I'm confused though. He used to call you all the time anyway."

Maria slapped her palm down on the table. "Yes, but I didn't have to answer it. I have an answering machine. I was his secretary, not his wife. What I do at my own home is my business. But he told me I couldn't turn the cell phone off. Ever! It had to be on all the time, so he could reach me. He said I had to sleep with it on my pillow. Do you know what that's like? He called me at midnight to tell me I had to get someone to fix his lawn mower. Another time, at three in the morning, he calls to tell me he caught a mouse in a trap. He was convinced it had some virus and I had to send it to a lab to be analyzed."

Kat cringed. "Eww. Gross."

"I know! Then another time he calls to tell me that a dog crapped in his front yard. He demanded that I get one of those pooper-scooper companies to come out and disinfect his precious zoysia lawn. And get surveillance equipment installed, so he could catch the perpetrator of the crime."

Kat grinned. "Oooh, illicit dumping. Call out the National Guard."

"Anyway, this went on for weeks. I didn't tell you about it because I know you were dealing with your own stuff. And that was some really heavy stuff. You had a lot going on." She paused. "Speaking of which..." she pointed at Joel, "You're not broken, right?" She pointed at Kat. "And you're not with kitten, right?"

They moved their heads simultaneously indicating *no*, and Kat said, "I already told you all that! Get on with the story. What happened?"

"I just wanted to establish the mood of the room." Maria swirled her wine in the glass. "So last week, I finally told Mark that I would have to quit if he wouldn't let me have a personal life." Maria shook her head and peered down into her wine. "He said I couldn't quit—that I'd never find another job. It was upsetting. He called me a lotta names and said I was stupid."

"That's not true!" Kat said.

"I know. But I didn't say anything back when he said that, because I felt like I needed that worthless job. And then that pissed me off. I was so mad at myself. That night I decided to quit, but I wanted to do it right." Maria grinned at Kat and raised her glass high. "I decided that it was time to organize an office party."

Kat looked at Joel, who raised an eyebrow and smiled. This was going to be good. "A party? How was it?"

Maria held up the back of her hand and examined her long red fingernails. "You know I do excel at party planning. But I did hear the word *legendary* bandied around after this one."

"Nice." Kat waved her hands. "Okay. Go on."

"Well, when the creepy D&D guys helped me move, they told me they had a Queen tribute band. They call themselves "Funkcan," which they think is hilarious, because it's a combination of Frank and Duncan."

Kat groaned. "Oooh, funky. Ugh. That's awful."

"Yeah, they're a pair of mutants, but it worked out because there's a song by Queen that truly expresses my innermost feelings about Mark. Freddy Mercury already wrote what I would have, so I didn't have to." She turned to Joel. "Do you have the *Night at the Opera* album?"

"I think so." Joel said.

Maria waved her hands toward the living room. "Put that baby on! I need musical accompaniment to give you a feel for the ambiance, so I can do justice to the re-telling of this experience."

Joel stood up. "Okay, if you want." He went over to the stereo and started rummaging through the pile of CDs.

"Anyway, I asked the guys if they'd be willing to play an office party." Maria smirked. "They were all over it. It's their first major gig, you know. I gave them their big break. So I feel good about that."

"Silver lining," Kat said.

"Once I had the band lined up, I moved into my full-on power-party-planner mode." Maria fluffed her hair for emphasis. "I printed up flyers and everything. I told Mark that the party was in his honor, to make sure he'd be there. I wiped out the petty-cash fund and got the best munchies ever. There was an open bar and everyone was having a great time. By the time Funkcan came in to play their set, most of the office staff was feeling really fine."

"I hesitate to ask this, but did Duncan dress up as Freddy Mercury?" Kat said.

Maria giggled. "Oh yeah. He had his skinny little ass in high heels and the full leather drag get-up. It was outstanding."

Kat could hear Joel chuckling from across the room as he sorted through CDs. "So then what happened?"

"Well I hired a stage-lighting crew and they set up the lights and a wooden platform in the corner, over near Mark's office."

"Wow. When you blow the petty-cash fund, you really go for it." Kat said.

"I don't like to do things halfway, girlfriend. Then someone turned off those horrible fluorescents in the office and the stage lights came on. It was like blue and purple streamers of light. Duncan got up on the stage and started singing Queen's "Death on Two Legs." They've got these serious speakers and amplifiers and Frank was just wailing away on the guitar, doing backup."

"I think I know this song." Kat looked over at Joel. "Did you find it?"

"Yes. It's one of Abigail's I think," he said.

Kat said to Maria, "Since Joel and I combined our CD collections with Abigail's, we have access to almost any classic-rock album made in the last thirty years. It's pretty impressive."

The song began to play and Joel walked back to the table. Maria said, "Mark was standing right next to the stage. Now imagine Duncan in full-on tranny drag, crooning these lyrics—comparing Mark to a leech and calling him an overgrown schoolboy."

Kat put her face in her hands and snickered. "Wow. There are no words."

"So the guys finish up the last few lyrics and Mark's kinda standing there looking confused, with his mouth hanging open. I'm not sure he actually got it." Maria grinned. "But everyone else did, since a lot of the women were waving their arms and screaming. People were holding up lighters. It was an experience, and I think Funkcan has a major fan base now.

After the mayhem died down, Joyce handed me the cake, which I had made up special by that great bakery around the corner. I got up on the stage, took the microphone from Duncan, and said, "You can kiss my ass goodbye," and then I handed Mark the cake, which said "I quit" in pretty purple cursive letters. It also had my cell phone sticking out the top like a wedding-cake topper."

"Nice touch." Kat said.

"It's all about the details, girlfriend." Maria took a sip of wine. "Then I left, grabbed some stuff from home, and came up here."

"I don't suppose anyone videotaped this, did they?" Kat said.

Maria shook her head. "I think Joyce had a camera, though."

"Make sure you get copies. I have *got* to see those pictures." Kat put down her wine glass. "Maybe tomorrow we can work on your resume."

Maria leaned forward, holding her glass with both hands. "I don't think I'm going to be asking Mark for a reference."

"Yeah, that probably wouldn't be a good idea."

Chapter 13

Friends & Robots

The next morning, Tracy was awakened by the feel of Rob running his hand up the back of her calf, up to where her leg was sticking out from under the sheets. She rolled over and looked up at him. He was holding two mugs of coffee by the handles in his other hand.

He sat down on the edge of the futon and handed her a mug. "Good morning."

Tracy sat up and took a sip of coffee. "Same to you. A girl could get used to this. I like this no-alarm-clock thing."

Rob set his mug down on the coffee table, put his hands on either side of her jaw, and kissed her. "Me too."

Tracy looked into his eyes. "Is something wrong? You look like you just lost your best friend."

"Not yet."

She sat up straighter. "What happened?"

"I woke up early and checked my e-mail." He pointed at his work laptop, which was sitting on the coffee table next to his glasses and coffee. "Sometimes real life has a way of intruding on your dreams."

Tracy smiled. "I thought almost the same thing not too long ago when I was driving back up the hill to Alpine Grove. I tried to pretend I was driving your car, and The Turd almost stalled out, which really interrupted my flow."

He took her in his arms and kissed her neck behind her ear. "Being here with you has been like a dream."

Tracy leaned back to look at him. "Except for that whole work part."

"No, even that was great. You make me laugh, and you're so beautiful and sexy. Plus, you're just fun to be around. Even when you're trying to avoid working."

She widened her eyes in mock horror. "I would never do that."

He reached over and grabbed his coffee again. "Well, you don't have to worry, because I got an e-mail from Ben Walsh. They gave the contract to some big firm in LA."

Tracy slumped down on the futon, cradling the coffee in both hands. "I guess that's not completely unexpected. But I think I secretly thought it would really happen. The last few days, I've walked through quitting my job in my mind probably a thousand times. Dr. C is always really nice about me quitting, and gives me free vet care for Roxy forever."

Rob stroked her cheek. "You certainly have a detailed fantasy life."

"Maybe we can change Ben's mind."

"I don't think so. Maybe it wasn't meant to be. I mean, what are the odds that you'd say your father's name wrong, anyway?"

Tracy sat up straight again. "You *do* think this is my fault, don't you? That I did that on purpose. I knew it! This is probably part of your theory of sabotage or whatever it is. You're the one who wouldn't stop laughing."

Rob held up a hand. "Hey, don't get mad at me. I'm just telling you what he said."

Tracy reached down to put her mug on the floor, flopped down on her side, and put her hand under the pillow. "You're being too nice about my screw-up again. Why are you being so reasonable? You should be mad. At Ben. At me. At somebody. I mean, come on. We did all that work for nothing."

Rob took a sip of coffee and peered over the rim of the mug. "Can I ask you a question?"

"Okay."

"Were you a cheerleader in high school?"

She rearranged her pillow. "What? Is this a trick question?" She fisted her hand and shot it up in the air. "Cedar County High School Rules!"

"That's what I thought. Let me guess. That guy you dated in high school. Neil or whatever his name was? He was on the football team, wasn't he?"

"Yes. He was the quarterback. So what?"

"Do you remember any of the guys who were in the chess club, the math club, or metal shop?"

She shrugged. "Not really, I guess. The high school draws from a pretty wide area actually, not just Alpine Grove. So it's not like I knew everybody."

"Those geeks in the math club were me. Some people go through life being sort of forgettable. Early on, you figure out you won't be dating the cheerleaders and they don't know you exist. Or if they do know, they just think you're really weird, and they *pretend* you don't exist. The end result is basically the same. That's why being with you is kind of like a dream for me. You actually talked to me in class that first day. And then you talked to me again."

Tracy sat up. "I would have noticed you in high school. Neil was in auto shop, remember?"

"I was not a jock. Just a tall, skinny weirdo."

"Okay, so what? Life is not high school. What does this have to do with anything?"

He leaned back and put his arm behind his head. "Sometimes you just have to accept that no matter how much you may want something or how hard you work, it's just not going to work out. You put yourself out there—you try. But some things are out of your control."

Tracy shook her head. "That is such a cop-out."

"No. It's just the way things are. Some people are born salespeople. I'm not. I hate presentations, speaking, and all that."

"So what? You can still do the work."

"Not if I never get the job. I knew it was a long-shot, but I thought having you there might help. I fix someone's network system and the next day they can't remember my name. That's one reason I've had so much fun being here. I go to the cafe and Betsy asks me about the project. When I see Joe, he talks about my hair." He pointed at the shelf along the wall, which the paint box was now sitting on. "And your mom gave me that shelf over there because she remembered something I said."

"Yeah, that was nice of her." She shook her head. "But I don't get why any of this makes any difference."

Rob sat up again, moved to the edge of the futon, and put his feet on the floor. "I didn't think you'd understand. From what you've said, you haven't ever wanted something bad enough to really work hard for it. If you know deep down that you never truly did everything you possibly could, you're never completely disappointed either."

"That's not true. I tried in college!"

"Couldn't you have switched majors, explored other options, or done something else instead of just quitting and going home to live with your parents?"

"I don't know. Maybe. Who knows? That was a long time ago."

"I'm just saying that different people have things that affect their lives. Different experiences. Baggage. All that has an effect on how you react."

"This is all too depressing. I don't want to have this conversation." She gestured toward the windows. "I screwed up at the meeting and you're just acting like it's no big deal. I mean, what are you, some kind of bizarre robot?"

Rob jerked away as if she'd slapped him, and stood up. He walked over to the coffee table and slammed his mug down on the edge of it with enough force that the ancient wooden legs on one side collapsed. The table fell and the laptop slid off and crashed to the floor, landing on Rob's glasses. One lens popped out of the frame and spun across the floor like a top. Roxy yipped, jumped up off Rob's shirt on the floor where she'd been sleeping, and ran under the futon.

Rob managed to keep from dropping his mug on the laptop, but coffee spilled on his hand. As he shook his fingers, droplets of coffee swirled off around the room. He picked up the lens off the floor and placed it deliberately on the counter. Turning to look at her, he growled, "No. I am *not* some type of robot."

Tracy pulled the sheet up to her chin. "I...I didn't mean that. Sometimes I say things without thinking."

"And because you're *you*." He waved his hand vertically, indicating the length of her body. "You can get away with it." Shaking his hand again, he moved to the sink and poured the coffee down the drain.

"That's not true!"

Rob turned and leaned back on the counter, waving the mug as he spoke. "I had this all figured out. We do a few screen layouts every night and no problem. But no—you refuse to work and spend your time going out with Mr. Gorgeous Trout Guy. And then...and *then* you have the great idea to stay up all night. I *knew* that wouldn't work. I can't deal with no sleep."

"But we finished the job. We did it!"

He turned back to face the sink. "And then I blew it because I was too tired to think straight." The muscles in his back tensed and he threw the coffee mug into the sink. It made an ear-splitting cracking noise as it shattered. Putting his hand over his eyes, he bowed his head. "It was stupid to think this would ever work."

"What do you mean?"

"I need to go." He walked over and crouched down next to the laptop on the floor. After slapping the lid closed, he began ripping the cords off the back. "The work e-mails I got were worse than the note from Ben. When I go back to my real life, it looks like I'll have to go to Iowa, then Oklahoma, then Nebraska."

"You have to go to *Iowa*?"

"Yes. Iowa." He stood up, holding the laptop. "Normally, I try not to think too much about work. Usually, I just blow things up."

"What?"

Rob pointed at the pile of boxes that contained the various components of his personal computer that he'd brought from home. "Video games. When I'm not working, I sit at home and blow things up. It's more socially acceptable to play video games in my dreary apartment than to throw things. I wired up my computer so it's attached to my huge TV. Blowing up stuff is better than spending too much time thinking about my job. But this place is so small, I can't even set up my computer." He shoved the pile of Tracy's clothes off the boxes, so they fell on the floor. Slamming the laptop on top of the stack of boxes, he said, "And now my computer seems to be your new laundry basket. Don't you *ever* put anything away?"

Tracy twisted the sheet in her hands. "Shouldn't you be careful with the laptop?"

"It's ruggedized. That's the word they use for laptops you can use in harsh environments. Like North Dakota in January, for example." His shoulders slumped and he closed his eyes. "Which is only slightly worse than Nebraska in November."

"I guess I didn't realize how much this meant to you."

"I know. I tried not to get my hopes up. But you weren't the only one with fantasies of quitting your job."

She got up off the futon and stood in front of him. "I have got to get ready for work. I'm going to be late. Please don't leave."

Shaking his head, he bent to pick up his glasses. "I have to fix these."

Tracy went to the bathroom and turned on the shower. She got in and began scrubbing shampoo into her hair vigorously as tears streamed down her cheeks. What just happened there? Was Rob just going to give up, leave, and never see her again? That idea just made her cry harder. She began sobbing, swiped at her face with her hand, and got soap in her eye. He was wrong. She *was* disappointed. And furious. And sad. All at the same time. She definitely didn't want Rob to leave, never to return. That was too awful to contemplate. But a long-distance relationship was dismal at best, and pointless at worst. The guy was never even at home. She'd never see him again.

Tracy got out of the shower and wiped the condensation off the small mirror. Yikes. Scary. She splashed some cold water on her face and looked again. Not much of an improvement. She still looked like an albino hamster with a bad case of pink-eye. Ugh. She opened the door and went out into the room.

Roxy was curled up next to Rob on the futon, which was back in couch configuration, the sheets neatly folded in a pile. The end of the coffee table was propped up on the paint box and her clothes were off the floor. Maybe he'd thrown them in the closet. Rob's clothes appeared to be packed away in his luggage. He sat petting the dog with one hand and holding a fresh mug of coffee in the other.

Tracy sat down next to him. All the anger seemed to have drained out of him and he had settled into morose silence. Tracy turned to face him. "I'm sorry. I feel terrible. I don't want to argue. You only have a couple of days before you have to go back to work. Please stay here. Today, I'll see if I can get some time off."

"I don't see the point. I should just go back to work. They're getting my flights set up. I should go home."

She touched his arm and felt him flinch. "That's a lot of miles. Why not just enjoy your last days of vacation?"

"I have racked up enough frequent-flyer miles, going to all these networking jobs, that I could take a free trip pretty much anywhere. Except I never do."

Tracy took his hand. "Just stay, then. Stop by the clinic at three. I'll make sure I'm done."

"All right." He waved toward the coffee table. "I'll go to the hardware store and see if I can find something to fix that."

She squeezed his hand. "I'd be happy to take some of those frequent-flyer miles off your hands this winter if you'd like to take me to the Caribbean."

He sighed deeply and took her in his arms. "We'll see." He kissed her gently. "If you actually still feel that way a few months from now, we'll talk."

~

At the clinic, Tracy had a lot of time to think because there weren't many appointments. She spent most of the day monitoring the anesthesia machine while Dr. Cassidy spayed and neutered animals.

The vet looked up from her stitches. "You sure are quiet today."

"I think I had a fight with Rob."

Dr. Cassidy snipped off a thread. "Don't you know?"

"Yes. I guess it was a fight. I said some things I shouldn't have. But mostly I think we were both just mad and sad because he found out we didn't get the web-site contract. He's more upset than I thought."

"Well, it sounded like there was a lot of competition." The vet pointed at the anesthesia machine with her needle.

Tracy leaned over and adjusted a dial. "I suppose. He's going to be traveling for work for ages. I'm not even sure when I'll see him again."

"At least you have a couple of days off. Maybe you can figure something out."

At three, Rob walked through the door. He half-smiled in a melancholy way. Tracy bit her lower lip as her heart did a little flip-flop in her chest. Not only did she not want him to leave now; she didn't want him to leave *ever*. She had fallen in love with him. That was the last thing she'd ever expected. Kat was right—these things didn't happen on a timetable. Hoping that Dr. C was still busy in the back room, she ran over, put her arms around him, and gave him a passionate kiss. "Let's go. I want to show you a place that's not in any of the guidebooks."

He looked startled and smiled for real this time. Holding out his keys, he said, "Wanna drive?"

With a whoop, Tracy grabbed the keys and ran out the door.

He followed her out to the car. "I guess that's a *yes*."

Tracy drove out to the peninsula on the lake near where Ben Walsh lived. She took a side road, and at the end of the pavement she stopped the car. "We have to walk from here."

Rob got out and looked up at the canopy of trees. "This is beautiful."

"We haven't gotten to the good part yet. Technically, it's private property, but the owner has known that kids come up here for years. It's one of those things where if no one does anything stupid to damage the place, he's fine with it. So far no one has, and he hasn't gated it off."

They walked down a trail that ended at a huge rock outcropping. Tracy started climbing up the first boulder, following along a well-worn path through the rocky crags. Rob followed, looking around. They continued to ascend the path. Tracy was getting tired, but she knew it would be worth it. At the top, she moved aside so Rob could get through the last craggy pass.

He stepped out onto a flat granite slab that jutted out over the lake about three-hundred feet above the water. "Whoa. That's incredible."

Tracy took his hand. "I know. This is my favorite place in Alpine Grove. Come on. There's a place over here where the rock is smooth and curved, almost like a chair. I like to sit at the edge, dangle my feet, and look out across the water."

They stood next to each other near the edge of the rock, gazing at the panoramic lake and mountain landscape. The lake stretched for miles in front of them pristine and silent, dotted with a few small islands. Along the shoreline other outcroppings of rocks sloped toward the water. A few clearings for houses were interspersed among the vast swaths of forest. An eagle flew overhead, the sound of its wings breaking the stillness. Tracy took off her shoes and sprawled on her back. She scooted down toward the edge, so she could swing her legs back and forth, letting her bare feet dangle in the light autumn breeze.

Rob took off his shoes, laid down next to her, and held her hand. "Thanks for bringing me here. You're right; the guidebooks definitely didn't mention this."

"They never do."

She pulled her feet in from the ledge and sat cross-legged, looking at his profile. Leaning over, she pulled off his glasses and peered into his eyes. "I need to talk to you."

Rob raised his eyebrows. "I think you are."

"Very funny." She laid the glasses next to the shoes and turned back to him. "I'm serious. You said that I didn't really look at all the options when I ditched college. Because I didn't really care. And maybe I didn't. Maybe I didn't care about getting the web site thing enough either. I mean, more money would be nice. Not wading through barf and dog hair would be cool too. But here's the thing. It doesn't matter if we didn't get the job because I screwed up or because you aren't a good salesperson. What does matter is that I do *not* want you to leave and never see you again."

He sat up. "Really? Are you sure? You mean that?"

"Yes, that's something I truly care about." She leaned to kiss him. "We need to look at the issues and possible solutions."

"Okay. This sounds very organized." He pulled his own feet in from the edge and sat cross-legged to face her, so their knees were touching. "Issue one. You live here. I live in LA, except when I'm in places like scenic Oklahoma."

"I hate that issue. How much do you like your job?"

"Not that much. But what else would I do? How much do you like your job?"

"Better than you like yours. But what else would I do?" She raised her hands, turning her palms toward the sky. "Oh, and I am basically destitute, except for the money I just got from you. And I have a dog that I can't leave anywhere, except with Kat. Which I can't afford on any type of long-term basis."

"Those are definitely issues." He scratched his chin and looked thoughtful. "I have an apartment that doesn't take pets. And it's in kind of a bad area, anyway. I don't think you'd want to live there. I never cared that much, since I don't spend much time at home. But I could move."

"Is there some other job you could do that doesn't require you to travel to the far corners of the country?"

"Maybe." He rubbed his eyes. "It would take me a while to find a new job."

Tracy sighed. This was hard. "I have an apartment that does take dogs. Or at least one small dog. My place is tiny, but it does have a super-low rent, thanks to the family discount. And it's in a good neighborhood. But it's located in an employment wasteland."

He reached over and took her hand. "Yes. I think you've tried out most of the available jobs."

"I know, and most of them I wouldn't wish on anyone, least of all you." She looked into his eyes. "Would you even be interested in living here, if you could?"

"And leave the smog and my bad neighborhood in LA?" He squeezed her hand. "Not a problem."

"Okay. So we didn't get the huge web-site thing. Maybe we could do something else. Other web sites, maybe?"

"Like I said, I'm not much of a salesperson. And most people in little towns don't have a lot of money for something like a web site. I don't think there's much of a market."

Tracy took his other hand in hers. "You're right. I mean, my mom probably has one of the more successful businesses in town, but if I asked her about a web site, she'd think I was nuts. She might not even know what a web site *is*."

"So where does that leave us?" He squeezed both of her hands gently.

"Confused."

"Yeah, I know." He uncrossed his legs and pulled her into his embrace. "I'm not sure there's an easy answer here."

Tracy kissed him and turned to lean back on his chest. She looked out across the water. "We haven't solved the immediate problem either."

"What's that?"

"I don't want you to go. What if you just didn't leave?"

He stroked her hair. "You know, I can't realistically do that. I mean, I have some savings, but not that much. If I quit, I need another job."

She gazed out over the expansive view of the lake in front of them. "I know. But if you got rid of your apartment, you wouldn't need a job immediately, right?"

"Maybe. I have student loans, though. And a car payment. That car you love costs money, you know." He pushed a windblown lock of hair back, away from her face. "What are you suggesting? Run away to Rio?"

"While that does have some appeal, if I don't quit my job and you stay with me, we can live cheap. Really cheap. I have vast experience with that."

"I suppose. But I draw the line at Cap'n Crunch. I'm not eating another crunch berry, ever. I could sell my car too."

She turned around to face him. "I'm going to try not to think about the car." She sighed. "This is sort of crazy, isn't it? I mean, I'm asking you to dump your whole life and trade it for mine, which isn't that great, unless you're fond of being broke. Taking a vow of poverty sounds a lot more romantic than it really is."

"Sometime crazy isn't so bad. It was kind of crazy for me to ask you to help me with the meeting back in LA. But if I hadn't, I wouldn't have gotten to know you." He hugged her shoulders and kissed her behind her ear. "Maybe your life doesn't seem that great to you, but the last few days have been better than most of my life in LA."

"Yeah. I whine about Alpine Grove a lot, but every time I leave here, I want to come back. It's home. Maybe that's why I didn't really care that much about staying in LA for school. It really is kind of a disgusting place. I mean, I talk about that whole Annette fantasy, but it isn't what I want. Not really. Sure, I'd love to be able to do something art-related, but mostly right now, I rather be with you than have paintings hanging in some dusty gallery."

"You won't get any argument from me. Particularly when I'm sitting up here with you, staring out at possibly the most beautiful view I've ever seen."

She turned in his arms to face him. "You know I love you, right?"

"I wasn't sure. But I hoped that might be the case." He kissed her. "Because I love you too."

"I was hoping that too."

He cradled her in his arms and kissed her again. "I'm glad we cleared that up. By the way, you never said. What is the name of this place?"

She put her hands around his neck and pulled him closer. "I'm not sure what the real name is, but we always called it Make-Out Rock."

He bent to kiss her neck and murmured. "Another reason it's not in the guidebooks."

"Nope. Only locals know. Get ready to be part of the Alpine Grove in-crowd."

~

Tracy was glad she had taken Friday and Saturday off from the clinic. She and Rob spent most of those two days either out hiking, walking Roxy, or curled up together planning Rob's exit from La-La Land.

Saturday night, Tracy was lying on the futon on her stomach with her arms hanging off the end. "I have no idea how you do that."

Rob rolled over and threw an arm over her back. "Do what?"

She turned her head to face him. "One kiss and I end up naked. I mean look at me. I'm exhausted. You really know how to show a girl a good time. For someone who claims not to have had much luck with cheerleaders, you certainly know what you're doing with this one."

"It's not like I've never had a girlfriend, you know." He looked thoughtful for a moment. "And yes, I suppose some of the ladies were rather complimentary about that particular aspect of the relationship."

"As well they might be. You are a very patient and methodical man."

He chortled. "Patience is a virtue. I guess being mechanically inclined helps too."

"What? Wait. Are you saying something disgusting?"

"No, I mean I've always been good at figuring out how things work. That's why I'm good at my hopefully soon-to-be-former job. I see network diagrams in my head. How things fit together. I wasn't that great at school—English classes were definitely *not* good. But I could fix things. The neighbors used to bring small appliances like toasters over to our house."

"You fixed the neighbor's toaster?"

"Among other things."

"What does that have to do with sex?"

"I read some books. I'm good at visualizing. It's not that complicated."

Tracy giggled. "I wish other men felt that way. There'd be a whole lot more happy women in the world." She kissed him. "I am going to miss you so much."

"I know. I'm going to miss you too. But I'll be back soon. I just have to go quit and deal with packing up my apartment. But right now, I don't want to think about that."

"Are you visualizing something?"

"Very much so."

The next day, Rob packed up the car and headed back home. Tracy waved as the Prelude disappeared down the street. She went back up the stairs into her apartment, which, now that it was clean, seemed a little larger than before. With two people living there though, it was a good thing Roxy was such a small dog.

Although she hadn't talked to Rob again about it, Tracy still was upset about the web-site project falling through. She had to do something. Talk to Ben. Explain that the screw-up with the presentation was her fault and that she and Rob could do the job.

She crouched down and looked into Roxy's face. "Okay, little dog. I'm going to do this before Ben leaves town and I lose my nerve. If I don't, I'll always wonder. You behave yourself, okay?" Roxy wagged, which was probably as close as Tracy was going to get to a vote of confidence.

After some forceful convincing, Tracy finally got The Turd into motion. It seemed the car had enjoyed its time off and was not eager to go back to work. Glancing up at the sky, she hoped that the weather would hold, otherwise she might have to walk or swim back from Ben's house on the lake.

She drove up the long paved driveway to the magnificent entrance and was again intimidated by the opulent house. She looked down at what she was wearing. Oh well. The car sputtered to a stop and quivered into silence. The huge wooden front door of the house was open and movers were taking things out of the house, to be placed in storage for the winter.

Most people with a summer cabin just locked the doors and left, but those places weren't filled with valuables worth more than the GNP of small countries either. If someone ripped off the cabin's Corelleware, the owners could just get more at a yard sale and call it good.

Tracy walked into the house and looked up at the ornate woodwork on the ceiling. She stopped a worker who was hoisting a ceramic elephant. "Is Ben here somewhere?"

"Yes, he's out back."

Tracy walked through the house, exited the tall French doors onto a patio, and took a path down to the lake. Ben was standing by the huge tree on the lawn, looking out at the view.

She walked up alongside him. "Hi Ben. Have you run across Miriam Gray yet?

The tall man turned and frowned at her, "What are you doing here? Tracy, right?"

"Yes. From the meeting. I wanted to talk to you."

"You came all the way out here to talk to me? You should have set up an appointment with my secretary. I'll be back in the office tomorrow."

"I thought it would be easier to stop by here. I want to apologize for...well...the meeting here the other day. I was so tired and I just sort of lost it. I know Rob would be able to do a great job on the site. He figured out the whole thing, down to the last detail."

"Yes, the proposal was very comprehensive. But we've already selected another company."

Tracy took a deep breath. "I know. But some big firm in LA doesn't care like we do. For them, you're just a number on a client list and they're creating a web site about some place they don't know anything about. With us, your project would be our priority. Alpine Grove is our home."

Ben glanced at her. "Rob said he lives in LA."

"Not anymore. He loves it here. He doesn't want to leave and he's moving here."

He looked out across the water. "I can understand that. I love this place too. My family has had so many good times on our vacations up here. Wonderful memories. We adore this house."

Tracy nodded. "It is beautiful. I live in town, but I can come out and see the lake whenever I like. Or hike the waterfall trail. Or just sit in the forest somewhere. This place and this project mean a lot to us. And think about it—you'd even be supporting the local economy!"

"I suppose."

"Selecting a local firm could be great public relations for your company."

Ben crossed his arms in front of his chest. "I don't think that's really necessary for us."

"Maybe not. I just wanted to let you know that Rob is really good at what he does and I know he wouldn't let you down."

Ben raised his eyebrows. "Apparently he thinks highly of you, as well. He sent me an impassioned e-mail telling me that you're a brilliant artist who knows Alpine Grove like no one else."

"He did? Well, we make a good team."

"That may be true, but we had to go with the other firm. They're in LA, but they have a lot of experience. Although their price was higher, we just felt more comfortable with them. It was a business decision. Nothing personal."

"Okay. Well, I just wanted to make sure you know how I feel before you leave town."

Ben furrowed his brow. "I know where I've seen you—the Italian restaurant! I didn't recognize you without that outfit."

Tracy shoulders drooped. "Yes. That was me. I've lived here my entire life, with the exception of some feeble attempts at higher education. That's why Rob said I know Alpine Grove so well." She waved at the lake, toward the general direction of town. "You can't get much more local than a townie like me."

Ben pressed his lips together and said, "Well, it's been nice talking to you, but I have to get back to the city now. Let me see you to the door."

"That's okay, I can find my way. Thank you for your time."

Tracy walked up the path to the house and out to The Turd. She got in and laid her forehead on the steering wheel.

Staring down at the filthy, worn floor mat, she turned the key and listened to the car's noisy protests as it attempted to turn over. This had been a complete waste of time. Not to mention humiliating. What had she been thinking?

She ground the key in the ignition again and finally the car cooperated with a gigantic cough of exhaust. As part of its deep unwillingness to move, it seemed to be having some new sort of convulsive catastrophe. At length, the engine finally settled down into its normal sputtering cacophony of automotive angst. She put the car in gear and steered it down the driveway toward home.

Chapter 14

Revivals

After her trip out to the lake, Tracy returned home and walked Roxy. She settled onto the futon with the dog and turned on the television. Time for some bad TV. She flipped through some channels and frowned. Sunday afternoon was not a good time to watch, unless you were a big fan of religious or sports programming.

She looked up at the easel standing near the corner next to the stack of Rob's computer boxes. The unfinished painting continued to sit where it had sat for months after she got stuck. Maybe if she just added some color in the corner, it would help. She started rummaging through the box of paints and supplies, lining them up on the shelf next to the easel.

Many hours later, the sun was setting and the painting was almost finished. It still needed something, but she wasn't sure what. Roxy barked angrily and Tracy looked down at the dog. "I forgot! You probably want dinner, don't you? Sorry."

Once she had fed Roxy, Tracy realized how late it was. How come Rob hadn't called? He said he would after he got to his apartment. Maybe he'd had an accident. What if he wasn't okay? How would she ever know? He could be lying in a ditch somewhere between here and Los Angeles. What if he had gone off the side of the mountain road? They'd never find him.

She went to the kitchen, got a bag of chips, and settled in front of the TV with Roxy, but she couldn't focus on the stupid sitcom rerun. What if Rob had gotten home and changed his mind about moving here? What if he was hurt? Should she call hospitals? The morgue? The phone rang and Tracy leaped straight up off the futon, slapping her hand to her heart. Maybe she should turn down the ringer on that thing.

She picked up the receiver and breathed a sign of relief when she heard Rob's deep voice on the other end of the line. She said, "How are you? I was starting to get worried." Okay, she'd been beyond worried—more like on the high road to serious freak out.

"I'm fine. It's been sort of a strange day."

"Strange? What do you mean, strange?" She sat down on the futon and moved the chip bag away from Roxy.

"You know how when a neighborhood gets fixed up they call it gentrification? What's the opposite of that?"

Tracy stroked the soft fur on Roxy's back. "I don't know. Slumification?"

"I think we should be glad that when we considered options, we ruled out living at my apartment. My neighborhood has slumified more than I thought."

"What do you mean?"

"When I got back to my place, the whole street was filled with police cars. I guess there was a shooting."

"What? Are you okay? Did someone die?" Tracy twisted the phone cord in her hand.

"I don't think anyone died. But someone shot at my apartment building. In the middle of the day. I guess they shot out a bunch of windows on the first floor. So the police were there and a bunch of neighbors were standing around out in front of the place. I tried to ask what happened and no one would talk to me. So I went up to my apartment."

"Did they shoot out your windows? Is there glass all over the floor?"

"No. I live on the second floor. But moving is going to be a lot simpler than I thought. Someone broke in and stole everything."

Tracy gripped the receiver. "What? Are they gone? Are you safe? You're not there, are you? What if they come back?"

"No. I'm not there. I decided my car and I would like to spend the evening in a better neighborhood. I'm at the office. I don't think gangs find office buildings particularly interesting. Plus there's underground parking. You need a card to get in."

Tracy relaxed her death grip on the phone somewhat. At least he was safe. "I'm glad you're okay. But they took everything?"

He paused. "Not everything, I guess. They took the TV, stereo—pretty much all my furniture. They dumped all my clothes and files and stuff all over the floor. I got some Hefty bags and threw everything in them. It's going to take forever to reorganize my files. Oh, and they left an end table that I found sitting on the curb when I first moved here. I had painted it green."

Tracy leaned back on the couch and covered her eyes with her hand. This was too bizarre. "So you're saying all you have are clothes and a green end table? And a Hefty bag filing system?"

"Pretty much. Oh, and there was a box of photographs. too. I'm so glad I left my computer in Alpine Grove."

Tracy dropped her hand and shook her head. "This is unbelievable."

"I took some of the bags down to my car and finally got the attention of one of the cops. So I spent most of the afternoon filling out reports about all the stuff I don't have anymore."

"I don't know what to say. I'm so sorry this happened." People she loved weren't supposed to have their home ransacked. It was just wrong.

"I really liked that TV. And my stereo. I guess I'm most sad to have lost all my music, though. They stole all the CDs too." He chuckled. "They'll be really pissed when they try to get those electronics to work, though. I rewired them to work with the computer. Without it, getting anything to turn on is going to be tough."

"At least you have your photographs. People always say that's what they miss the most after their house burns down."

"Yeah. I'm just relieved that you weren't here. After I took all the Hefty bags downstairs, I gave my landlord my notice and turned in my keys. I'm never going back there."

"Are you sure you're okay?"

"Yeah. I'm just gonna sleep on a couch here at the office and then tomorrow morning I'll hand in all my work keys, laptop, and stuff. It's all sort of surreal. Everything I own now fits into a Honda Prelude."

"It's a pretty small car."

"I know. Sad, isn't it?" He sighed. "So that was my fun-filled day in the city. What did you do?"

Tracy paused. She wasn't going to mention the humiliating trip out to Ben Walsh's place. "Mostly I just hung out here with Roxy. Watched some bad TV. Spent some time worrying about what happened to you."

"You worried about me? That's sweet."

"Hey, I love you. We just got that figured out. I don't want anything to happen to you. And I really want you back here."

"I love you too. I'll be back in Alpine Grove tomorrow sometime. I have your key. Unfortunately, all that laundry I was going to do here isn't going to get done."

"After you return, maybe we can have a romantic trip to the Alpine Grove laundromat. It's another local hot spot filled with fascinating human dynamics."

He laughed warmly. "That sounds great. I'll see you tomorrow."

"Roxy and I will be here. Be careful."

"I will."

~

The next day, Tracy returned from work at the clinic and found Rob sprawled out on the futon. Given the dachshund-size dent in the comforter, Roxy had obviously been curled up next to him, but she stood up to bark when Tracy entered the apartment. Six Hefty bags were strewn around the apartment and the green end table sat next to her easel. She sat down on the futon next to Rob. He looked more disheveled than usual, even for him. He sat up. "Sorry to just dump my stuff all over the place and crash. I was tired."

She placed her hand on his cheek and ran her fingers through the hair behind his ear. "You may have noticed I'm not a stickler for tidiness." She leaned to kiss him. "I'm really glad to see you."

He wrapped his arms around her. "Me too. I missed you. It's good to be back here. Your mom waved to me through the store window. Even Roxy was nice to me."

Tracy kissed him again and grinned. "I see that! You seem to have a small furry friend up here on the futon."

"She's figured out that if she stares up at me and looks sad, I'll pick her up and let her hang out."

"You're such a soft touch. Don't get too complacent, though. You'll do something to piss her off and then she'll turn on you and my pots and pans will be all over the floor again."

He looked over at the recumbent dachshund. "I'll keep that in mind."

She stroked his arm. "Are you officially a member of the ranks of the unemployed now?"

"Not exactly. That didn't really go as planned."

She pulled away to look at him. "You're not going to Nebraska, are you?"

"No. But my boss was shocked that I was quitting. I suppose I didn't give them much warning. My boss—Jim— he's a nice guy. Even though I don't really like what I do, it's been an okay place to work in a lot of ways. It's not really fair to not give them any notice."

Maybe she could give Rob some pointers on quitting. She had lots of experience. "I thought you had so much vacation, you could just leave."

"Well, technically I could. But there was begging. Lots of begging."

"Really?" She ran her fingertips along the contours of his shoulder, tracing his trapezius muscles. "I guess you were right. I'm not the only one who benefits from the whole visualization thing."

He gave her a quick kiss. "True. Jim tried to talk me into doing a few more jobs and I told him that I'd given up my apartment and was moving here. That kind of threw him."

"I'm getting the impression that you aren't known for making spontaneous major life changes." She outlined his clavicle with her fingertip and kissed his neck.

"No. I've worked there doing the same thing for years. Jim refers to me as Mr. Reliability. I can fix the stuff no one else can."

Tracy pulled away from him and tickled his ribs. "I knew it. You *are* Dudley Do-Right."

"Yeah, yeah. I know. Cut that out." He caught her hands and moved them away from his midsection. "Jim wouldn't let me give back my laptop. Or my keys."

"He wouldn't *let* you quit? I've quit a lot of jobs and never had that problem." More like don't let the door hit your butt on the way out.

"Jim gave me an incentive, I guess you'd say. A whole lot of money to do a networking job in Napa. Double my normal rate. I have to connect a group of wineries."

"Napa? As in wine country?" She put her arms around his neck. "That's a heck of a lot nicer than Nebraska."

"The extra money would mean I could keep my car for a little while longer, until I figure out something else." He brushed her lips with his. "I was thinking you could go with me. We could drive there."

Tracy smiled widely. "You want me to go on a road trip to Napa. Really?"

"Yes, really. But only if you want to. They're putting me up at some swanky place. Can you get the time off? Do you think Kat will take Roxy?"

Tracy moved her hands to either side of his neck and kissed him eagerly. "*Want* to? Are you kidding? Kat had better take Roxy. There is no way I'm not going."

"I'll have to work, but you could have the car." He grazed her cheek with his lips and murmured in her ear. "It's very hilly there. You could drive around through vineyards."

She wrapped her arms around him and hugged hard. "When do we leave?"

"Next week."

Tracy released her hold and stood up. "I'm calling Kat now. And Gail. She can take my shifts at the clinic." She clapped her hands together quickly and stomped her feet. "Wine country! Whee!"

The next morning when Tracy opened her eyes, Rob was sitting on the edge of the futon caressing her cheek with one hand and holding mugs of coffee in the other. "Hi."

Tracy sat up, leaned over to kiss him, and took a mug of coffee. "You are truly the best alarm clock ever."

"Thanks." He pointed at the painting. "You didn't tell me you worked on that. It's beautiful. I like what you added."

She ran her fingers through her tousled hair. "It's still not done. But it was getting late. Roxy wanted dinner. Like I said, it's a good idea to comply with her demands."

"I fed her breakfast."

"Thanks. I guess I have to go earn my six dollars an hour now. We need cereal and you have vetoed Cap'n Crunch. It's still on sale, you know."

"Yeah, it's all my fault." He kissed her. "Speaking of which, if I sell the Prelude, that just leaves your car. Before it gets any colder, maybe I could take a look at it. I might be able to do something to keep it from dying completely."

"I think Joel said it needs spark plugs." Tracy waved her hand. "I don't know. The stupid thing doesn't run in the winter. Or in the rain. And now it's not fond of cloudy weather either. I have no plans to drive it for the next six months or so, after it goes into its winter hibernation." She shrugged. "It's sunny today, though. Do whatever you want to it. You can park it out in the field again, for all I care."

Rob looked down into his mug of coffee. "No. We might need it. After I unpack a little, I'll take a look at it."

"I thought you didn't work on cars."

"I said I don't *like* to. Not that I can't." He took a sip from the mug. "I don't have much else to do today, anyway. I'll go to the library and see if they have the *Chilton's* for that era of Subaru."

Tracy put her coffee mug in her lap, holding it with both hands. "What's a *Chilton's*?"

"A car-repair book."

"Nothing you could possibly do to the Turd could make it run any worse than it does. When I took it out yesterday, I didn't think it would make it home."

Rob paused before taking a sip of coffee and looked over the rim of the mug at her. "I thought you didn't go anywhere."

"I...uh...went for a drive." Tracy took a big gulp of coffee. "But I changed my mind, since The Turd was uncooperative."

"No fantasy driving flow happening, huh?"

"Not even."

~

When Tracy got home from work, Rob was sitting on the floor in front of the futon with his laptop on the coffee table. His hair was wet and he was squinting at the screen. She put down her bag, grabbed his glasses from the green table, and handed them to him. "That looks uncomfortable."

He put on his glasses. "Thanks. It's better now that I put Roxy on the futon. Having a dachshund in my lap was problematic."

Tracy sat down on the futon next to Roxy and ran her fingers through his damp hair. "I thought you were supposed to put the computer in your lap. It's a *lap*top."

"You think this looks uncomfortable? That's worse. Laptops can get hot."

She leaned over and kissed his neck. "Hmm. That could be bad. I didn't think about that."

He turned and smiled up at her. "Life is full of trade-offs. How was your day?"

Tracy leaned back on the futon, slipped off her shoes, and put her feet on the coffee table next to the laptop. "Nothing unusually disgusting or heart-rending. Just kind of an average day. I'm tired."

Rob extracted himself from under the coffee table and sat next to her on the futon. "I took a look at your car."

Tracy stared at the ceiling. "Ugh. Is it terminal? Can we shoot it?"

"No. Sorry. It does need some work, though." He pointed downward in the general direction of the gift store. "I took out the carburetor. It's soaking in a bucket in a corner of the storeroom."

Tracy closed her eyes. "Eww. Soaking in what?"

"Carburetor cleaner."

"Yuck." She turned her head to look at him. "Does my mom know this?"

"Yes. Actually she was very supportive of my efforts to revive the car. I learned a little more about its colorful past."

Tracy sat up straighter. "My mom told you? She's never told *me*. No one ever told me the car was a way-out hippie-mobile. I never would have known if I hadn't seen that photograph again."

"Your father painted it."

Tracy's eye's widened. "You've got to be kidding me. That *Alice in Wonderland* stuff was incredible. I didn't even know he could draw, much less paint like that. And then he painted over it with that ugly brown paint? How could he do that?"

Rob took her hand. "Your mom said that's why they left the commune. He had tried to sell his art in a lot of different ways, and it just didn't work out. You were getting older and they started worrying that they wouldn't be able to take care of you. So they moved into town and got jobs."

"My dad was an artist?" Tracy looked down at the floor and shook her head. "He's the one who drilled it into my head that you can't make money as an artist. I can't believe they didn't tell me."

"I think your father didn't want her to." He interlaced his fingers with hers. "Your mom likes me."

Tracy leaned back on the futon again. "I think she's just relieved that I'm with someone who actually has all his teeth."

"The fact that your father couldn't sell his artwork does explain why he was so against you doing anything art-related."

She closed her eyes. "I don't know what to think about all this." She opened her eyes and turned her head to look at him. "Thanks for working on The Turd, though."

He squeezed her hand. "That is one dirty car. The engine is a study in grime. I was so ready for a shower by the time I was done."

"I know. I try not to touch The Turd unless I absolutely have to."

"Well, there's a sentence that could be taken the wrong way. You're too hard on that car. It's just old." Rob released her hand and readjusted his glasses. "By the way, I also went to the store and bought food. I had some ideas for ways we can eat inexpensively and not die from malnutrition."

Tracy opened her eyes, leaned forward, and kissed him. "Have I mentioned that I love you lately?"

"Not really."

"Well I do. What's for dinner?"

"Pasta and veggies. Cheap and not filled with scary chemicals."

Tracy grinned. "Are you secretly a health nut?"

"Not particularly." He waved toward the kitchen area. "I just prefer food that does not include made-up names like crunch berries. What is a crunch berry? It doesn't even make sense. Berries aren't crunchy."

"Sometimes you can be a little too literal, you know that?"

He gave her a kiss and got up. "Let me check my e-mail, then I'll figure out dinner." He rearranged himself on the floor, with his legs back under the coffee table.

Tracy stretched out on the futon, pushing Roxy to one side so she could put her feet up on the arm rest. She closed her eyes. It was so nice to not be standing up anymore.

Rob tapped her shoulder. "Hey. Look at this! This is—wow—I don't believe it. They changed their minds!"

Tracy propped herself up to look over his shoulder at the laptop. "What are you talking about?"

He pointed at the monitor. "Ben Walsh. He says that you were right. He wants to give us a chance!"

She put her feet on the floor, put both hands on his shoulders and leaned around to get a better look at the screen. "What about the LA people?"

"I don't know. It sounds like they had the project kick-off meeting and it didn't go well." Rob turned to look up at her. "What does he mean, you were right?"

"I went to talk to him." She raised her hands, palms up. "At the time, it seemed like he wasn't really listening and just thought I was an idiot. And he remembered that I worked at the restaurant, which was embarrassing. I thought going out there was a waste of time. But I wanted him to know that you know what you're doing and that we could do the work."

Rob took off his glasses and scuttled out from under the table onto the futon. He wrapped her in his arms and hugged her. "You're amazing."

"I'm glad you think so. When I talked to him, he also said you sent him what he referred to as 'an impassioned e-mail' about me."

He stroked her cheek with his fingertips. "I guess I did do that. But I wanted him to know that you are a great artist and know the subject matter really well."

"Maybe you're a better writer than you think." She patted his shoulders with excitement. "Do you know what this means?"

He tilted his head. "We're not going to be totally broke this winter?"

"That too." She gripped his shoulders. "It means I don't have to worry that I'll be driving your car for the last time in Napa."

"Something would have worked out. We still have your car."

Tracy released her hold on his shoulders and leaned back on the couch. "Ugh. Now that we're not going to be destitute, do we get to shoot it?"

"No. I'm going to get it working better again." He leaned back next to her. "The Turd is part of your family history, Rainbow."

"Fine. I'll drive your car. I love your car."

He reached over and pulled her into another hug. "I'm sure it loves you too. I know I do."

∽

The following week, Tracy and Rob got into The Turd to take Roxy out to Kat's place. Roxy was in the back of the car gazing out the window, apparently looking forward to another car ride. Tracy put the key in the ignition and turned it. The car started with only a few extra sputters of complaint. She turned to Rob. "You had an ulterior motive in fixing this hunk of junk, didn't you? You don't want to subject your car to Kat's road."

"The thought did cross my mind."

She reached over and poked his arm. "You are *such* a planner." Tracy steered the car out of the parking lot, down the alley, and out to the main street. She pointed at one of the buildings. "Look, there's some new business going in there. I guess that real-estate guy finally gave it up. He had the same listings hanging in the window for years."

"I guess they didn't sell?"

"They didn't look terribly appealing. I'm okay with rustic and as you know, I'm definitely not a neatnik, but I draw the line at falling-down shack. A roof is important. As is indoor plumbing." She turned her head to glance at him. "If we ever move, just so you know, running water is a non-negotiable feature. I don't do outhouses. I still have some nightmares about the one at the commune when I was little. Spiders around here can grow really large."

"I'll keep that in mind. Spider nightmares sound bad."

"You don't want to know."

Later, they bumped their way down the driveway to Kat's house. A group of people and dogs were standing outside the house talking. Tracy recognized Kat, Joel and the librarian who had helped her do research. She was standing next to a seriously gorgeous man. Like male-model-level gorgeous. He should be on a poster. Yowza.

Tracy parked the car and waved to Kat.

Kat walked over. "Hi Tracy. Hi Rob." She waved toward the people and dogs. "I think you know Jan. She's one of the librarians at the Alpine Grove library. That's Michael. The furry white dog is Swoosie and the black lab is Rosa."

Tracy waved at the group. "Wow, this is quite a crowd you have going here." She opened the back door, removed Roxy from the car, and put her on the ground. The other two dogs started straining at their leashes to get a look at the exciting new mini-canine.

Jan walked over with Rosa, who engaged in some reciprocal sniffing with Roxy. "Hi Tracy. How did the meeting go? Did the research I did help you? It was fascinating learning about human interaction with computer interfaces online."

"Yes. I sounded a lot smarter than I was. Thanks again for your help," Tracy said.

Rob said, "Yes. Thank you. She did great. We actually got the contract."

Joel said, "I thought it fell through. That's why you're doing the networking job."

Rob shook his head. "They changed their minds. But we're still going on the trip."

"There's no way I'm giving up the opportunity to drive the car all over winding roads through vineyards." At Joel's expression, Tracy pointed to The Turd and added, "Not this car. Rob's car."

"She likes my car," Rob said. "A lot."

Michael walked closer to the group with Swoosie and asked the dog to sit. She looked up at him eagerly and he gave her a treat. "Driving around Napa is fun. It's like you're driving through the set of that old TV show *Falcon Crest*."

Tracy said, "I'm okay with that. Maybe I'll find Lorenzo Lamas wandering among the grapes. Would it be okay if I pet Swoosie? I love Samoyeds—and she's adorable."

Michael nodded and Jan said, "Actually, the exterior shots of *Falcon Crest* were filmed at the historic Spring Mountain Winery, which is near St. Helena. The Victorian mansion from the show is called Miravalle. You could still visit it when the TV show was on, but the winery changed hands and now it's closed to the public."

Tracy crouched down to dig her fingers into the deep soft fur on Swoosie's ruff. "That's too bad." She looked up at Jan. "I'd love to see the real *Falcon Crest* house."

"You never know. Maybe they'll open it up again someday," Jan said.

Michael pointed at Kat, "So did you decide what to name the boarding kennel yet?"

Kat said, "Well, Maria suggested Poopenbarker's, which technically may be accurate, but I'm leaning toward Wag on Inn, which sounds a little more welcoming. She turned to Joel. "Could you put Roxy's crate in the house? I'm going to show Jan and Michael the new, improved door to the Tessa Hut." She waved toward the outbuilding. "Come on."

Joel got the crate, and Jan and Michael followed Kat and the dogs across the driveway to the outbuilding, leaving Tracy and Rob standing next to The Turd.

Tracy looked at Rob. "I guess Roxy still gets to be a special inside dog."

"You don't really think she'd put up with staying outside, do you?"

She grinned. "No. And there are no pots and pans to play with out there. What would she do?"

"I'm sure she'd think of something."

Chapter 15

Epilogue

Two weeks later, Rob and Tracy were walking Roxy down the main street of Alpine Grove. Tracy recognized Michael, who was standing outside the former real estate office. He had his hands in his pockets and was staring at the large plate-glass window.

Tracy waved. "Hi Michael. It's nice to see you again."

He turned and gave them a welcoming smile. "Hi, you guys. How was Napa?"

"Better connected now." Rob said. "It was a fun trip, but it's good to be back home."

Tracy stopped and convinced Roxy to pause in her march down the sidewalk. "Yes, it was the best trip ever! Hey, I never asked you. Where were you going? Someplace fun?"

"Russia." Michael waved his arms expansively. "It was incredible. Jan did research on all the history about the places we went. It was like having my own tour guide."

"I've never been to a foreign country," Tracy said.

"It was for work. One of my clients is based there and I talked Jan into coming with me."

"That wouldn't take much convincing for me," Tracy said.

"You'd be surprised. But we had fun." He grinned and raised his arms in a gesture of victory. "And the best part is that Kat is still speaking to me, so Swoosie must have behaved herself."

Tracy laughed and looked down at Roxy, who was sniffing at a particularly fascinating leaf on the sidewalk. "Yeah, so did Roxy! Or Kat just didn't tell me if Roxy did something awful. Sometimes she doesn't."

Michael nodded. "Yeah, she told me Joel decided to take up running. I'm pretty sure Swoosie helped with that decision."

Tracy pulled Roxy back over to her. "So you have a client in Russia? What do you do?"

"I'm in advertising." Michael inclined his head toward the building. "This will be our office after I get some work done on it. I was wondering what your contract was about, actually. It sounded like a good thing. Congratulations."

Rob said, "We're creating a data-driven web site about Alpine Grove. It will connect to the local multiple-listing service and show houses for sale." He waved his hand. "And a bunch of other stuff. We're just starting on the project. We need to find office space."

Tracy gestured toward the gift store. "We tried setting up one computer in my apartment and it didn't go well. We have a spatial-relations situation. Either we can sleep or use the computer. It's complicated and a lot of cords are involved."

Michael pointed at the brick wall in front of them. "I just bought this building. My offices will be downstairs, but the upstairs has offices that I'll be renting. I can't put up the sign until the sale is final and I get the keys."

Tracy looked up at the two-story structure. She had always thought of it as "the old Frederickson's," since years

ago it had housed a department store by that name. "You bought the entire building?"

Michael said, "Yeah. I was going to rent space, but then my house in San Diego sold. So I decided to invest."

"That must have been some house," Rob said.

"It was nice and right near the beach. But I was ready to leave." Michael looked at Rob, then at Tracy. "Maybe we could talk about web sites sometime. I'm working on the marketing plan for that client in Russia. They make vodka, and we've been talking about getting the business online. It's a global company and they're excited about the whole worldwide aspect of the web."

Rob smiled. "Sure. Any time. And we're definitely interested in the office space too."

"Okay. The place should be mine in about a week. Feel free to stop by then and take a look."

Tracy and Rob agreed and continued down the street, holding hands. Roxy charged ahead of them, her feathery tail waving happily in the breeze. They went up the stairs to the apartment and Tracy unlocked the door. Roxy rushed in and stood by her food bowl. Ignoring the dog's plaintive look, Tracy examined the painting on the easel. "I know what it's missing."

Rob sat on the floor and turned on the laptop. "You should finish it."

She pulled out paints from the box and picked up her paintbrush. She began working as Rob quietly tapped the keys on the laptop.

A few minutes later, she stepped back from the easel and put down her brush. Rob looked up at her. "Done?"

"Yes. It's finally done."

He extracted himself from under the coffee table and walked over to stand next to her. They gazed at the painting, which was a landscape showing the view over the lake from a rocky ledge. Tracy had added two people holding hands silhouetted at the edge of the outcropping.

Rob put his arm around her shoulders. "You really captured the feel of the place. What are you going to call it?"

"The Heart Never Lies."

Rob wrapped her in his arms and kissed her. "That sounds like a greeting card."

"Maybe. But it's true."

Thanks for Reading

Thank you for dedicating some of your reading time to *The Art of Wag*. I hope you enjoyed the adventures with Tracy, Rob, and Kat and I wanted you to know that I'll be writing more books that will feature Kat, Joel and various other residents of Alpine Grove who bring dogs to the new boarding kennel. The fourth novel, *Snow Furries*, is available, along with ten other books in the series.

If you would like to be notified by email when I release a new book, you can sign up for my New Releases email list at SusanDaffron.com.

I know that not everyone likes to write book reviews, but if you are willing write a sentence or two about what you thought of *The Art of Wag*, I encourage you to post a review at your favorite book vendor site or share a message with your social networking friends.

If you would like to share your thoughts about the book with me privately, you can reach me through the contact page on the SusanDaffron.com web site.

I look forward to hearing from you!

~ Susan C. Daffron

Acknowledgements

Writing a novel is never easy and I'd like to thank my husband James Byrd for his support and encouragement throughout the writing and publishing process.

Thanks also go to Daniel R. Marvello and Caroline Grimm for their contributions to the scene that includes the name of the boarding kennel. (Kat thanks you too.)

I'd also like to thank my alpha and beta readers for their eagle-eyed reading and great feedback:

- James Byrd
- Cynthia Daffron
- Dian Chapman
- Kathy Goughenour
- Kate Turner

Finally, a special kudos to our ancient Coleman generator for providing electricity during an extended power outage. Being able to use my computer definitely aided in the completion of the manuscript.

About the Author

Susan Daffron is the author of the Jennings & O'Shea series and the Alpine Grove romantic comedies, a series of novels that feature residents of the small town of Alpine Grove and their various quirky dogs and cats. She is also an award-winning author of many nonfiction books, including several about pets and animal rescue. She lives in a small town in northern Idaho and shares her life with her husband and three really cute dogs.